SOME KIND OF HATE

SARAH DARER LITTMAN

Scholastic Press / New York

Library of Congress Cataloging-in-Publication Data available

ISBN 978-1-338-74681-5

1 2022

Printed in the U.S.A.   23
First edition, November 2022
Book design by Maeve Norton

For Hank,
who is my happy place

Some Kind of Hate was a hard book to research and write—perhaps the most challenging and personal for me of all the books I've written. I want to give you fair warning: It isn't an easy book to read, either.

The contents include white nationalist ideas based on antisemitic conspiracy theories, Islamophobia, racism, misogyny, and violence.

I do not condone these ideas—in fact, they go against everything I believe in. They are included for two reasons: because they are necessary to understanding Declan's journey, and because it's important to recognize coded language and rhetoric used to promote hateful ideas when you encounter it in everyday life and online spaces.

Reading about these ideas might cause you some discomfort, and that's normal. I'd be more worried if it didn't. We aren't supposed to feel comfortable when we encounter those who hate entire groups of people based on religion, ethnicity, skin color, gender, or sexual orientation—the danger is in allowing such ideas to be normalized. If it makes you uncomfortable to read about this kind of hate, try to imagine how it feels to be the target of it in your life, not just in a book.

Still, if at any point the discomfort starts to feel overwhelming, please put this book down. Take care of yourself. You can always come back to it if you choose to.

As always, thank you for reading my books.

Sarah

FRESHMAN
YEAR

JUNE

JULY

AUGUST

DECLAN

The pop of the glove is my favorite sound in the world—especially when it's followed by an umpire calling a strike after I've thrown the pitch.

I could listen to it all day.

We're warming up for the most important game of the season. The Stafford's Corner Sabres are about to play the Tilbury Tigers for the New York State high school baseball championship.

"That's it, Declan, give that arm a rest," Coach Kriscoli shouts out.

"Just a few more, Coach, please?" I beg him.

"A few," Coach K says. "But don't push it."

"I won't," I promise. I have to protect my pitching arm, because baseball is life.

Not only that, it's the ticket out of my town, where if you drive not too far in any direction you'll find a house or a barn with peeling paint and a caved-in roof about to fall down and not much else.

I make one more warm-up toss. My best friend and practice partner, Jake Lehrer, catches it effortlessly.

If anyone on this team knows me, it's him. We met playing T-ball, and we've spent more hours playing together than I can count.

He rushes over, throws an arm around my neck, and pulls the brim of my baseball cap down over my face. "Nice job, Dec. Keep it up during the game."

"I will, if Coach puts me in," I say in a low voice, taking off my cap and running a hand through my hair. My parents have been after me to get a haircut, but I'm superstitious and won't cut it until after the championship.

"Come on, Dec. You know he will," Jake says, detangling from me to wipe the sweat off his face with his arm.

"Mateo Molina is a sophomore. He's got seniority."

"Yeah, but you're the closer," Jake says. "You're the guy with the golden arm—and hair."

He reaches his hand out to mess with my hair, but I bat it away. It's not even worth trying to retaliate, because his dark curls are definitely a matted mess under his own hat. Before he can open his mouth, I say, "If you call me Goldilocks, I'm going to beat the crap out of you, Jake."

He flashes me a grin. "Oh, no you won't," he says. "Because you want us to win, and for that to happen, we need me at first base . . . Goldilocks."

I try to punch his arm, but he's too quick for me. He's already taken off running, his laughter floating back to me on the breeze.

"Yo, Goldilocks, is Jake being an idiot again?" one of my other friends, Cody Miller, asks as he walks over. You can smell the sunscreen on him from like a mile away. He's got that seriously pale ginger look going on, so it doesn't take much to turn him into a lobster.

I grit my teeth. "Stop calling me that!"

Cody grins and says, "I'll stop if you win us the championship."

"You know I'm gonna try."

"Yo, Declan! Over here!" It's hard to miss my twin sister Kayleigh's voice from the stands. I see her waving like the weirdo she is, next to my parents, who have actually taken the day off work to watch me play in the championship. June is one of my mom's busiest times as a hairstylist, what with proms and weddings. And Dad's been taking all the shifts he can at Pinnacle Metalworks because there's a new general manager being transferred in from out of state to "streamline production," which apparently is corporate speak for layoffs. My parents have been even more stressed out about money than usual. They missed the quarterfinal and semifinal games, but at least they're here now. Mom waves, and Dad shouts, "Knock 'em dead, Dec!"

Coach has to put me in. Otherwise, they took off work for nothing.

Jeff Seale pitches the first three innings and gives up two runs—but so does the Tilbury pitcher. Coach and Mr. Morrison are conferring about who to put in to relieve him. I'm gutted when Coach calls out, "Molina! You're up!"

By the bottom of the fifth, we're ahead by one run, and I'm starting to feel sick to my stomach as I pace the dugout. Is Coach going to let Mateo pitch for the rest of the game without even giving me a chance? I might be a freshman, but I proved myself in the quarterfinal and semifinals.

We're still ahead by the time Mateo's struck out two batters. But I can tell he's flagging, and the bases are loaded. It's my turn. It's gotta be.

Coach doesn't even look at me.

I hold my breath as Mateo winds up for the pitch. As soon as the ball leaves his hand, I know we're in trouble. Sure enough, instead of the pop of the ball in the catcher's glove, there's the loud ping of it hitting the aluminum bat. It sails over the outfield for a homer.

I kick a helmet, but even the satisfying thunk of it hitting the wall doesn't make me feel any better. We're going to lose, and I'm just standing around on the sidelines when I could win this for us.

By the time Mateo strikes out the next batter, our dugout is like a wake. Mateo comes in from the mound, pulling his cap down lower over his face. Coach squeezes his shoulder, then shouts the five glorious words I've been waiting to hear: "Taylor, you're up next inning."

JAKE

"Strrrriiiike two!"

It's the bottom of the seventh, and Dec has managed to hold the Tigers scoreless so far. We pulled ahead by one run during our time at bat.

If he can strike this batter out, we win the state championship.

Don't choke, Dec, I think, watching the Tilbury guy who's on first with me out of the corner of my eye. He's creeping off like he's about to steal.

Suddenly, the ball is zooming toward me. I reach out my glove and feel the thud as the ball lands. By the time I go to tag the guy out, he's already back on base.

I nail the ball back to Declan, along with a you-got-this smile.

He shoots me his usual cocky grin, then turns to home plate, throwing the ball into his mitt and staring at the batter like he can win this game just from the glare of his ice-blue eyes.

His arm draws back, his leg bends, and as his body travels forward, the ball rockets from his hand at an insanely fast speed. It sails straight over home plate into the catcher's mitt with the sweetest pop I've ever heard.

"Strrrriiiike three!"

He did it! I let out an earsplitting whoop before racing to the mound and jumping on Declan, who is grinning like the Cheshire Cat. The rest of the team runs in from the outfield and out from the dugout, until we're in a massive, pulsing huddle of elation.

After shaking hands with the other coach, Coach Kriscoli jogs out to join us, his suntanned face creased in a broad smile. Players release their hold to let him into the huddle until he reaches Dec.

"Great job, Goldilocks!" Coach says. "I've got my eye on you, kid."

Declan is stunned enough that he doesn't even complain about being called Goldilocks. "Wow . . . Uh . . . thanks, Coach."

"A lot can happen between now and next season," Coach says. "Take care of that pitching arm, especially when you're playing travel this summer. I want you back in the spring in top form."

I didn't think Declan's smile could get any wider, but it does.

"Dec, you did it!" Kayleigh shouts as she runs onto the field trailed by their parents, who are beaming with pride.

"Jake!" Mom shouts, jumping up and down so I can see her over my teammates.

Dad reaches over Mom's head to pull off my baseball cap and ruffle my curls. "Nice work, Jake!"

"At least the party tomorrow won't be a total bust now," my older brother, Ben, says, grinning.

Having a dad who is a building contractor means we have a pool, so I get volunteered to host parties. I knew it would be either a celebration or a commiseration, but either way it would be a party to end our season. Winning state is definitely a reason to party.

"Are you going to take the bus home with the team or come with us?" Dad asks.

For a nanosecond, I'm torn between the comfort of my parents' car and being on a foul-smelling bus with my boys.

"Nah, I'll take the bus," I tell them, wanting to enjoy the post-game high with my teammates.

"Okay," Dad says, and they head to the parking lot.

Back on the bus, we're still pumped and getting ridiculous. Ken Borsuk starts singing "We Are the Champions" and everyone joins in, deafeningly loud and not particularly in tune, but who cares, because we *are* the champions, right?

By the time we're back in Stafford's Corner, I've pretty much lost my voice from all the singing, but it's worth it. I wish this feeling could go on forever.

"You invited Megan Moran to the party tomorrow, right?" Declan asks me as the bus pulls into the lot at the high school.

Dec has had a crush on Megan for, like, three years, but he's never acted on it. For someone who is such a big presence on the mound—and lives with a sister like Kayleigh who kills it on the soccer field and everywhere else, for that matter—he's weirdly shy when it comes to girls.

"Of course I did!" I tell him. "You finally going to actually ask her out? I mean, come on, you're Declan Taylor, MVP of the state championships. How could she possibly say no?"

"Maybe," he says, pushing me down the bus aisle. "You'll just have to wait to find out, won't you?"

I grin. "See you guys tomorrow!" I call out to my teammates as we tumble off the bus.

"Party at Lehrer's house!" Cody shouts. "Be there!"

The next morning, I'm up early—well, early for me on a Sunday-after-winning-the-state-championship, that is.

"Hey, champ!" Ben says when I walk into the kitchen. "I'm making some chocolate chip cookies for the party."

"Awesome!" Ben makes the best cookies. I go get a spoon and steal some batter, while he tries to swat me away.

"Mmmmm. Breakfast of champions," I say.

Just then, Mom comes into the kitchen, phone in hand. "I've invited a new family from the synagogue to the party," she informs us. "The Kramers. They moved here a few days ago from New Jersey, and they have a daughter your age, Jake. Her name's Arielle."

"Watch out, Jake, Mom's trying to make a shidduch," Ben says, winking at me.

"Oh puh-leeze, Ben. She's not trying to marry me off. I'm fifteen," I remind him.

"She's not *yet*," Ben replies. "But wait till you go to college and Mom and Dad are like, 'So-and-so's brother's cousin's daughter is going there, too! You should meet her!'"

"Ugh, Mom! Is that what this is?"

"No! Don't listen to him," Mom says, flashing Ben a look. "When I spoke to Molly Kramer about joining Congregation Anshe Chesed, she told me Arielle was unhappy about the move. That she's homesick for New Jersey and anxious about having to start at a new school as a sophomore. Just be nice to her, okay?"

"You know, instead of the jerk Mom thinks you are normally," Ben adds.

"That's not what I meant!" she protests. "I meant be extra nice. Help her meet some people. Apparently, Arielle's a soccer player, so you could introduce her to Kayleigh."

"Don't worry, Mom, I've got this," I promise her.

A little while before the party is supposed to start, Mom tells me to go set up the food and drinks outside.

"Yo, Goldilocks, come help me bring out food," I shout to Declan when he walks into the backyard with Kayleigh.

"Kayleigh, he's talking to you," Dec says, nudging her with his elbow.

She laughs and grabs his arm, pulling him toward the kitchen door.

"No way, Goldilocks," she says. "I'll help, but you're just as capable of carrying a tray as I am."

Declan exhales a loud, exaggerated sigh, then takes the tray of guacamole and chips I'm carrying.

"That last pitch of yours yesterday," I say. "I bet it was over a hundred miles per hour."

"Maybe," Declan says with a sly grin. "Someone had to close the deal. I figured it might as well be me."

"It was pretty fricking fast." I grab a handful of ice from a nearby bucket of soft drinks. "I think you should ice it," I say as I shove it down the back of his shirt.

He almost drops the guac, which would have sucked, but he manages to dump it on the table before shoving me into the pool. I grab his hand as I go and pull him in with me.

When we both come to the surface, laughing, Kayleigh is on the side of the pool holding a tray of sandwiches, shaking her head. "Typical. I turn my back for two minutes to help Mrs. L, and you guys are already acting like idiots."

I swim to the side just as Mom comes out with a family I don't know. Must be the Kramers.

"You're supposed to be helping, not swimming!" she says, throwing up her hands in despair.

"Dec pushed me in!" I protest.

"Yeah, after you shoved ice down the back of my shirt," Dec says, grinning.

"Are you two in kindergarten, or are you going to be sophomores?" Mom asks.

"More like sophomorons," Kayleigh says, provoking a giggle from the two kids with Mom.

"Oh, Arielle, I wanted you to meet Kayleigh," Mom says to the girl, who I can't help noticing is a super cute white girl with greenish eyes and long, dark hair. "Kayleigh's on the soccer team. Arielle is a soccer player, too."

Mom introduces us to Mr. and Mrs. Kramer, and Arielle's little brother, Bobby, who's going into fifth grade.

"Arielle, that blond bozo over there is my twin brother, Declan," Kayleigh says. "As you can probably tell, I got all the brains."

"And I got all the looks," Declan retorts, flicking back his golden mane.

Kayleigh opens her mouth, probably to shred him, but then seems to remember that parents are standing there. She closes her mouth and smiles so sweetly at Declan that I start cracking up.

Arielle laughs, too, and waves to Declan, who swims over.

Mom invites the Kramers inside to get a drink. I pull myself out of the pool. Declan follows. I notice he winces slightly as he does. When he's standing, he rubs his right shoulder for a moment.

Kayleigh gives him a concerned glance. "Are you okay?"

"I'm fine," Declan tells her.

I meet Kayleigh's eyes behind his back as he starts talking to Arielle.

As his twin, she knows him better than I do. But still—I've known him practically forever, and we're both expert enough in Declan to know he's lying.

DECLAN

The new girl, Arielle, is cute, but not my type. Megan Moran, on the other hand . . . she is totally my type, and I'm waiting anxiously for her to arrive. I wonder, if I flirt with Arielle, will it make Megan jealous, so she'll pay more attention to me? I read this thing online that said it's a good strategy because you should always keep girls off balance.

"So, Arielle, what brings you to the middle of nowhere?" I ask, flashing her my state-championship-pitcher smile.

"My dad got a promotion," she says with a sigh. "He's taking over as general manager at Pinnacle. Which is great for him . . . and sucks for me."

I feel the smile freeze on my face.

Kayleigh glances over at me. "Our dad works for Pinnacle," she says.

"Really?" Arielle says brightly. "That's so cool."

She obviously doesn't have a clue what her dad's arrival could mean for families like ours. My parents made it to the game, but they're back at work today while Arielle's parents are hanging around the pool laughing with the Lehrers.

"So, Kayleigh, tell me about the soccer team," Arielle says. "I miss my girls back in Jersey. But I'm psyched to try out for the team here."

"What position do you play?" Kayleigh asks her.

"Defensive midfield. You?"

"Center forward," Kayleigh says. "Are you good? We have to win the state championship next year, otherwise I'm never going to hear the end of it from this guy." She elbows me in the ribs.

I elbow her back, and we start to wrestle each other toward the edge of the pool until Jake puts his fingers in his mouth and lets out a shriek of a whistle, then yells, "Taylor twins! Time-out for breaking pool safety rules!"

Kayleigh and I release each other and turn to him sheepishly.

"Sorry, Jake," Kayleigh mumbles.

"Yeah, sorry," I mutter.

Jake's busy explaining to Arielle how his parents are sticklers about pool safety.

"Makes sense," she says. Then she asks us what we're doing for the summer. "I was all excited because I'd lined up an internship with a local radio station in New Jersey," she explains. "But then Dad said we were moving here, so now I'm looking for a job. Any job."

"Come work at the Burger Barn!" Kayleigh exclaims. "You, too, can come home smelling like a french fry!"

"I can attest to that," I say. "And she doesn't even bring any home for me."

"Sheesh, Kayleigh, what kind of sister are you?" Jake says.

"Wow, the chance to come home smelling like I'm wearing eau de fries . . . how can I resist?" Arielle says with a grin.

"Stop by tomorrow," Kayleigh says. "I'm working from eight to three. I'll put in a good word for you. I can't say it'll be fun, exactly, but most of the people who work there are pretty cool. It's the customers who drive me crazy."

"I'll do that!" Arielle says. Then she turns me. "So, Declan, what are you doing this summer?"

"Playing travel baseball and working at Stafford's Corner Youth

Baseball with this loser," I say, jerking my thumb over my shoulder at Jake.

"Travel baseball sounds fun," Arielle says.

"Yeah, it's gonna be dope," I say.

"It's a lot more fun than the online summer school I have to do this summer," Jake says, a gloomy shadow passing across his face. "If I don't get my grades up, I'm off the team next spring. Dyslexia sucks."

Jake's smart, but we've had to do way more reading in high school than we did in middle school, and that's never been his strong point.

"You'll do it," I say. "There's a big brain under that mop of hair you've got going there. When are you gonna get a haircut?"

"Ugh. My parents have been nagging me to get a haircut for, like, a month now," he says.

"Justifiable nagging," Kayleigh says, smiling. "You look like a sheep that's way past due for shearing."

"Oh my god, you're right!" Arielle says, before making baaing noises.

"Stoooooppppp!" Jake groans. "I can't help it if my hair grows like a weed!" He gives me a sideways glance. "Maybe we should go for a haircut together, *Goldilocks*."

Just then, Megan Moran comes into the backyard with her best friend, Melodie Carter, and I get that familiar stomach flip. I've known Megan pretty much all my life. It wasn't till the first day of seventh grade, when she walked into school without braces, and with curves in places she hadn't had at the end of sixth grade, that my feelings for her changed. It was like being sucker punched. I still feel a less violent version of it every time I see her long hair swishing behind her as she walks.

"Hey, congratulations!" she says, walking over with a big smile, which feels like it's directed right at me, especially when she leans in and gives me a hug. She smells like summer, a mixture of coconut and flowers. She pulls back, and I'm forced to let her go. "I hear you were the hero of the last inning!"

I feel heat rising in my face. "I just did what pitchers do."

"Dec's being modest," Jake says. "He was awesome."

"We're proud of you guys," Melodie says. The beads in her braids are red and white, our school colors. "Stafford's Corner baseball state champions. I like the sound of that!"

"Hey, M-Squared, meet Arielle," Kayleigh says. "She just moved here from New Jersey. Arielle, meet Melodie and Megan."

"Hi!" Arielle says, giving them a little wave. "Great to meet you both!" She grins. "M-Squared. I like it!"

"It's because they're inseparable," Jake says.

Don't I know it. Every time I think I've got the courage to ask Megan out, Melodie is there. It's impossible to get the girl alone.

Everyone's chatting, and I'm tongue-tied, trying to figure out what to say to Megan. Why does being near her turn me into a dork? My hands clench into fists, and I shove them into the pockets of my board shorts. What is the matter with me?

"Is it time to swim yet?" Melodie asks. She fans the sweat beading on her mahogany skin. "I'm about ready to melt."

"Me too!" Megan says. I try not to stare like a creeper as she takes off her shorts and T-shirt, revealing a red-hot bikini. She dives into the pool and swims a lap underwater, the sunlight painting patterns on her body as it refracts through the water.

"I'm going to get a drink," I mutter so I don't make a fool of myself.

When I come back, Megan is lying on a pool float, looking totally hot. Jake and Melodie are hanging off the side of the float, inches from her face, and they're all having this animated conversation.

13

Megan giggles at something Jake says, and I feel a rush of irritation. He knows I'm into Megan. Why is he flirting with her?

Before I can think better of it, I cannonball into the deep end, hoping to grab Megan's attention. I land a little closer to Jake's head than I probably should have. When I come up from underwater, he's wiping his face and he looks pissed.

"What the heck, Declan?" he asks.

"Lighten up," I say. "No one got hurt!"

"Although we did get plenty wet," Melodie points out.

"That's the whole point of a cannonball," I say, flashing a grin at Megan, who unfortunately doesn't seem all that amused.

"That wasn't cool, Dec," she says.

"Sorry," I say, hanging on to the float. I try to look apologetic, hoping for forgiveness.

But the three of them carry on their conversation like I'm not even there. I finally let go and submerge myself with growing frustration. I'm the MVP who won the game. I'm supposed to get the girl, aren't I?

The sounds of muffled voices and laughter travel through the water as I swim away from them toward the shallow end of the pool. I'm surrounded by people, and yet I couldn't feel more alone.

I break the surface and flick back my hair.

"Hey, Goldilocks, think fast!" Cody shouts, throwing a soaking-wet Nerf football at my head.

I catch it, and he gives me a golf clap.

"Yo, Jake!" I call out. "Incoming!"

I pull back my pitching arm and launch the ball. As I do, I feel a weird twinge in my shoulder. I gotta ice it properly when I get home.

Jake hurls himself away from the float and almost catches the football but misses by an inch. At least he's in the game now and not flirting with Megan.

Later, after we've eaten, I see him go into the house and I follow.

"Hey, what's with you flirting with Megan?" I say, unable to keep the anger out of my tone.

Maybe he's putting it on, but if so, he's a good actor, because Jake seems genuinely confused. "What do you mean flirting with Megan? I was just talking to her and Melodie about a cooking show we all watch."

"It sure looked like you were flirting with her," I mumble.

Jake shakes his head slowly. "C'mon, bro, you're my best bud," he reminds me. "You think I'd flirt with a girl I know you're really into?"

I can read the hurt on his face. "Okay, fine," I say grudgingly. "You weren't flirting. But just . . . back off Megan, okay?"

Jake stares at me. "Are you telling me I can't even talk to her about a TV show? Because that's literally all we were doing—and Melodie was there, too." He offers me a tentative smile. "C'mon, Declan, chill. I'm not going after your crush."

He puts his hand out to do the elaborate secret handshake we made up when we were in T-ball. I look him straight in the eye, and all I see there is hope and friendship. Maybe I am overreacting.

"Sorry, bro," I say, bumping his fist and swiping our palms and all the rest of it. "Guess I'm just jealous that she was talking to you instead of me."

"Dude . . . relax. You're the GOAT," Jake reassures me. He gives me that lopsided grin of his. "And pro tip for dating: Start watching *Eat, Bake, Love*."

"Why would I do that?" I ask. "It's a cooking show."

"Duh! Because Megan loves that show, and it'll give you something to talk about," Jake says.

I think about what he said as we head back out to the pool. But there has to be something I can talk to Megan about besides some dumb cooking show. I just gotta figure out what it is.

DECLAN

Having finals so soon after the state championship sucks, like we were able to concentrate on anything but baseball before them, and then for the two weeks afterward we were all still on a high from winning. But somehow, I manage to make it to the last day of school.

I don't even know why they bother making us go to school today, especially with it only being a half day. Everyone's already checked out mentally anyway, including the teachers. That's why we're sitting in the auditorium watching a dumb movie, when we could be swimming in the quarry at Seward State Park. A bunch of people from the baseball team are going—and so's Megan.

Maybe this is the day things will finally happen between us. If this stupid movie ever ends.

The PA system crackles to life just as the credits start rolling. "Have a great summer, everyone!" Principal Gardiner says. "Keep cool and be safe!"

"Finally," I say, standing up and stretching. "Let's bounce."

Cody pulls his car key out of his pocket and waves it in our faces. He's a sophomore, so he's not only got his license, he's also borrowed his mom's minivan, which we've christened Mario.

We follow him out to the parking lot, where we're meeting the other people who are going.

Megan looks especially cute today in a pair of cutoffs and a tank top. I sidle over to her.

"Hey, you should come with us in Mario the Minivan," I say.

Megan laughs. "How can I say no to riding in Mario?" she says. "There's room for Melodie, too, right?"

What is it with girls that they always seem to come as a set?

"Sure," I say, even though there really isn't. Kayleigh is going to have to find a seat in someone else's car.

We pile into Mario, and I make sure that Megan sits next to me. Her leg touches mine, and she doesn't move it away. That's a good sign, I think. I hope I'm not too sweaty. I'm going to make this happen today if it kills me.

Melodie, Jake, and Parker squeeze in after us. When Kayleigh finally shows up, she sticks her head in and sees we're full. "Wow, thanks for saving me a seat, bro."

"You snooze, you lose, sis," I say, earning myself a glare as she slides the minivan door closed a little harder than necessary.

"Oooooh, Declan's in trooooouble," Jake says, like we're still in kindergarten.

"Shut up!" If things go well with Megan, Kayleigh will totally understand. Teasing me about my crush is one of her favorite pastimes.

But as usual, now that I'm sitting next to the object of my dreams, our legs touching for the twenty-minute ride, I can't think of what to say. Megan's talking to Melodie a mile a minute about the latest episode of that stupid cooking show Jake told me to watch. I'd rather play video games than sit through that. Cooking shows are for chicks—and Jake, apparently.

"Did you see the one where Janelle makes monster brownie cookies?" he says, sounding almost as excited as he did about my winning pitch at state. "I'm definitely going to try to make those over the summer!"

Megan turns in the seat, and her knee pokes into my thigh. "Oh my god, if you do, you have to invite me over for quality control!"

I clench my hands on my knees and stare out the window at the passing cars. Fricking Jake, man. Just two weeks ago he swore he wasn't even into Megan and claimed he'd never break the bro code that way. Now look at him. Laughing about making stupid cookies with her.

"You better invite me over to eat them," I say in a tone that's probably snarkier than it should be.

"Of course!" Jake says. I don't turn around, but I can almost feel his *C'mon, bro* look on the back of my neck.

He better step back and let me talk to Megan when we get to the park. Why can't they just shut up about that stupid show? Seriously, are they going to analyze every single episode?

They're still at it when Cody pulls the minivan into the parking lot. As much as I've enjoyed having Megan's leg pressed against mine, maybe now that we're getting out of the van, I can talk to her about something other than baking.

The group that was in Mateo's Jeep is already there waiting for us. That includes Kayleigh, who flicks her towel at me, catching me on the leg. "That's for not saving me a seat!"

"Ow! Hey, I hope you are all witnessing this sibling abuse!" I exclaim. "Help me!"

Jake laughs and holds up his hands. "No way am I getting in the middle of a Taylor twin fight."

"Wise decision, Jake!" Kayleigh says.

"Traitor," I mutter at Jake. He smiles, but I'm only half joking, especially when he, Megan, and Melodie start up again with the baking show, and now Kayleigh joins in.

I'm stuck walking behind them with Cody.

"You pumped for travel baseball?" he asks.

"Yeah. Except for having to listen to my parents complain about how expensive it is all the time," I say. "Dad didn't want me to do it. He wanted me to get a full-time job. Mom was the one who finally persuaded him, after I told her that doing travel baseball would help me get a scholarship when the time comes."

"I didn't do it between freshman and sophomore year because my parents couldn't afford it," Cody says. "They made me work and save up money so that I could do it this year."

"I wonder what it's like to have parents who can afford to pay for all this stuff without even thinking about it."

Cody laughs. "I'll never know. Unless we win the lottery or something."

"Same. Like that's ever going to happen."

"Why so glum? You're killing it after that strikeout at state."

I nod to the group in front of us. "He knows I like Megan," I say in a low voice, not that Megan and Jake would hear us, because they're too busy flirting. "I told him to back off at the party. And what's he doing? Flirting with her!"

Cody looks from them back to me. "Uh, dude . . . you know I'd level with you, right?" he says quietly.

"Yeah," I mumble.

"Jake isn't flirting with Megan," he says. "He's acting toward her the same way he is toward Melodie and Kayleigh. Do you think he's flirting with your sister?"

"No, but—"

"Seriously, Declan, chill. We all know you're into Megan."

Just then, Jake and Megan start laughing, loudly. It feels like they're laughing at me.

I've got to do something to get her attention, to make her look at me instead of Jake.

There's a rock face up ahead, and I decide that's where I'm going to make my stand. I'm going to show Megan what a real man does instead of watching baking shows.

I jog around Jake and the girls and, ignoring the No Climbing sign, I start my ascent, finding holds with my hands and feet, moving swiftly up the wall of rock.

The first voice I hear is my sister's. "Uh, Declan, can't you read? It says no climbing!"

But Parker is cheering me on. "Go for it, Dec! I'm getting this on video!"

"You can do it!" Cody shouts. "But be careful, man!"

"This is excellent content!" Parker calls out. "Keep going!"

I keep climbing. I feel strong, invincible. My muscles flex, and I hope Megan is paying attention.

"Dude, come on! Get down," Jake shouts.

He's probably mad that Megan is watching me instead of him now.

I climb higher and higher, and glance down to make sure she is watching. She is, and I'm so pumped by that that I don't pay enough attention to the next hold, which is too shallow and not secure. It starts crumbling beneath my fingers.

Suddenly, my entire weight is hanging from the fingers of my right hand, straining the muscles and shoulder of my right arm. My shoulder is on fire, but I have to hold on. My fingers scream for mercy, but there is none.

I scrabble for a hold with my left hand, but then it happens: Something in my right shoulder gives, and all I feel is intense pain, pain, pain like I've never felt before. I'm falling . . . falling . . . . I hear screaming . . . and everything goes black.

JAKE

As soon as I see Declan lose his grip, I start sprinting, like I'm going to catch him.

But I don't.

He lands with a sickening thud.

"Declan!" Kayleigh screams.

"Someone call 911!" I shout, and drop to my knees beside him, carefully feeling for the pulse in his neck. "His heart's beating," I reassure Kayleigh.

She clings to me and points. "Oh my god, look at his arm!"

I gaze down and almost puke. Dec landed on hard, rocky ground and his arm is bent in a really disturbing way. There's literally a bone fragment sticking out through the skin. It looks unreal, but it's not.

"We need an ambulance . . . Seward Park . . . He was climbing a rock face and he fell," I hear Cody saying. "No, he's not conscious . . . I think he hit his head. There's some blood under it . . . His arm looks totally messed up . . . Okay, we won't move him . . . Yeah, one of us will meet the ambulance at the trailhead."

"How long?" Kayleigh asks, her face contorted with fear.

"They didn't say, but an ambulance is on the way," Cody says. "I'll run back to meet them. They said not to move him, and if we need to administer CPR, we have to be really careful about tilting his head to open the airway."

"Does anyone know how to do CPR?" Kayleigh asks.

"I'm certified," Megan says. "Did it to be a camp counselor."

"I'll go with Cody," Melodie says.

She and Cody go racing back down the trail to the parking lot.

"Declan, wake up!" Kayleigh begs softly, her hand on his cheek. When she doesn't get a response, she switches to threats. "Listen to me, loser— if you don't wake up, I'm going to punch your lights out!"

Megan puts her hand on Kayleigh's shoulder. "The ambulance will be here soon," she says, then kneels on Declan's other side, carefully looking around his head and ears. I'm not sure what she's looking for. Then she gently runs her hands down his body, avoiding the obviously messed-up arm, checking for other broken bones.

I can't help thinking that Declan would have been so into Megan's hands on him if it had happened for different reasons and he were conscious. But given what his elbow looks like right now, it's probably better that he's not.

"We should call your parents so they can meet us at the hospital," I suggest to Kayleigh.

She nods slowly—probably in shock. It's so different from her normal full-speed-ahead self.

"Do you want me to call them?" I ask.

"No, I can," she says. She pulls her phone out of the outside pocket of her backpack and presses Mom.

I hear it ringing, but it goes to voice mail. Kayleigh grunts. "Mom, Declan fell at Seward Park. The ambulance is on the way. Call me."

She tries her dad. That goes to voice mail, too.

Kayleigh lets out a frustrated scream. "Why are they always at work when we need them? It's like we have to parent ourselves."

"Hey," I say, trying to sound calmer than I feel. "We're all here, and we've got your back."

Kayleigh crouches over Declan, and Megan's regularly checking his pulse, and we're all watching his chest to make sure it's still rising and falling.

It seems like we've been waiting hours before we see Cody and Melodie coming up the trail with the ambulance crew. They've brought a body board, and after putting a collar around Declan's neck, they strap him to it and carry him out.

He comes to, groaning in pain, just as they're loading him in the ambulance.

"Declan!" Kayleigh exclaims. "Thank god you're alive, you idiot!" She starts to climb into the ambulance, but they won't let her.

"Come on! He's my twin brother!" she pleads with them, but the EMT guy says, "I'm sorry, you'll have to follow us to the ER in another vehicle."

She opens her mouth to argue, but Cody puts his hand on her shoulder. "C'mon, Kayleigh. Dec's in pain. Let them go. We'll follow."

"It's because he's in pain they should let me go with him," she says, but Cody guides her to Mario the Minivan, and we take off after the ambulance.

Cody tries to follow as best he can, but the ambulance has lights and sirens, and we don't. By the time we get to the hospital, Declan's already been taken into an ER room.

"Can I go in with him?" Kayleigh asks. "I'm his sister." The nurse at the desk nods, and Kayleigh turns to us. "Keep an eye out for my parents."

An ER nurse takes her back to stay with Declan, while the rest of us take seats in the corner of the waiting room.

"Why would Declan do something so stupid?" I mutter under my breath.

Cody glances over at where Megan is standing a few feet away, on the phone to her mom. "He was showing off for her," he says softly to Melodie and me. "He was pissed because he thought you were flirting with her again."

"What?"

I'm louder than I should be because I'm so surprised that Declan would think that even after our talk at the pool party. People look in my direction, and I lower my voice.

Melodie shakes her head, the beads at the bottom of her braids clicking. "Because we were talking about a baking show? Was I flirting with Jake, too?"

"Look, I'm not saying that he's right," Cody says, holding up his hands. "I'm just saying that before he did it, he was complaining about that."

"But I wasn't flirting with her!" I protest.

"I know that," Cody says. "I told him that you were acting the same way toward Megan as you were toward Melodie and Kayleigh, but . . ."

Melodie rolls her eyes. "Did he really think that showing off like that was going to make Megan like him better?"

I put my head in my hands. "Did you see the bone sticking out? That's his pitching arm. And he did that because . . . he thought I was flirting with Megan?"

"Ugh—why, Declan?" Melodie says, shaking her head.

Just then, Mrs. Taylor bursts in through the doors. She's so intent on getting to the desk that she doesn't see us in the corner.

"My son, Declan Taylor, was brought here," she says. "Please—is he okay?"

"I'll take you back," the nurse says. She buzzes Mrs. Taylor into the medical area.

We sit there for a long time, long enough for Megan and Melodie to have to leave and for Kayleigh to finally come out, her face grim.

"Any news?" I ask.

"Well . . . the good news is that they haven't found any damage to his spinal column. Although he might have a concussion."

"And the bad news?" Cody asks.

"His arm is a mess. It's going to be a long wait. He's being prepped for surgery," she says with a wobble in her voice. "They're going to have to try to rebuild his elbow with pins or screws or something. The surgery today is to clean everything out, and then they have to do another one in a few days to close it all up."

"That's not good," Cody says.

"You guys should probably go home," Kayleigh tells us.

"Are you sure you don't want us to stay?" I ask.

"I . . . I . . ." She looks at us helplessly, so unlike her normal self. "What if he can't play baseball?" Kayleigh whispers, like she's afraid to even voice it in case it comes true.

I've been worrying about the exact same thing. Declan lives, eats, and breathes baseball. Like basically he's all about baseball, video games, and being into Megan Moran.

"There's nothing we can do now except wait," Cody says.

"And pray," I say. "I have to go to synagogue tonight for Shabbat services, so I'll . . . you know."

"And I'll say a prayer to Saint Raphael," Cody says. "He's the patron saint of healing—or so my grandma tells me. She set up a shrine to the dude when my grandpa had cancer."

"Thanks," Kayleigh says, her eyes glistening. I bend down and grab some tissues from one of the many boxes that are strategically placed around the room to mop up all the tears. It freaks me out that there are so many of them. It's a sign that nothing good ever happens here.

"I mean it," she continues, wiping her eyes. "You guys should go. My dad's supposed to be here any minute."

I'm wondering why he didn't get here sooner. Kayleigh called him when we were waiting for the ambulance, which seems like a century ago.

"He's so freaked out about the possibility of losing his job in the stupid reorganization at work that he felt like he couldn't ask to leave early, even though his kid is in the ER," Kayleigh says, like she read my mind. "How messed up is that?"

"Very," Cody says.

She's talking about the reorganization that Arielle's dad is in charge of.

"But . . . you met Arielle's dad at the party. Do people at Pinnacle really think he's so awful that he wouldn't let someone leave early to go to the ER to see their injured kid?" I say.

"Jake, you know what it's like around here. If my dad loses his job . . ." She shudders, shaking her head. "I can't think about that right now."

The doors to the waiting room open, and Mr. Taylor walks in as if summoned. His hair is sticking up like he's been running his hand through it.

"Dad!" Kayleigh exclaims, running toward him and practically knocking him over with the force of her hug.

"Any news?" Mr. Taylor asks.

Kayleigh pulls away and shakes her head. "Not since I last texted you."

She turns to Cody and me and gives us a watery smile. "Thanks for being here."

"Keep us posted, okay?" I say.

"I will," Kayleigh says. "As soon as there's anything to tell."

My heart is heavy as Cody and I walk out to the parking lot. Declan has to be okay. I can't imagine Declan without baseball—or me playing baseball without Dec.

DECLAN

I hear people talking in low voices. Am I still in that nightmare I was having about falling? I make out a few words. *Fracture . . . baseball . . .*

There's a soft beeping noise, steady like a heartbeat. It starts to beep faster, like it's an alarm, telling me it's time to wake up.

But my eyelids are weighted; I have to make a superhuman effort to raise them. There's a flash of light and then they close again.

"Mom! Dad!" I hear Kayleigh say. "Look! Dec's waking up!"

"Declan? Honey?" Mom's voice is soft and trembly.

"We're here," Dad says, his voice rough with emotion.

Okay, here we go. Engage eyelids . . . and . . . liftoff . . .

The sudden influx of light blinds me. Gradually, I'm able to focus on the faces around me. My mom, dark smudges under her eyes, smiling bravely. Dad, biting his lip. Kayleigh, her hair sticking out of her ponytail, looking like she's played a full match with no time-outs.

It makes me dizzy to turn my head, but I do, and the sight that greets me makes me wish I were still unconscious. My arm's in a splint, and there's a bandage with these bead things over what looks like an open wound. Seeing it wakes up the pain receptors in my brain. My arm hurts. It's my pitching arm.

My head feels like someone hit me with a baseball bat, and I'm sick to my stomach.

"What . . . happened?"

"For reasons that have yet to be explained, you started climbing the rock face that had a big No Climbing sign," Kayleigh says, her voice laced with anger. "You fell."

Dad puts a warning hand on my sister's shoulder.

"My arm . . ."

"You landed on it," Mom says. "There's serious damage to your elbow. Multiple fractures."

"Your bone was sticking out of your skin, Dec," Kayleigh says, looking like she's going to either cry or pass out just from thinking about it.

I close my eyes, not wanting to remember.

"Hurts," I breathe out.

"I'll go get the nurse," Mom says.

"I'll do it," Kayleigh says. "I need to get out of this room."

I manage to drag my lids open again once she's gone. "How long?"

"How long what?" Mom asks.

"Before I can play?"

My parents glance at each other.

"It's going to be a long recovery, Declan," Dad says. "You're not playing any baseball this summer, for sure."

"You have to have another surgery the day after tomorrow to close things up," Mom says.

I feel like I'm going to barf, but only a choked sound emerges from my mouth. My throat is raw and hot, like I've been screaming.

Maybe I have. I feel like doing it now.

"Try taking a few sips," Mom says, holding a straw to my lips. "Just little ones so you don't vomit."

Kayleigh comes back with a nurse in dog-print scrubs. "Hi, Declan, I'm Rania, your overnight nurse. Can you point to your level of pain?"

She shows me a chart with all these smiley and frowny faces, and asks me to rate my pain from one to ten. I point to the frowny face of number nine.

"Okay, let me give you something that should make you more comfortable," she says.

I close my eyes while she does whatever it is, then slowly drift back into the comforting fog of oblivion.

When I wake up, I'm alone in the room and bursting to pee, but there's a drip attached to my left hand.

How do I get a nurse? "Hello?" I call out, my voice croaky. No one comes. "HELLO?" I try again, louder. That's when I notice there's a thing that looks like a remote control positioned close to my left hand, and it's got a red button labeled *Call Nurse*. I push it and wait, hoping that I can hold it, but I'm starting to sweat from the fear of pissing myself. I still remember the one time it happened in nursery school and how everyone called me Pee-Pee Head until Kayleigh stepped into the sandbox and stood next to me, and together we threatened to hit the next kid who said it.

Finally, a different nurse from the one last night comes in. "Hi, Declan, I'm Sabrina. What's going on?"

"I have to pee," I say.

"Do you want a bottle or to try walking to the bathroom?" she asks.

"Walk," I tell her, a decision I regret as soon as she starts helping me to sit up. Everything hurts. My head spins.

"Easy does it," she says. "Rest if you need to. I'll move the IV for you." She sees my face. "I can still get you a bottle or a bedpan."

"No, I'll get up." If I can't even walk, there's no way I'll be able to play baseball. But after taking the few steps to the bathroom, I feel like I went twelve rounds in a prize fight and lost.

Then I catch sight of myself in the mirror and gasp. Half my hair has been hacked off, and there are stitches on the side of my head. Well, at least no one is going to call me Goldilocks anymore. I look more like Frankenstein's monster.

"What happened to my hair?"

"They had to shave off the area around the wound so they could put the stitches in," Nurse Sabrina says. "You did quite a number on yourself."

She positions me in front of the toilet and starts to lift my hospital gown. "Whoa," I say, trying to hold it down with my left hand.

"I'm not looking," she says. "I'm just going to tuck up your gown between your torso and your arm."

Reluctantly, I release the gown, and averting her gaze, she does just that, then points out the call button in case I need her.

As soon as she steps out of the room, it's an instant waterfall, and I exhale a sigh of relief. But it's quickly followed by anxiety. How am I going to do this at home? Who is going to help me? There's no way I'm gonna let Mom or Kayleigh do it, and Dad's hardly ever around.

And how long do I have to wear the splint and sling? When can I play baseball again? I had my whole summer mapped out, and now there are just endless questions circling my woozy brain.

Sabrina helps me back into bed, then takes my vitals. "Anything else I can get you?"

Answers. That's what I need.

"How long do I have to wear this thing on my arm? When can I play baseball again?"

"Dr. Molina will be making rounds this morning, and you can ask him all those questions," she says, giving me a pitying look that feels like she's saying the answer is never.

In that moment, I hate her. I turn my face away from the pity, because I cannot, will not, believe what her sorrowful gaze is telling me.

If it's true, my life is over.

Mom shows up an hour later, while I'm sitting around miserable and uncomfortable, half watching cartoons.

I'm glad to see her until she starts fussing over me. "Are you comfortable? Have you had breakfast? Do you need me to get the nurse? Has the doctor been by yet?"

"Mom, stop!" I snap.

A shocked, hurt expression crosses her face, but then she swallows and says, "Sorry."

She slumps into the seat next to the bed. "I can only stay until ten. I was booked to do hair for a wedding today, and I can't cancel. But Kayleigh promised to come visit when she gets off work. And Dad will be here tonight. He took on an extra shift this morning to make up the hours he missed yesterday."

"Okay, okay, I know it's all my fault," I say. "I'm the world's biggest screwup."

"No, Declan—"

"You and Dad must be happy you won't have to spend money on travel baseball this summer," I say. "One less expense to worry about." I know I'm taking my frustration out on her, but I can't seem to stop.

"Declan, we would have managed, somehow," Mom says. "We know how important baseball is to you."

That's not what they said when I first brought up playing travel this summer. Back then all they seemed to care about was how much it cost.

"What if I can't ever play baseball again?"

"Let's take one day at a time," Mom says, stroking my hair back from my brow. "Dr. Molina said that the first surgery went well, but they'll know more after tomorrow's surgery. Right now, you need to rest and focus on healing."

Just then the nurse brings in my breakfast—not that I'm hungry. It gives Mom something else to fuss about.

"You have to eat to keep up your strength," she says.

I force myself to eat some lukewarm scrambled eggs and a rubbery pancake. It's hard because I'm used to holding my fork in my right hand, and that arm is immobilized.

I finally throw down my fork in disgust.

"Are you in pain? Do you want me to feed you?" Mom asks.

"I'm not a baby!" I snap. "I'm just not hungry, okay?"

She gives me a reproachful look. "I'm only trying to help, Declan."

"Sorry, Mom," I mumble, feeling terrible. "It's just . . ." I trail off, not knowing how to explain.

"I know," she says. "We'll get through this, Dec."

I wish I could be so sure—especially when Dr. Molina comes in for the morning rounds. The surgeon who happens to be Mateo's dad.

Mateo, the other relief pitcher on the team.

"Good morning, Declan," Dr. Molina says. You can see the resemblance to Mateo; they're both tall and muscular, with thick dark hair and light brown eyes and skin. "This definitely isn't the place I wanted to see you after that amazing job you did at state."

"It's definitely not the place I want to be, either," I tell him. "No offense."

He gives a small smile and says, "You're lucky. If you'd landed differently, you could have been paralyzed."

34

"But I'll be able to pitch again, won't I?"

I catch the worried glance Mom shoots Dr. Molina and wonder what they're hiding from me.

"I can't make you any promises, Declan. But the first surgery went well. We cleaned out the wound and tried to fix the damage with plates and screws. Tomorrow we'll close things up. Let's see how things go, okay? Recovery will take time."

He's avoiding my question, but at least it's not a hard no. Still. I'm stuck in a long, dark tunnel right now, and it's hard to see any light at the end of it.

JAKE

Kayleigh calls me the following week to tell me that Declan's finally home from the hospital after his two surgeries.

"How's he doing?" I ask.

"He's in a lot of pain," she tells me. "And one hundred percent miserable. Honestly? Leaving and dealing with obnoxious customers at Burger Barn is a vacation. Especially now that Arielle's working there, too."

"Yeah, she texted me to tell me she got the job," I say. "So . . . is Dec up for visitors?"

"That would be awesome," Kayleigh says. "My parents and I have been trying to schedule our shifts so that someone is home with him, but it's not always doable." She sighs. "And none of us can afford to give up any hours because the medical bills are pouring in. My parents are so stressed about them, and that's with health insurance. I can't even imagine what it would be like if we didn't have it."

I've never thought much about health insurance. I mean, yeah, I've heard my parents complaining about how it costs crazy money because they both have their own businesses, but I didn't realize you have to pay so much even when you've got it.

"That sucks," I say. "I'll see if I can round up a bunch of guys from the baseball team and stop by."

"Um . . . maybe not too many people right away," Kayleigh says. "He's . . . not in a good place."

I wait for her to explain more, but she doesn't.

"It's not surprising," I say. "He's got to be in a lot of pain still, and then having to miss travel baseball this summer—I'd be miserable, too."

"I know, but . . . it's like he wants to push everyone away." There's a beat of silence. "Even me."

That surprises me, knowing how tight Declan and Kayleigh are.

"I'll be over tomorrow," I promise her. "Baseball camp doesn't start till next week, so I've got time to hang out."

When the call ends, I'm left wondering just how bad things are at the Taylor house.

The next morning, I ride over to see Declan. I pull my bike up to the garage and slip in through the kitchen door, like I've done so many times before. I can hear Declan upstairs shouting something about watching out for land mines. I grab a glass out of the cabinet, fill it with cold water, then take the stairs up to his room.

"Nooooooo! Kill him!" Declan is saying as I walk into his room. Someone's moved his gaming console so he can play propped up on the pillows in bed, with more pillows under his arm, which is in a sling.

"Hey, it's good to see you," I say, trying to hide how shocked I am by how different he looks. Goldilocks is gone. One side of his head is shaved, and the other side's been trimmed short. He's wearing a pair of loose shorts and no shirt, and there's a distinct odor of unwashed guy.

Dec looks up briefly to acknowledge my presence, then focuses back on whatever it is he's playing.

I get it. I hate being interrupted when I'm in the middle of a game, especially if I'm playing with other people. Even so, Declan keeps playing for longer than I consider cool.

To keep myself busy, I walk around the room, looking at all the reminders of how long we've been friends: the trophy we won playing T-ball and a picture of our littler selves looking so proud in our Stafford's Corner Cheetahs T-shirts. Those had *Sponsored by Pinnacle Metalworks* on the back. I wonder if Pinnacle is going to keep sponsoring stuff like T-ball after the "restructuring" Arielle's dad is implementing. I hope so. Pinnacle hasn't just employed a lot of people around here; they've been a big part of the local community.

There's another trophy from middle school, when we won the regional championship. Next to it is a picture of Dec and me grinning from ear to ear; we've each got one of our arms around the other's neck and our outside arms flexed to show how mighty we felt.

Finally, Declan says, "Hey, I gotta go. Yeah. Thanks."

He rips off his headset with his good arm and says, "Sorry. Was in an intense battle in *Force and Fortune*." Looking down at his sling, he mutters, "Not that I'm much good at gaming with this thing on." I flop down on the end of his bed as he adds, "Not that I'm much good at anything right now. I keep getting this tingling feeling in my fingers, and sometimes they don't work right." He grimaces. "I'm useless at baseball *and* gaming."

Wow, Kayleigh was right. There's a major black cloud vibe going on here.

"C'mon, Dec, give yourself a break," I say. "Healing from injuries like you had is gonna take a while."

"Yeah, yeah, I know. And I'm lucky and I should be grateful—blah, blah, blah," Declan grumbles. "I get that from my parents and Kayleigh every fricking day."

The image of Declan lying on the ground, bone sticking through his skin, blood under his head flashes through my brain like a scene from a horror movie.

"Dec . . . I've got to tell you . . . seeing you lying there . . ." I feel a lump rise in my throat and swallow it down, telling myself to pull it together because me losing it isn't going to help. "I was afraid you'd . . . you know . . . died."

"Maybe it would have been better if I had," Declan says, picking at a thread on his comforter.

Whoa. How am I supposed to respond to that? Is he serious? Should I be worried? Do I need to tell someone?

"Dec, I know you're feeling like crap now, but you don't really mean that, do you?" I ask, choosing my words carefully. "My life definitely wouldn't be better if you died, man. Like . . . maybe you should talk to someone if you feel that bad."

He groans. "Not you, too!" He looks me in the eye. "I'm talking to you, aren't I?" The corner of his mouth turns up in the shadow of a grin. "Aren't you someone?"

"Heck yeah, I'm someone," I say, figuring if he's trying to joke, I should, too. "And not just anyone, either."

The shadow grin turns into a fully realized one. It feels like a victory. A small one, but I'll take it.

"So . . . a bunch of guys from the team are going to the July Fourth fireworks on the town green," I say. "You should come. You're gonna come, right?"

I see Declan start to shake his head no. "Dude," I say, "it'll be good for you to get out. Cody can come pick you up. I'll take care of all the snacks. You won't have to do anything except show up."

"Nah, I'm good," Declan says.

"Come on, Dec, we always go to the fireworks together," I remind him, but he gives his head another quick shake.

"You know what's gonna happen if I go?" he asks me. "Everyone's going to see this"—he gestures angrily to the sling on his arm—"and they're going to ask what happened, and that's the last thing in the world I want to talk about right now, okay?"

I hear what he's saying, but still . . . it's got to be better than being alone, feeling sorry for himself, while everyone else is out having fun. I try to think of what might convince him to come, to get out of his room and his misery and let me and the rest of the team cheer him up.

"I bet you anything Megan will be there," I say, thinking that might give him incentive.

Wrong.

His face clouds over. "Megan's the reason I'm in this mess," he says. "If I hadn't been so busy trying to impress her, I'd be starting camp and travel baseball with you next week instead of going to physical therapy."

Suddenly, everything is awkward, and I can't help wondering if he blames me for his accident, too. After all, I was talking to Megan when he started climbing the rock face. Not that there's anything wrong with talking to her, but Dec was pissed about it at the pool party. I thought we were cool, but now I'm not sure.

"Okay, so other girls will be there," I say, desperately reaching for something to change his mind.

"Jake, enough already! Just STOP!" Declan explodes suddenly. "Stop trying to pretend that everything is the same for me!"

"I'm not. I just—"

"C'mon, Jake! What girl is going to want to be with a guy with a busted arm?"

It's like there's no arguing with him. He's made up his mind, and that's that. I raise my hands in surrender. "Okay, okay, fine! I won't say another word about it."

"Good," he says. "Now pick up a controller and let's play so I don't have to think about reality. That's what's going to make me feel better right now."

I grab a controller, and we play *Force and Fortune* for a few hours. It's been a while since we've spent an afternoon goofing off and playing video games. It's kind of a blast to just hang with my best friend like this, and Dec does seem a little brighter by the time I have to leave.

"Thanks for coming by," Declan says. "I'm spending a lot of time by myself these days." Then he shrugs and starts fidgeting with the controller, like he can't wait to get back to the game instead of talking to me.

It hurts, but I guess I can't blame him. If I were worried about not being able to play baseball again, I'd be heavy into whatever would help me forget, too.

"I'll try to stop by as much as I can," I promise him.

He just grunts, and before I'm even out of his bedroom, Declan's back in the game. I close the door behind me, leaving him to escape reality the best he can.

JAKE

I hitch a ride to the fireworks with my parents and Ben, but there's no way
I'm going to sit with them. Tonight's for hanging with friends. "See you
later," I say, grabbing my lawn chair and snacks.

"Have fun!" Mom says. "Meet us here when it's over."

When I find Cody, Jeff, Parker, and Mateo, they've nabbed a good
spot on the green, far enough away from the gazebo so we won't be
blasted with the marching band tunes from the sound system but still
with a good view. Kayleigh and a bunch of the girls from the soccer team
are nearby—with Arielle, I notice, happy that she and Kayleigh seem to
have hit it off.

As soon as I've set up my chair, I head over to say hi.

"May the Fourth be with you," I say.

Kayleigh shakes her head. "Come on, Jake! You're geek enough to
know that doesn't work in July."

"I was just testing that you're geek enough to tell me that," I say with
a grin.

"Sure you were," Kayleigh says, exchanging a glance with Arielle, who
is looking super cute in an American flag T-shirt.

"Dec didn't change his mind about coming?" I ask Kayleigh. "I
tried . . ."

Her smile fades. "No. He was being his usual stubborn self, and then
Mom felt like she had to stay home, which meant Dad did, too, and they
ended up fighting with Dec and each other about it."

"Ugh," I say. "Bet you're glad to be here, then, huh?"

"Oh yeah!" Kayleigh exclaims. "But it sucks for them, because it's not like Dec's going to do anything but sit in his room gaming anyway."

"How's his arm?" I ask. "When I was over there on Saturday, he said he was getting these weird tingles in his fingers."

"That's one of the reasons Mom wanted to stay home," Kayleigh says. "He's been having problems with his wrist, too. Like it kind of droops and then he can't raise it."

"Wow. That doesn't sound good," I say. "Especially for baseball."

"I know," Kayleigh says. "Though right now, Dec's pissed about how it's limiting his gaming."

"Can they fix it?" I ask.

Kayleigh shrugs. "Who knows. But Mom says Dr. Molina sounded concerned. Like that it might complicate Dec's chance of making a full recovery. He's definitely going to need a ton of PT."

"That sucks," I say.

"Yeah," Kayleigh says, frowning. Then she shakes her head. "Okay, enough about my pain-in-the-butt brother. I'm out of the house, and I'm determined to have fun, even if the rest of my family isn't."

"And I'm going to help you," Arielle says. She takes a plastic container out of her bag and opens the lid, revealing some really amazing-looking bars drizzled with chocolate. "Try one of these. It's an *Eat, Bake, Love* recipe."

"Comfort food for the win!" Kayleigh says, taking one.

"You had me at *Eat*," I tell Arielle, grabbing one for myself. I take a bite, and it feels like my eyes roll back in my head from ecstasy. "This brownie slaps."

Her answering smile is as great as the brownie. Better, even.

I catch Cody waving at me from the corner of my eye. "I'm being summoned," I tell them. "See you later."

Weaving my way back to my chair while avoiding people's picnic blankets, I see Ben sitting with some of his friends from high school a little farther back, and off to the side my parents sitting with friends from the synagogue.

I think Dec and his parents must be the only people in Stafford's Corner who aren't here. I feel a pang, thinking back to how many fireworks displays we've been to together. I wish he'd come.

"You did good getting such a forward spot," I tell the guys as I drop to my seat.

"Thanks," Cody says. "So . . . how's the new girl? What's her name again?"

"Arielle," I remind him.

"I saw you over there making googly eyes at her," Cody says.

"Googly eyes? My eyes do not google," I say. "They observe."

"Okay, so we saw you observing the new girl," Parker says, grinning. "She is quite . . . observable."

Why does that make me clench my teeth?

"Give it a rest," I tell them. "I was being friendly. She just moved here, and she doesn't know a lot of people."

Parker and Cody exchange a glance and start cracking up.

"What? What's so funny?" I ask, starting to get annoyed.

"'I was being friendly,'" Cody says, in what must be the worst imitation of me I've ever heard.

I ignore them and turn to talk to Jeff and Mateo. I *was* just being friendly. Okay, I noticed she was cute, but that doesn't mean anything. Kayleigh's cute, too, but they don't think I have a crush on her.

The sun sets behind the horizon, and when the sky deepens to an inky blue, the lights on the field dim, patriotic music starts blasting from the loudspeakers, and the fireworks begin: loud bangs, followed by colorful bursts of bright light that fizzle into nothingness until the next one comes. It's July Fourth and I'm hanging with my friends, exactly as it should be— except that Dec isn't here with us.

When I get back to the car after the show, my parents are standing with their friends and Ben. None of them look like they enjoyed the fireworks very much.

"What's going on?" I ask.

"Someone left these on all the cars while we were watching the fireworks," Ben says, handing me a piece of paper. It's got some symbols I don't recognize and says *Globalists will not destroy us or replace us! Save our civilization and heritage!*

I look around and see that they are stuck under the wipers of most of the parked cars.

"What does this even mean?" I ask, feeling uneasy, although I'm not sure why. "Who are these globalists they say are going to destroy our civilization and heritage?"

The adults exchange glances, and I feel like I'm missing something they all know.

"They mean us," Dad says finally.

"What do you mean 'us'?" I ask, confused.

"Us," says Mrs. Greenberg from our synagogue. "Jewish people."

It's like a gut punch. "Are you serious?"

"I wish I weren't," Mrs. Greenberg says. "This is straight out of a conspiracy theory concocted in Russia during the early 1900s called *The Protocols of the Elders of Zion*. It's one of the most widely circulated antisemitic conspiracy theories of modern times. Hitler and Stalin both used it in their propaganda."

Great. People hating on us from both sides. "What did this protocols conspiracy say, exactly?"

"They were allegedly the secret minutes of a group of Jews who were plotting to take over the world by manipulating the economy and controlling the media," Dad says. "But they've been proved to be fake, more than once, by historians and in different courts of law."

"And yet people all around the world are still spreading it to incite hatred," Mr. Greenberg says grimly. "Extremist groups have been pushing it online—and offline, too." He rips the flyer in half.

"But . . . it doesn't say Jews," I say, still feeling like I'm missing something.

"Exactly," Dad says. "They know it would make a lot of people uncomfortable to come out and say they hate Jews."

"That's why when they're recruiting, they use code words like *globalist* or they make a well-known Jewish figure like George Soros or members of the Rothschild family into the bogeyman," Ben says. "Someone put up flyers about that at my college."

"That is beyond messed up," I say, getting a queasy feeling when I realize there are people around here who hate us enough to put these nasty flyers on all the car windshields while we're celebrating the Fourth of July.

"I know, right?" Ben says. "Way to ruin a fun evening."

"If we let them ruin our evening, then they win," Mom says, crumpling up the flyer and squaring her shoulders. "I say we go home and have some ice cream."

But even my favorite ice cream won't take the bad taste of this out of my mouth.

DECLAN

Another day alone at home, feeling like trash, knowing that my friends are all starting travel baseball training tonight . . . and I'm not. I'm glad I didn't go to the Fourth of July celebrations last night. It would have been too hard to listen to the guys talking about baseball when I'm not even sure if I'll be able to pitch again.

Every morning when I wake up, I think I can't possibly feel worse than I did the day before. And yet . . . I do.

I'm getting my stitches out next Monday and starting PT on Tuesday, which will add a new layer of torture to my life given how much my arm already hurts, not to mention this whole wrist drop thing.

Still, I've got to do what it takes so I can pitch again.

Even gaming is hard, because I can't move my right thumb fast enough, but I still spend every moment I can playing. It helps take my mind off everything. But that's a sore point between my parents and me. When Dad left for work this morning, he stood in the doorway while I was lying in bed trying to drift back into the comfort of unconsciousness.

"I don't want to come home and find out you spent the whole day in your room gaming, Declan," he said. "Go outside. Take a walk. Your legs are still in working order. It'll do you good."

Mom wasn't a whole lot more sympathetic. "I'm working late because I've got a trial bridal appointment for a wedding next month. I ran the dishwasher, so please unload it when it's done."

I started to protest, but she cut me off. "Everyone has to pitch in right now, Declan. Including you. And you've got one good arm that can unload a dishwasher, so do it."

At least Kayleigh just said, "Later, Dec. Try not to injure anything else while I'm slinging burgers."

I threw sweaty socks at her and pulled the pillow over my head, hoping to get back to sleep once everyone was finally gone, but no such luck. My brain keeps going around in the same vortex of what-ifs: What if I can't get back to what I was? What if I can't play baseball competitively again? What if I can't afford to go to college? What if I end up like my dad, working at a place my entire life and then having to live in fear that I'm going to get laid off when I'm older?

I finally give up trying to sleep and fire up *Force and Fortune*, pulling on my headset. I'm glad to see some names I recognize—it makes me feel less alone.

"Yo, FastBaller49 in the house!" FenrirLupus says.

FenrirLupus always seems to be online. I wonder if his dad ever gets on his case, telling him to stop gaming and go take a walk.

"I'm always in the house since the accident, much to the disgust of the parentals," I tell him.

"Accident? What kind of accident? You okay?"

"Climbing accident. I fell and messed up my pitching arm. Bone sticking out and everything," I tell him.

"Dude . . ." he says.

In the chat he posts a meme of a skeleton that says *Life sucks. Might as well play some sick games, listen to dope music, and make the best of it.*

FenrirLupus is majorly into memes. Like I think he'd be happiest if he could communicate using them instead of using actual words.

He posts another meme of a cat hanging from a branch that says *Hang in there.*

But then he asks me to tell him what happened, so I tell him how it went down.

He posts a meme of some sculpture of a naked guy thinking—*If all men are the same, it stands to reason that women must be the problem*—and another one of a disgruntled-looking guy with *Don't try to understand women. Women understand women and they hate each other.*

FenrirLupus doesn't seem to like women a whole lot. But his memes make me laugh.

At the same time, they prick a hurt place I don't want to admit is there.

Megan sent me one stupid text asking me if I was okay—duh, Megan, of course I'm not fricking okay—and she hasn't come to visit, either. Mom and Kayleigh are more sympathetic than Dad, but they're still basically telling me to get off my butt and do stuff to help around the house. You'd think being female, they'd be more, you know, nurturing.

"I'm sorry you gotta deal with this crap," FenrirLupus says after his meme drop. "I'm gonna DM you a link to a hot new game to take your mind off things. I only share this with the coolest dudes."

It's good to know someone still thinks I'm cool.

"See you there. Same screen name," he says.

"I'll have to change mine," I say. "Since I can't throw a fricking fastball now."

"Sucks, man. Let me know the new screen name, okay?"

I tell him I will, and we continue playing.

I think these are the most words FenrirLupus has ever said to me. It's like he's actually being a person instead of the meme lord of all he surveys.

My stomach waits till about eleven thirty before rumbling—or at least that's when I finally become aware that I'm starving, because I've been so wrapped up in the game. I have a bowl of cereal in front of the TV. I skip around trying to find something that's not news or women on a couch arguing or some PBS kids' show for five-year-olds. Too bad it's not Saturday morning cartoons. Too bad we don't have anything but basic cable anymore, because my parents have been so worried about money lately that they've cut back on "everything but the essentials."

I think they wish they could cut back on me. I keep overhearing them talking in low, anxious voices, doing addition and subtraction, trying to figure out how and where they can find money to pay off the bills from my ER visit, and now for my PT.

I thought the whole point of having health insurance was that you didn't have to worry about the bills if stuff happened. But seeing how stressed my parents are, seems like I was wrong about that.

When I'm done with my cereal, I click off the TV in frustration. Nothing to watch. Nothing to do. No one to talk to. Just me, my useless arm, and my thoughts in an empty house.

I go to put the bowl in the dishwasher, but it's clean. I remember Mom told me to empty it, but I can't face doing it right now. It's bad enough having to unload the dishwasher with two hands. She won't be home for hours. I'll do it later.

The quiet surrounding me is dangerous; in the silence, my mind starts getting lost in a maze of negative futures. I'd much rather be lost in a game than in that mess. I leave the bowl and spoon in the sink and head upstairs to check out the link FenrirLupus sent.

Turns out, it's for a private server for a different MMORPG game called *Imperialist Empires*, one that I've never played before. It's all about the Crusades. I pick an avatar that's tall, with the muscles of a superhero, who wields a massive sword and has a wicked-looking mace dangling from his belt.

Best of all, he's whole. Uninjured. Strong. Everything that I'm not right now.

I google famous fighters from the Crusades and decide to name myself after Richard the Lionheart, but of course that's already taken, as are a bunch of other versions of it. I finally get Lionheartttt, and then I'm in.

Almost immediately, someone named OdalRune88 says, "Hey, looks like we've got a new brother in arms. Welcome, Lionheartttt. Where'd you get the link?"

"FenrirLupus dropped it in the chat when we were playing *Force and Fortune*," I say.

"Excellent! FenrirLupus is a good soldier. Look around and explore," OdalRune88 says. "Then join us to attack the infidel hordes. We have Damascus under siege."

"Cool! Will do," I tell him.

The graphics in *Imperialist Empires* aren't as slick as the ones in *Force and Fortune*, but it doesn't bother me too much because it kind of lends to the historical vibe of the game. I haven't really learned that much about the Crusades—we do that sophomore year in world history. I hope I get Mr. Morrison again. I had him for social studies last year, and he was cool. He made stuff interesting and seemed to care what we thought about things. He's also into baseball—he helps out Coach K with the school team and coaches travel ball over the summer.

Travel baseball that I can't do anymore.

I push that thought away and focus on the new game. There's lots of cool weaponry like scimitars and broadswords and maces and stuff.

People are using what I thought were catapults, but I quickly learn are something different called trebuchets, to throw huge boulders at the walls of Damascus. OdalRune88 asks me if I have any questions and sends me links to different videos about the various weapons and the history of the Crusades in the chat.

I watch them when I take a break for lunch, and can't wait to get back to the game.

I'm so absorbed with learning all this stuff and playing something new that I have no idea what time it is until suddenly my room smells like fried food. I glance up and Kayleigh stands in the doorway in her ugly Burger Barn uniform.

I ignore her, hoping she'll go away and let me stay in Crusader world. No such luck.

She comes over and pulls the headset away from my ear. "How are you doing?" she asks.

"I'm fine," I say, pausing the game. "Just playing."

"What's that game?" she asks.

"It's called *Imperialist Empires*," I say. "And in case you didn't notice, I'm trying to play it."

"Well, okay, then," she says, laying on the snark. "Just trying to show you some, you know, love and concern. But since you don't seem to need it, I'll go remove the hideous uniform of my corporate overlord and shower off the stink of fried food."

"Good," I say. "Because now my entire room smells like fries, and I note that you weren't concerned enough to bring some home for your wounded brother."

Kayleigh laughs and walks to the door. "Sorry, Drama King. I'll bring you home some fries tomorrow."

As much as I'm into playing, there is something I've been thinking about doing since I got out of the hospital—one of the many things that it's impossible to do with one hand.

"Wait!" I call as she's walking out my door. "Can you help me with something?"

She turns back to me. "Like what?"

"Can you shave off the rest of my hair?"

She gives me a quizzical look. "Uh . . . you realize that Mom actually cuts hair for a living, right?"

"Duh," I say. "She already trimmed the non-shaved parts. But I still look ridiculous, and you know Mom'll try to talk me out of going full bald."

"True, but . . ." She exhales. "It's just that you've always been so vain about your hair. It seems kind of drastic."

"Vain? Wow, thanks a lot," I say. The anger that never seems far from the surface these days takes over. "Get out and leave me to my game, okay?" I pick up my controller.

Kayleigh's still there, leaning against the doorjamb. "Fine, I'll do it," she says. "But this isn't a satisfaction-guaranteed deal, okay? If you hate it, that's on you."

"It can't be any worse than this."

She nods, then goes to get one of Mom's old hair clippers from downstairs before meeting me in the bathroom. When everything is set up, she waggles her eyebrows and grins. "Are you sure you're willing to trust me with these? Last chance to change your mind."

"Go for it."

She does, avoiding the area around my stitches, which is easy because that's already shaved.

"What made you decide to do this?" Kayleigh asks as a hunk of hair falls into my lap.

"I don't know. I guess since, like, part of my head is already shaved, I might as well do the rest of it."

Kayleigh shrugs and continues clipping. "Mom's gonna freak and you know it."

"Yeah. But it's my head." I know I shouldn't say this, but I've heard my friends joking about it online, and I can't resist the opportunity to rile up my sister. "You know, 'my body, my choice.'"

She takes a step away from me and frowns. "You did not."

Her reaction is so predictable, and it's weirdly satisfying to be able to provoke her like this, like making her mad helps me feel less so. "What?" I say, playing dumb. "It's what you say. Women need the right to control their own bodies . . . so why not men?"

I want it to go on, to see her get super riled, but she just shakes her head, mutters "How can I be related to such an idiot?" and finishes shaving my head. I feel . . . cheated.

When she's done, she carefully folds up the towel; then she takes a step back and looks at me. "It makes your eyes look bigger and bluer. But personally, I think you look better as Goldilocks."

Hearing my team nickname feels like she pushed a blade through my heart.

"I'll grow it back when I can play baseball again," I say, even though I haven't had the courage to look at myself yet.

She sighs, drops the folded towel on the counter, and says, "Get rid of that." As she leaves, I take a deep breath and then brave the mirror.

Rubbing my hand over my hairless scalp, I wonder if it was the right decision. The Declan in the mirror is different. Harder. It suits my mood.

I take a selfie and post it, captioning it *new look*.

Then I go to my room and check in to *Imperialist Empires*.

"Welcome back, Lionheartttt," OdalRune88 says. "Where'd you disappear to?"

"I just had my sister shave my head," I say.

"No way!" OdalRune88 says. "Share a pic."

I drop the selfie in the chat.

"Niiiiiice," OdalRune88 says. "You look very Aryan—you'd be a hit in the Lebensborn program."

I have to look up what that is, and when I do, I'm not sure if it's a compliment or an insult. He's basically telling me I look like a perfect Nazi.

Before I can figure out how to respond, Kayleigh shouts from downstairs. "Hey, Baldilocks! You better empty the dishwasher before Mom comes home, or you're going to lose the other arm!"

"Got to go," I tell OdalRune88.

"See you soon, my brother," he says.

Then I grab the towel from the bathroom and head down to empty the dishwasher, because Kayleigh's right: Mom's going to freak out enough about my hair. If she comes home and sees that I not only didn't empty the dishwasher but also left my dishes in the sink, I'm toast.

JAKE

There's a heat haze over the baseball diamond at the high school when Mom drops me off for the first travel team practice. Summer didn't slide into home gently—it hit us with high temperatures and humidity.

"Make sure you stay hydrated," Mom says.

"I know, I know," I say, holding up my two water bottles: one with ice water and one with Gatorade. I'm already sweating as I turn and walk over to my teammates.

It's weird to be here without Declan. His absence feels concrete.

Our social studies teacher from last year, Mr. Morrison, coaches the travel team. He was a star baseball player at our high school, back in the day. He got a scholarship to some fancy college but was in a bad car accident his junior year, and that was the end of that. Now he's stuck teaching us instead of being in the pros like everyone thought he'd be. Still, everyone fights to get into Mr. M's class, because he's cool and makes learning not suck.

"Hey, Jake. Where's your sidekick?" he asks me with a broad smile. "Or are you Declan's sidekick? I still haven't figured that one out."

I stare at him, surprised. I assumed everyone had heard about Dec's accident by now. It was all over social media; it seems impossible to have missed it. Unless you're old, I guess.

"You didn't hear? He's out for the summer, at least. We're hoping it's not for good," I tell him.

"No way!" Mr. M exclaims. "What happened?"

I tell him the story of Declan climbing the rocks and falling. My stomach clenches when I get to the part about how badly he was injured.

"Wow, that's awful," Mr. M says, adjusting his cap to push his hair back from his sweaty forehead.

"I saw Dec a week ago . . . He doesn't seem too good," I say. "I guess I wouldn't be, either, if I were him."

"I'll reach out to him to see how he's holding up. I know from experience how hard it is to deal with a potentially career-ending accident." Mr. M looks at his watch, shaking his head. "We gotta get this practice started." He blows his whistle so everyone gathers around. Then, after giving us a start-of-season pep talk, he says, "Okay, warm up with three laps around the field."

I take off with the rest of the guys. It feels good to be playing ball again, even if it's not with the school team.

After practice, Cody and I head to the Burger Barn for milkshakes. Arielle is behind the counter, and although it's a challenge to look good in a Burger Barn uniform, she pulls it off.

But Arielle doesn't seem her usual self. She's serving some guy, and while he seems all chatty, she's got this strained, fake smile on her face.

At least until she sees Cody and me standing in line.

"Jake! Cody!" she says, her icy pseudo-smile transforming into a genuine one.

The guy turns around, a disgruntled expression on his face, like he's pissed we've interrupted his ordering process, even though we were just standing here waiting. I'm sure I've seen him around town somewhere, but I can't remember where.

"That'll be $12.79," Arielle tells him. "I'll get your order."

The guy's gaze seems to be following her with laser precision as she puts together his fries and burger and gets him a soda cup. When it's all assembled on the tray, he hands over some cash and I see a weird expression cross Arielle's face. She counts out the change and puts it on his tray instead of handing it to him. "Enjoy your meal!" she tells him with the fake smile.

"Think about it," he says to her as he takes his tray and walks away.

Arielle waits till he's out of earshot and then leans on the counter closer to us. "I am so glad to see you two! Kayleigh warned me about that guy, and he's just as much of a creeper as she said he was."

I feel a rush of disgust. "What did he do?" I ask Arielle.

"Creepy Chuck? Oh, he asked for my phone number. Even though he's, like, thirty or something."

"Gross," Cody says.

"That is so wrong," I add.

"And then when he gave me the money, he was, like, stroking my palm with his finger," she says, shuddering. "Ugh. He weirds me out. Kayleigh said he does stuff like that with her, too."

I feel a rush of anger that this guy is acting like that toward my friends. I want to go over there and punch him, but I've had it drilled into me since nursery school that I should use my words, not my fists.

"Did you report him to your manager?" I ask.

"Yeah," Arielle says. "So has Kayleigh, but he said that Creepy Chuck is a regular here, so we should just ignore it." She rolls her eyes. "Easy for him to say."

"That's wrong," Cody says. "There are supposed to be laws about that, aren't there?"

"I know," Arielle says. "If it keeps up, I'll try again. But I don't want to lose my job."

"Your manager should lose his job if he doesn't do something," I say. "He should at least give the guy a warning. Like he'll be banned from coming in if he doesn't stop or something."

"You'd think," Arielle mutters. "Anyway, what can I get you?"

We order our shakes, strawberry for me and chocolate for Cody.

While Arielle's making them, Cody and I turn around and glare at Creepy Chuck, who is eating his burger and fries like he didn't just act all pervy with our friend. But then he glances up as he puts a fry in his mouth, sees us giving him the hairy eyeball, and stops midbite. I would laugh at how ridiculous he looks, but the cold, angry expression in his eyes raises the tiny hairs on the back of my neck. There's something off about the guy, but also something familiar. I hate that Kayleigh and Arielle have to put up with him on a regular basis.

I don't turn back to the counter, though, until he finally turns away. It seems important somehow.

Arielle comes over with our milkshakes. "Here you go," she says. Then she peeks over our shoulders, to where customers are lining up to order. "Sorry, guys, I have to get back to work. See you soon."

"Hope so," I tell her.

We're hit by a wall of humidity as soon as we push open the door and step out of the air-conditioning. As we walk back to Mario the Minivan, I notice that Creepy Chuck is glaring at us through the window of Burger Barn.

"So, what do you think about Dec's new hairstyle—or should I say total lack of hairstyle?" Cody asks as I take a sip of my milkshake.

"What do you mean?"

Cody stares at me. "You haven't seen it yet? He posted it last week."

"I've been too busy with camp and summer schoolwork to look at that stuff."

"Hold my milkshake," he says, shoving it into my empty hand. "You've got to see this."

He whips out his phone and scrolls, then holds out Dec's post for me to see.

"Holy crap!" I exclaim. "Guess we can't call him Goldilocks anymore, huh?"

"I know, right?" Cody says. "It just doesn't seem like Dec, does it? He looks so . . . I don't know . . ."

I hand him back his drink and take his phone so I can look at the picture more closely. I can't believe how different Dec looks without his hair.

"He looks like an MMA fighter," I say.

"It must suck to be him right now," Cody says, and I nod.

On the way home, I send Dec a text: Like the bald look. Makes you look fierce.

When he finally responds, my heart sinks.

As fierce as I can look when I can't pitch . . .

How am I supposed to respond to that? Do I say, *It'll get better?*

I want to say something encouraging, but I saw his arm.

Still, I'm not a doctor. What do I know?

So I write: If anyone can come back from a busted arm, it's you. 💪

The three dots show he's typing back, and then they disappear.

I feel bad that I haven't been over there since last Saturday. Being at practice today seemed weird without Dec, and I'm worried because he seemed so down last week.

I'm going to try to get over there to see him soon.

DECLAN

I'm falling . . . falling . . . falling . . .

I wake up gasping, my skin clammy with sweat and heart pounding against the wall of my chest, and I force myself to breathe in three . . . two . . . one and out three . . . two . . . one until it slows.

Grabbing my phone from the nightstand, I see that it's 2:47 in the morning. Even the birds who normally wake me up at god-awful hours are smart enough to be asleep right now. But me? I'm waking up at least three times a week because the accident keeps replaying itself in my sleeping head. If only it had all been a bad dream instead of my inescapable reality.

I start PT today. I've been taking off the sling and doing the gentle mobility exercises Dr. Molina gave me. It makes me sick to see the pathetic weakness of my pitching arm. The exercises are painful, too. But I've got to suck it up and do what it takes to get back to top form.

When Dr. Molina took out my stitches yesterday, I asked him, "How long till I can play baseball?"

He wouldn't give me a straight answer. "It's early days, Declan. The important thing is to get into PT so that we get the arm moving. At the moment, I'm concerned about the drop wrist, which could mean nerve damage. That's why I've given you the brace to wear."

I wasn't going to let him get away with a nonanswer like that. "Can't you just give me an estimate?"

Dr. Molina pursed his lips. "I really can't make you any promises right now," he said. "It's usually about six months out from the accident before we know if you'll be able to get back to top form."

"So six months means the end of December, right?" I asked. "Being able to pitch again would be the best Christmas present ever."

He held up his hands. "Slow down, Declan. You need to be doing PT a minimum of three times a week, preferably four, to help you regain strength and range of motion. But even if you do that, and do all the exercises at home, I can't promise that you'll get back to where you were. We're just going to have to wait and see."

Ugh. Pulling a pillow over my face to blot out the memory, I try to go back to sleep, but end up logging in to *Imperialist Empires*. It feels good to be back as my noble, strong alter ego. It feels good to be someone besides me.

"Yo, Lionheartttt, how goes?" FenrirLupus says.

"What brings you here at this hour, my brother?" OdalRune88 asks. "Isn't it zero dark thirty where you are?"

"Yeah, but I can't sleep," I tell them.

"Something on your mind?" OdalRune88 asks. "Maybe we can help."

I hesitate. *Imperialist Empires* is the place I can escape from my miserable reality. I don't want to ruin that.

Still, these guys are offering to listen. Jake and Cody haven't been coming by much; they're too busy living the summer that was supposed to be mine.

Here, they only know me by my screen name, which makes it easier to be honest.

"I told FenrirLupus this, but I had a bad accident a few weeks ago."

"Yeah? What happened?" OdalRune88 says. "Only if you want to share, that is."

The fact that he gives me the option not to, that he's not pressing me to "express my feelings," makes me want to do it. So I tell them about going to Seward Park and how things went down.

"And then I climbed up this rock face to impress Megan—"

"Love it! Warrior mindset . . ." OdalRune88 says.

"Yeah, except then one of my holds crumbled, and I fell. Let's just say I didn't get the girl *and* I wrecked my arm."

"Women. They're always at the root of our troubles, right?" says FenrirLupus.

"Women and Jews," says this guy IOKTBW, who logged on a few minutes ago.

Wait, what? Where did that come from?

"Trust me, when trouble happens for white guys like us, Jews are usually at the heart of it," IOKTBW continues.

Jake's Jewish and he's one of my best friends. IOKTBW seems kind of out there.

"My parents keep telling me I'm lucky that I wasn't more seriously injured. But if I can't play baseball anymore, then what's the point?" I say.

"Lionheartttt, I've been where you are, my brother. Down on my luck. In a bad place, facing a bleak, uncertain future," OdalRune88 says. "But I came through it."

I've only been playing with OdalRune88 a little while, but he seems like someone who's really together. It's hard to believe his life was ever as bad as mine is right now.

"*How* did you get through it?" I ask him. "I don't see any way out."

"Check out Jarred Stonepen's videos," OdalRune88 says. "His stuff helped me a lot."

"Stonepen's one of the few people at those elitist universities who isn't a Marxist tool. He knows his stuff," FenrirLupus says. "Start with 'The Ten Rules of Manhood.'"

"Will do," I say.

"Okay, therapy session's over, ladies," IOKTBW says. "We've got enemies to kill."

IOKTBW seems like he gets off on being a troll or something. OdalRune88 and FenrirLupus tell him to shut up. He says, "Jawohl, mein Führer!" posting a picture of Hitler in the chat while we get back to the game. What a tool.

Finally, around five in the morning, tiredness sets in. I say good night to the guys, crawl back into bed, and crash.

By the time I wake up again later, the rest of the house has gone to work. There's a note from Mom on the table, saying that she'll pick me up at four to go to PT.

Great, now I have to feel guilty for her missing more work, since I know she's normally not done until seven on Tuesdays. I crumple the note in my fist and grab a Pop-Tart, because it's easy to do with one hand. I manage to pour milk into a glass left-handed without spilling any. It feels like a small victory, until I realize how fricking pathetic that is. Declan Taylor, the golden boy with the bullet pitch, now getting excited because he can pour milk without spilling, something a six-year-old could do.

I slump into one of the kitchen chairs, wondering how much worse it's possible to feel. Then I remember that OdalRune88 told me about those Jarred Stonepen videos that helped him when his life was the pits. I pull them up and start watching.

I thought Stonepen would be some super macho dude, but he's a nerdy-looking guy with a high, reedy voice, giving a lecture in one of those university classrooms that looks like a mini stadium. "Western civilization was created by men of action," he says.

I snort, imagining Kayleigh's reaction to that statement. She would go totally bonkers.

He goes on, saying that "modern society has feminized us. We need to reclaim our masculine energy, otherwise civilization is doomed."

For real? Still, I keep listening, because OdalRune88 said this stuff helped him, and he seems so together.

"Stand up straight with your feet grounded on the earth. Don't slouch. Slouching decreases your masculine energy. Put your shoulders back and stand tall, like you believe in your own competence. It will start a virtuous cycle of positive interactions, which will give you more confidence, and so on."

I straighten my back in my chair and take another bite of Pop-Tart. This is something I can do with a busted arm—or at least the part about putting my shoulders back and standing tall. Believing in my own competence . . . that's not so easy right about now.

"Don't blame the world for your own problems. Perhaps it's not the world that's at fault; perhaps, just perhaps, it's you."

Okay, this is making me want to stop watching. I thought OdalRune88 said this helped him. This just sounds like more of the same crap I'm getting from my family. Do I have to listen to this Stonepen guy getting on my case, too?

I decide to give it another minute or two. Time is the one thing I have plenty of right now.

"Don't use this as an excuse to despair. You don't have to be stuck here.

In order for our civilization to prevail, you have to do your part—take hold of yourself and meet the challenges in your own life head-on so that you can contribute to solving society's ills."

Okay, that's legit.

"Start with the little things. Make your bed every day. A tidy room helps to create an ordered mind. A logical, ordered mind helps defeat the chaos that surrounds us."

I think about my bedroom. I've never been the neatest guy, but I'm pretty good about putting dirty clothes in the laundry basket, if only to keep Mom off my back. Now my room looks like a bomb hit it. It's such a struggle to get dressed and undressed with one arm, the last thing I feel like doing is picking up stuff from the floor afterward.

But after listening to Jarred Stonepen's video, I resolve to throw all my laundry into a neat pile in the corner instead of leaving it where it lands. It's a start. A first step.

I'll see if Mom notices.

At about 4:10, Mom honks from the driveway. I run downstairs, and when I slide into the passenger seat, she's clearly frazzled.

"My last client was late and didn't even bother to call," she says. "Some people seem to think I exist just to serve their hair needs and have no life of my own."

"Jerks," I say. "Now we're going to be late for PT. And I need all the PT I can get if I'm going to get my arm working well enough to get back on the team."

Mom doesn't say anything, and when I glance over at her, her face is scrunched up as if she's in pain, her lips tightly pursed.

"What?"

"Declan . . . honey . . . you need to have realistic expectations."

The air disappears from my lungs, like my own mom just gave me a sucker punch to the gut.

"You . . . don't think I can do it?" I say slowly. "You think my baseball career is over?"

"It's not that I don't think you can do it, Declan," Mom says. "You're a fighter, and I know you'll do whatever it takes to get better."

"So what exactly are you saying?" I ask. "That Dr. Molina screwed up my arm?"

"No!" Mom says. "Why would you think that? But I just want you to prepare yourself in case it's not enough."

I can't prepare myself for that. I won't. I have to get better, because I can't imagine my life without baseball. It's what I do. It's who I am. Mom knows that.

That's when it hits me. "This is about the money, isn't it?" I say, anger flooding my chest. "Did Dr. Molina tell you that it's not worth spending the money on PT because my arm is too mangled? Bet that would be a big relief for you and Dad." Then I think about the team. "Dr. Molina probably told you that so Mateo definitely gets to be first string next year."

"Declan!" Mom exclaims. "How could you say such a terrible thing?" She gives me a look that's so full of hurt, a tiny twinge of guilt pricks through my anger. "You know Dad and I are doing everything we possibly can to make sure you get the treatment you need. We're working ourselves to the bone to pay for it all."

I stare out the window sullenly as she continues. "And Dr. Molina is an excellent surgeon. To accuse him of something that absurd is ridiculous." We sit in uncomfortable silence.

"Look, Declan," Mom says finally. "I know you're upset about not being able to play baseball this summer—"

"Or maybe ever."

"Or maybe ever. But whatever the outcome is, it's no excuse for you to say terrible, untrue things about people."

She's probably expecting me to apologize to her, but I don't. I just sit in the passenger seat, seething, until she drops me at PT. I'm going to prove everyone wrong.

DECLAN

Amazingly enough, we're all home for dinner on Thursday for the first time in weeks. If Dad's not working overtime, Kayleigh's doing a late shift at Burger Barn, or Mom's taking on an extra client. But tonight, we're all sitting around the table, eating a tuna casserole. I'm not a big fan of tuna casserole, but Mom says it's all about stretching the food budget right now. I'm busy trying to pick the tuna out and push it to the side of the plate with my fork so I can just eat the pasta when Dad says, "Declan, your mom and I have been talking, and it's time you start thinking about a job for the summer, since baseball camp isn't happening."

I look up from my plate, where I'm about two-thirds done with my tuna evacuation project. "Who is going to hire me with a busted arm?" I ask.

"They're looking for people at Big Value. There was a sign up when I went in while you were at PT," Mom says. "One of my salon clients is the store manager. I asked her if you could do a cashier job even without full strength in your arm and she said yes. She wants to see you tomorrow morning."

"Wow. I just got out of the sling and you're already telling me to get a job?"

"I want you to go in and apply tomorrow morning," Dad says. "We've all got to do our part."

"I'm still in pain and Dr. Molina said the tingling and wrist thing might be nerve damage. That's why I have to wear this stupid brace. He said I need a lot of PT if I'm ever going to get back to pitching. It's like you all don't want me to get better or something."

Kayleigh is uncharacteristically quiet, her gaze moving from Dad to me like she's watching a tennis match.

"Don't be ridiculous, Declan. You can't sit around in your room playing video games all day for the entire summer," Dad says. "Your brain is going to rot. Besides, how do you think we're going to pay for all this PT? We're already up to our eyeballs in hospital bills."

"I was *supposed* to be earning money helping teach little kids to play baseball," I point out. "You make it sound like I *want* to be in my room playing video games. And even that's not easy, because my fingers are doing weird things."

"Maybe it's because we don't see you doing the simple chores we ask you to do around the house while we're all at work," Mom says. "Your room looks like a tornado hit it."

"I've been trying to keep it neater!" I say, pissed that she hasn't even noticed I'm making an effort. I watched a bunch more Jarred Stonepen videos, and in one of them he talks about how women are so busy being told they should focus on careers and equality that they've devalued motherhood. Like Mom. She's so focused on her hairdressing career instead of being our mom that she never notices the things I actually do, only the things I don't.

"By 'neater,' he means he's organized a few piles of dirty clothes, not that he's actually doing his own laundry," Kayleigh says.

I give her a dirty look and cough "Suck-up" under my breath.

"I'm not a suck-up," she says. "It's the truth. Have you done a single load of laundry since the accident?"

I don't want to admit she's right, but she is. "No," I mutter, staring down at my plate. "But you try doing it with a busted arm."

"Funny how you manage to play games all day with a busted arm, but anything to help out your family is too hard," Dad says.

"Because for one thing, gaming is a lot less strenuous, and for another, I'm not just doing that all day," I say. "Do you realize how many exercises I have to do for PT if I want to have a hope of playing again?"

"Dec, honey, I understand how much you want to play again, but as I said earlier, you need to prepare yourself for the possibility that it might not happen," Mom says.

"Nice. My entire family is ganging up on me," I say, angrily shoving a forkful of tuna-less pasta into my mouth.

Dad blows out an exasperated snort. "We're not ganging up on you," he says. "We're working to pay off the medical bills from your little stunt."

You'd think that being injured, I'd get a little sympathy, especially from my family, but apparently that's too much to ask.

"That's right, Dad," I say. "It's all my fault. I'm just a stupid loser with a bum arm."

Dad slams his fork down on his plate. "Enough with the self-pity, Declan. I want you off your butt and down at Big Value tomorrow morning applying for that cashier job."

"Fine," I say, pushing my chair back and storming out of the room. I'm on the second stair when I hear Mom sigh loudly and say, "He couldn't even put his plate in the sink."

Feeling like I'm about to explode, I go upstairs and log in to *Imperialist Empires*, tugging on my headset.

"Yo, Brother Lionheartttt. What's good with you?" OdalRune88 asks.

"Nothing. Just . . . my family sucks," I tell him.

"Been there," Xtiansoldier503 says.

"We all have at some point," FenrirLupus adds.

"Jarred Stonepen has a good video about dysfunctional families," IOKTBW says. "He says to get out as fast as you can."

"I'm only fifteen," I confess. "And I can't afford to get out, anyway."

"I'm fifteen, too," IOKTBW says. "I hang out at a friend's house as much as I can so I don't have to deal with all the crap at home."

I wonder if IOKTBW is really fifteen or if he's just saying that. Either way, I wish I had somewhere to hang out that wasn't home right now.

"Having a family that sucks makes you appreciate your friends more, though," he continues.

"Too bad all my so-called friends are busy playing baseball," I say, my jaw clenching as I think about it. "And I can't because . . . my arm."

"Remember, Lionheartttt . . . you've got us," OdalRune88 says.

He's right. The *IE* crew has been keeping me sane lately. Well, sane-ish, anyway. Without them, I'd be drowning.

The next morning, on her way to the hair salon, Mom drops Kayleigh at the Burger Barn for her shift and me at Big V to apply for the job. As I'm walking to the customer service desk, I hear someone call out, "Hey, Declan."

I turn around and there's a gangly-limbed white guy who looks vaguely familiar, but I can't place him at first. Luckily for me, he's wearing a badge with *Finn* on it pinned to his Big V T-shirt. Now I remember him—Finn McCarthy. He goes to my school, not that I've ever really hung out with the guy.

"Yo, Finn, what's up? I didn't recognize you with the short hair."

"I barely recognized you with the bald head," he says, grinning. "I like it. You look like a skinhead. All you need is a pair of Doc Martens."

Huh. That wasn't the look I was going for, but I'll take it. It's better than a loser who can't play baseball.

Finn's been in a couple of my classes. He's kind of quiet, except when he lays out a snarky, I'm-smarter-than-all-of-you comment. I think his entire wardrobe consists of dark hoodies with gaming or anime logos. From what I've heard, he's some kind of computer wiz. He's always had long, lanky-looking hair, but now he's got a high and tight cut.

"How long you have worked here?" I ask.

"I started weekends in January, and now I work as many shifts as I can get," Finn says. "They make sure to keep us under the number of hours where they'd have to pay benefits, though, because of course they do."

"Typical," I say. "What's it like? I'm here for a cashier position."

"It's a job, right? The customers can be jerks, especially the summer people." He shrugs. "But most of the guys who work here are okay." He glances at a woman with auburn hair and coppery skin, also wearing a Big V badge, who is giving him a stop-socializing-and-get-back-to-work look over the top of her metal-framed glasses. "Well, except for her. I gotta go. Good luck."

I head to customer service and tell the person on duty that I'm applying for a job.

She calls a lady named Rita, the one who was giving Finn the hairy eyeball. She glances at my arm, which I'm holding close to my side.

"My mom said that there was an opening for a cashier, and that you said I could do it, even with my arm being messed up," I tell her.

It's like someone turned on the friendly switch—her whole demeanor changes. "Oh! You're Andi Taylor's son, right? One of the twins."

"Yeah. Declan."

"Your mom, Andi, is the best," Rita says. "She's been doing my hair forever. I heard about what happened. Such a shame about your baseball career."

Her words are a slap across the face. Has Mom been telling everyone in Stafford's Corner that I'll never play again?

Fury bubbles in my belly like molten lava, and I feel sweat prickle at the back of my neck, despite the air-conditioning. But Rita doesn't seem to notice. She keeps babbling on about Mom, and how great she is, and how happy she is to be able to help her out because she works so hard, like I'm a pathetic charity case. She asks me a couple of questions about my previous jobs, how I would handle a difficult customer, and if there are any times that I can't make due to PT.

"Okay, Declan, report for training tomorrow," she says finally. "Please bring your social security card and ID so we can get all your paperwork taken care of."

I see Finn on the way out and tell him I got the job. I wonder if he got hired on his own, or if he was hired as a favor to his mom, too.

As I pass by Burger Barn, I think about going in to get a soda before heading home in the heat and humidity, but I don't want to see Kayleigh. Instead, I make my way along the hot pavement, and when that runs out, the thin margin on the side of the state road. I'm tired and dripping with sweat by the time I get home. But the heat on the outside is nothing compared with the rage on the inside—and that's got nowhere to go.

•　　•　　•

74

The training at Big V the next day is easy, just boring. The hardest part is having to smile and be nice to all the customers, especially when it's the last place I want to be.

Alejandra, the lady who is training me, seems to enjoy talking to them—even the entitled summer people Finn warned me about. I don't know how she does it. By the time I get a break, my cheeks hurt from the effort of keeping the Friendly Cashier Smile on my face. How am I supposed to do it all day every day?

I'm sitting in the break room in the back, eating a bag of chips, when Finn comes in with this dude who looks like he's in his thirties, with brown hair that's showing a small white patch of bald in the back.

"Hey, Declan," Finn says. "This is Charlie. He works in the meat department."

"How's the first day going, buddy?" Charlie asks.

"Okay, I guess," I say. "My feet hurt, though."

"Gel inserts," Charlie says, pointing to his feet. "They help when you're standing all day."

"Thanks for the tip," I tell him. "Got any advice for how to keep smiling when people are jerks?"

Finn laughs. "That's why I'd rather stock shelves than be on the cash register. As a general rule, people suck."

"When I get a bad customer, I imagine all the painful ways they could die," Charlie says.

I stare at him for a second. I can't tell if it's a joke or if he's a total psycho.

Finn starts cracking up. "Your face, Taylor . . ."

"Relax, buddy, it was just a joke," Charlie says with a sly smile.

"Oh." I grin. "I'm an idiot."

"Nah," Charlie says, clapping me on my uninjured shoulder. "It's all good."

It might have been a joke, but the next time there's a rude customer, I try imagining them dying in some awful way. Strangely enough, it helps me to keep a smile on my face.

JAKE

I get a text from Dec on Sunday morning, asking me if I want to hang out. I feel bad because it's been a while since I've seen him, but my summer school homework is hanging over my head, and I've been too tired to tackle it during the week after dealing with little kids all day at camp.

Sorry. Got too much homework to get done, I text back.

He doesn't respond, and I wonder if he's pissed at me. I add: Would MUCH rather hang with you.

It's the truth, even if Dec isn't exactly a laugh riot right now.

My stuff is downstairs, so I head down to work at the kitchen table. I've struggled through answering one question on my English assignment when Ben comes in.

"Hey, will it disturb you if I try to make those salted caramel deluxe brownies they made on the last episode of *Eat, Bake, Love?*"

"You had me at salted caramel," I say. "I have no problem with being disturbed by brownies."

"You sure?" Ben asks.

"Yeah," I say with a sigh. "It's so unfair. It's supposed to be my vacation, and I've got all this stupid homework. Why'd I have to be the one to get the dyslexia gene?"

"Why'd I have to get the bad-at-sports gene?" Ben says. "You've never had to suffer through being the last one picked for every team sport." He smiles. "You know what they say: 'Sometimes you're the windshield and sometimes you're the bug.'"

"Who are you—Dad?" I ask. "What does that even mean?"

"I don't know, it's from some Dire Straits song Dad was listening to in the car," Ben says. "It seemed appropriate."

"Definitely feeling more buggish right now," I say, turning back to my assignment.

The smell of melting chocolate wafting through the kitchen doesn't do a lot for my concentration, but I force myself to focus. It's hard not to feel resentful of my brother sometimes—how he can sail through school with good grades, doing seemingly no work. Okay, that's not fair. Ben does study. It's not totally effortless. But he doesn't have to agonize over every reading and writing assignment. Luckily, I get accommodations like audiobooks and extended time. Before I was diagnosed, he'd finish a book in two days while I was stuck on chapter one.

Ben puts the tray of brownies in the oven, then looks over my assignment. "I can help you if you want," he says.

I nod, and he spends the forty minutes we're waiting for the brownies to bake going over my summer school stuff with me.

"It's so much easier when you're here to break stuff down," I say with a sigh. "What am I going to do when you go back to college?"

"Dude, it's not like I'm on the moon," Ben says, ruffling my hair. "There's this cool gadget called a phone, which has all these handy-dandy apps on it, and there's one where you can video chat with me so it's almost like we're in the same room." He grins. "I just won't be able to share the brownies."

"Yeah, you're going to be too busy being Genius Kid to help me," I say. "That's when you're not out partying."

"What? I never party!" Ben says with such a straight face, I do a spit take over my work.

"Nice," he says, blotting it with a nearby napkin. "But seriously, Jake . . . you're just as smart as I am."

"That's not what the report cards say."

"Not every kind of smart can be measured by report cards and those fill-in-the-bubble tests," Ben says. "Trust me. I go to a 'good school'"—he uses air quotes for emphasis—"but there are kids who can barely seem to get through basic life functions. I had to show a few guys on my floor how to do laundry."

"Learning how to do laundry is easy. Do you remember how I had to drill stuff over and over to get through my bar mitzvah?" I remind him.

"C'mon, Jake, that just shows how determined you are, doesn't it? It's that same ability to drill stuff over and over that made you such a good baseball player, right?"

"I guess," I reply. "But it sucks that I have to work so much harder than everyone else, and I still get bad grades in everything except for math." I sigh. "It would suck even more if I get kicked off the team because I can't get them up."

"You'll do it, Jake," Ben says. "Besides, Coach K knows you've got dyslexia. He's not going to punish you for it."

Just then, I get a text from Arielle.

Hey . . . are you around? Want to hang out?

Unfortunately, Ben sees the text before I can hide my phone.

"Ooooooh. The New Jersey Cutie wants to hang out!" he says. "Mom is going to plotz. Jakey hanging with a nice Jewish girl!"

"Her name is Arielle, not 'the New Jersey Cutie,' and you aren't going to tell Mom, right?"

He rubs his hands together like a cheesy evil villain.

"I mean it, Ben! Don't say anything to Mom and Dad."

The oven timer goes off.

"Fine, I'll keep quiet. But you owe me," Ben says, taking the brownies out of the oven.

"And you owe me a brownie," I say, texting back Arielle. Sure! I need a break from trying to figure out themes and metaphors. How about I take you on a bike tour of all the hot sights of Stafford's Corner. Like all 2 of them.

Arielle: LOL. Perfect.

Me: See you in 15 mins

Arielle: ☺

I smile and organize my work into a neat pile on the corner of the table. Then I put my phone in my pocket and grab one of the brownies off the cooling rack.

"Off to meet the New Jersey Cutie, by any chance?" Ben says with a grin.

"Maybe. Remember. Keep this between us."

He's laughing as I head out the kitchen door to get my bike.

Halfway to Arielle's house, I wonder if I made a mistake suggesting a bike ride. It's one of those hot, humid July days where I feel like I need a shower again even though I already took one this morning.

Arielle, on the other hand, looks cool and unruffled when she comes to the door.

"So . . . are you ready for your Magical Mystery Tour?" I ask her.

"Oh yeah. I can't wait to see all the wild hot spots of Stafford's Corner," she says over her shoulder in a voice as dry as the Sahara, going to get her bike from the garage.

"So, what's on our itinerary?" she asks.

"We're just going to see where the road takes us," I tell her. "But we'll definitely end up at Mocha Jenn's, because pastries and muffins."

"A perfect plan!" she says with a wide smile that does something to my insides.

I push off on the pedals, and she falls into my slipstream like a pro cyclist.

"To our right, you will see the historic Stafford's Corner cemetery. It's such a hot location, people are dying to get in there!"

Arielle snorts. "Aren't you a little young to be making dad jokes?"

I clutch my hand over my heart. "You know how to hurt me."

She laughs. "Sorry, but that was really corny."

"I'll attempt to recover as we ride to the next landmark," I say.

After an hour of cycling, showing her what passes for tourist attractions in Stafford's Corner, we end up at Mocha Jenn's. We both get iced tea, and I get us a double-chocolate-chip cookie and a coffee-cake muffin, two of Jenn's specialties. "To share," I tell Arielle.

"I knew there was a reason I liked you," she says.

We find a table by the window. Arielle takes her half of the coffee-cake muffin, breaks off a piece, and then pops it into her mouth.

"Okay, this might make me a little more up for living here," she says with a grin.

"Wait till you try the double-chocolate-chip. You won't miss New Jersey at all!"

"No cookie can be that good," she says, the smile fading from her face. "I'll always miss it—especially my friends."

"So . . . what's it like to live in a place where there's a decent-size Jewish community?" I ask. "I've lived in Stafford's Corner my whole life, so I wouldn't know."

Arielle shrugs. "I don't know—I mean, the biggest difference I notice right now is that it's so much more rural here, and there's a choice of, like, one synagogue."

"When you live in a bigger community, do you still get those moments where you go along thinking you belong and then someone says a dumb thing that reminds you that you're different?"

Arielle takes a sip of iced tea, then leans back in her chair, her face thoughtful. "Sure, there were kids who said things. Like 'Really? You don't have a Christmas tree? How do you celebrate without a tree?' and 'You don't put out cookies for Santa? How do you get presents?' You know, like they can't imagine that someone wouldn't celebrate Christmas. Like how you must be from another planet if you don't."

"Did you mostly hang out with other Jewish kids?" I ask. It's hard for me to picture having an option to do that, anywhere except at synagogue, and even then, there aren't that many kids my age.

"I had a lot of Jewish friends, but at school I hung out with all kinds of people. Especially being on the soccer team." She leans forward and puts her hand on her chin. "I guess I never thought about it much, because I took it for granted. Like I'd still go to the mall in November and see the huge Christmas displays with a tiny little hanukkiah next to a tiny little kinara stuck in a corner somewhere—but at least I had friends to notice that along with me."

"At least they *had* them stuck in a corner. Around here you'd never know anybody celebrated anything *but* Christmas," I say. "That's why I love youth group—because at least there I know people get the Jewish part of me without me having to explain it all."

"I can see how that would be hard," she says. Then she starts waving excitedly. "Look! It's Kayleigh and her mom!"

I glance out the window and see the two of them coming into Mocha Jenn's.

"Crap," I mutter under my breath.

"What's the matter?" Arielle asks.

"Dec texted me this morning wanting to hang out today, but I had summer school work to do, so I said no. Then Ben helped me, and I'd mostly finished by the time I got your text," I confess. "But now it's going to look like I blew him off so I could hang out with you instead."

"And you feel like a jerk?"

I nod, just as Kayleigh comes over. Her hair isn't up in its usual ponytail—it's all blown out.

"Wow, Kayleigh, your hair looks great!" I exclaim.

"It does!" Arielle agrees. "You look like you're about to do a cover shoot."

Kayleigh strikes a pose. "Thank you, fans!" she says in a movie star voice. "My stylist—aka Mom—just gave me a cut and blow-dry at the salon." Reverting to her normal posture, she adds, "I had to make it up to her for shaving Dec's head. Anyway, I'm glad I ran into you two so you saw it, because it'll look like this for like half an hour and then it'll start to drive me crazy, and it'll be back up in a ponytail."

"How is Dec?" I ask.

A shadow falls over her face. "The same." Then she tells us the latest from Dr. Molina.

"Wow. That's sucks," I say.

Arielle glances over at me, and I feel even worse about being here instead of hanging out with Declan. I wonder if I should ask Kayleigh not to tell him she saw me here with Arielle, but I can't think of a way to do it without sounding shady.

Ugh. I'm the worst.

I'm about to open my mouth and confess that when Mrs. Taylor comes over with their drinks. She looks really tired, like she's aged in the month since the accident.

"Hi there," she says. "Good to see you, Jake."

"Mom, this is my friend Arielle," Kayleigh says. "She works with me at the Burger Barn, and she's trying out for soccer next week."

"Nice to meet you, Arielle," Mrs. Taylor says. "Kayleigh, I need to get home." She looks at us apologetically. "I haven't had a day off in a while. It's busy hair season," she tells us. "So much to catch up on."

"See you!" Kayleigh says, following her mom out to the car.

I watch them through the window and sigh. "I feel bad about Dec."

"I'm sorry," Arielle says. "It's okay if you want to blame it on me. You can tell him I begged you to show me the exciting sights of Stafford's Corner."

"Nah, I'm big enough to own it," I tell her. "But it's nice of you to offer." I pick up the straw wrapper from the table and start rolling it up into a tight ball. "And if I'm honest, I'm having a really good time with you."

A hint of pink tints Arielle's cheeks. "Me too," she says with a shy smile.

"Should we ride some more?"

Arielle nods, and we head out to our bikes. We're unlocking them from the small bike rack when I realize how close we are—Arielle's lips are just a few inches from mine. My heart starts pounding wildly, and I realize I want to kiss her. I move my head to close the distance, stopping just far enough away to ask softly, "Can I kiss you?" I feel her breath on my face, a mixture of coffee and chocolate, and our eyes meet. She bites her lip, then closes the distance. As her lips press mine, I feel it hit me in the chest, like when the bat connects with the ball and you just know it's a home run. I lean into her, deepening the kiss. We pull apart, and she gives me a small smile.

Wow. I feel bad about Dec, but . . . as we ride off, I can't hold on to that, because I'm grinning too much.

DECLAN

One . . . two . . . three . . . four . . . five . . . ugh . . . crap!

I'm supposed to do ten reps of this stupid exercise, and I can barely manage five. How am I ever going to get back to normal at this rate?

I flop back onto my bed, discouraged. It's tempting to give up and play *Imperialist Empires*. To just lose myself in the game and forget about the pain for a while. But when I raise my head, I see all my shelves of baseball trophies. I hear Jarred Stonepen's voice, saying how it's important to orient myself toward my goal and to keep to a schedule or else I won't achieve it. I put reminders to do these exercises in my phone. I have to do them.

I drag myself off the bed and start over, determined to do all ten reps.

One . . . two . . . three . . .

I smell french fries, and sure enough, Kayleigh's standing in the doorway. "Hey, Dec!" she says. "How's it going?"

Four . . . ugh.

"Not good," I say, holding my arm close to my body. Will it ever stop hurting?

Kayleigh's brow furrows with concern. "Do you want me to get you an ice pack?"

"Yeah, thanks," I mumble.

She runs downstairs and comes back a few minutes later with an ice pack—and Mom.

"Do you need some pain medication?" Mom asks.

I nod. I've been trying not to take the stuff, because you hear all these news stories about student athletes who started taking it for injuries and ended up getting addicted. I thought that by doing my PT exercises religiously, I could get back to where I was without taking any. It's like having to swallow another defeat, in a long string of them, just this time it's in pill form.

Mom brings back a glass of water and one of the pain meds. She and Kayleigh watch me for any hint of a grimace.

I'm pissed because I know neither of them believe I can do this. Mom's been telling people as much.

"Stop it!" I snap at them both.

"Stop what?" Kayleigh asks, confused.

"Looking at me like that! Like I'm totally pathetic and I'll never play again," I say.

"Declan—" Mom starts, but Kayleigh cuts her off.

"Are you for real, Dec?" she asks, and storms out of my room.

I hate the look I see in Mom's eyes. Like I've disappointed her—again.

"Declan, we love you. We're concerned about you. Your friends are concerned about you," she says. "We bumped into Jake and Arielle at the coffee shop, and they were both asking how you were doing."

The flame of rage inside me, which had been on simmer, flares to high.

"You bumped into Jake? With fricking Arielle?"

Mom's brows knit together in confusion. "Yes. Why are you so upset?"

"Nothing," I say. "I'm fine."

Mom's shoulders droop as she exhales a loud sigh. "Declan, bottling everything up isn't going to do you any good. I'm worried about you."

"So worried you told Rita I'd never play baseball again?"

Mom looks down at her feet. "I didn't say that. I just explained what Dr. Molina told us." Raising her gaze, she says, "Nothing would make me happier than for you to be able to do the thing you love most again, Dec.

I want that for you. I will do whatever I can to help you achieve it." She sighs. "I'm praying for a miracle. I really am."

I lie back in bed and turn my face to the wall. I can't even look at her right now if she thinks it'll take a miracle for me to play.

I hear her sigh again, and then the door closes behind her, leaving me alone with my rage at her, at Jake, and at life.

At least I've got my online friends—and, strangely enough, Finn, who it turns out is pretty good company.

The next day at work we're both on a lunch break at the same time, and we start talking about video games because apparently he's a big gamer, too.

"My favorite game used to be *Force and Fortune*," I tell him. "But lately I've been playing a lot of *Imperialist Empires*."

He stares at me. "For real? I play that, too!"

"Yeah, it's awesome. I've gotten really interested in the Crusades since I started playing it."

Finn's still looking at me like he's totally shocked that I play *IE*.

"Why are you so surprised?" I ask. "It's a great game."

"I know, it's just . . . how did you get the link?"

"This guy I play *Force and Fortune* with gave it to me," I tell him.

"Cool," Finn says with a huge grin. "*IE* is sick. What's your username?"

"Lionheart with four *t*'s," I tell him.

"Oh! I should have put two and two together when you talked about baseball," he says. "Mine's IOKTBW."

"Huh. So is IOKTBW random letters, or does it mean something?"

"It means It's OK To Be White, because I'm sick of being told that I should be ashamed of my skin color and how I have all this 'white privilege' and all the rest of that 'social justice warrior' crap." He uses air quotes. "It's just me and my mom and her jerk boyfriends. What kind of privilege is that?"

"Makes sense to me. Unfortunately, my sister is one of those social justice warriors," I say. "But enough about her. I'd rather talk gameplay."

We're still comparing notes on *IE* when Charlie comes in, blood spattered all over the plastic apron he wears.

"You look like the psycho killer from a slasher movie," Finn says.

"Cutting up and packaging beef and pork will do that to ya," says Charlie.

"So get this, Charlie—Declan plays *Imperialist Empires*," Finn tells him.

Charlie turns from the coffee machine and smiles. "Shut up! How'd you hear about it?"

I repeat what I told Finn. Charlie seems super pumped about me playing a game—so over-the-top excited about it that I feel like I'm missing something. Given that he's closer to Dad's age than mine, it's weird—and at the same time kind of dope—that he's so into me gaming instead of telling me all the ways it's going to rot my brain.

Charlie finishes making his coffee, then leans back against the break room counter, sipping it.

"Finn, I'm thinking we should take Declan out to meet Ronan," he says.

Finn raises his eyebrows, then nods slowly. "Yeah. Definitely."

"Who's Ronan?" I ask.

"Ronan's awesome," Finn says. "I hang out at his place a lot. Learned more from him than I ever did from my deadbeat dad."

So that's the place IOKTBW was talking about, where he gets away from his family.

I vaguely remember Mom saying something about Finn's dad leaving, back when we were in elementary school. Mom hears everything working at the hair salon. I mean, everything.

"Ronan's a man's man like us," Charlie says. "Not like those entitled, soy-latte-drinking summer people we have to put up with."

Hearing that I'm included as a man's man makes me sit up taller. But then I look up at the clock. "Crap, my break's over."

"I'll take you out to meet Ronan soon," Charlie promises. "You'll like him."

As I head back to the register, I feel a little lighter than usual. Maybe it's because I've finally got something to look forward to for a change.

I've just finished ringing up a customer near the end of my shift when I look up and see Mr. Morrison is next in line.

"Declan, good to see you," he says as I start scanning his groceries. He chuckles. "You chose to go bald. Meanwhile, I'm trying to cling to the hair I have left!"

"It was already half shaved from surgery anyway," I say, figuring he heard about the accident just like everyone else.

Morrison frowns. "Jake told me about what happened when I saw him at practice."

The fury, always at a slow simmer beneath the surface, boils to life at the mention of practice. I should be there. I should be pitching. Instead, I'm stuck here scanning groceries. Whole wheat bread. Eggs. Healthy cereal. Tampons.

Ugh, what is Mr. M doing buying those? I'd have thought he had more self-respect.

"How are you doing?" he asks. "We miss you at baseball."

"Not as much as I miss being there," I say. Low-fat yogurt, skim milk, bananas.

"Dec, I know this has got to be really tough for you. I've been there. If you ever want to talk."

Is Mr. M implying I'm never going to be able to play baseball again, like what happened to him? What exactly has Jake been telling him?

Blueberries, peanut butter, apples.

"I'm doing PT," I say, trying and failing not to sound defensive. "It's not like my career is totally over. I just have to work hard to get my strength and my range of motion back."

"Right. Sure. I hope you do it," he says as he bags his groceries. But it sounds like maybe he's just saying that.

I'll show him. I'll show all the doubters.

Mr. M puts his bags in his cart. "Take care, Declan."

My teeth are clenched so hard from anger for the rest of my shift, my jaw hurts by the time I finish.

I listen to a Jarred Stonepen podcast as I'm walking home. This one is about why people aren't happy lately.

"There's a tremendous amount of uncertainty, instability, and complexity in our lives today," he says. "Instead of one parent working, you've got two parents working like hamsters on a wheel. No one is home with the kids, making sure they do their schoolwork and eat nutritious meals. Kids feel alone and unloved. Men feel emasculated when they can't work, when they can't provide for their family like they have traditionally. Women feel trapped by the pressures to 'have it all' while feeling like they're terrible mothers. It's all a matter of pride and identity.

"All we hear about is how the patriarchy is wrong and oppressive, but it's worked well for thousands of years of Western civilization," he says. "Yet every day, there is more confusion about what it means to be a man. The things that made men strong, that gave them purpose, are now labeled 'toxic.' And in a life that's characterized by suffering and heavy burdens, young men need to find direction and purpose, or they become angry and destructive. Meanwhile, young women are trying so hard to compete with men that they lose their natural femininity. Finding direction and purpose starts with taking responsibility for oneself."

I get a charge thinking about how much Kayleigh would hate this guy.

Still, if you'd asked me a month ago if I thought life was characterized by "suffering and heavy burdens," I would have laughed. But now? "Suffering and heavy burdens" doesn't even begin to describe it.

JAKE

"Another day, another game won," Cody says as he slides into the seat next to me on the bus. "Three weeks into the travel season and we define awesome."

"We do," I agree. "But let's not get cocky."

Cody rolls his eyes. "What are you, Coach or something? I can be cocky for the ride home, can't I?"

I laugh. "Yeah. Even until next practice."

The one good thing about the long bus rides is that they give me a chance to listen to audiobooks so I get my required summer reading out of the way—at least till Cody wants to talk and pulls out one of my earbuds.

"Have you heard from Dec lately?" he asks.

I feel a major-league guilt pang. "Not for a few weeks. I've been so beat, what with working at camp, travel practice, and summer schoolwork." I hit pause on my audiobook. "I'm a crap friend."

"So am I," Cody admits. "We should go visit him."

"I'm gonna text him right now."

Hey, Dec! Up for a visit from Cody and me?

Declan: If I can work at Big V, I'm pretty sure I can handle a visit.

"Salty," I say, showing Cody the response on my phone.

Jake: Sorry, man.

Declan: nbd

Even though he's said it's no big deal, from what he wrote I can't help feeling like it actually is.

Jake: We're on the bus back from a game, and you were def missed.

The dots show he's typing, but then they disappear.

"Maybe he's pissed because we've all been MIA recently," I say.

"Yeah," Cody says. He shrugs. "But it's not like he's texting us."

"I know. But still."

Jake: You around tomorrow afternoon?

Declan: Working. Monday?

Jake: K, see you after camp.

"We're on for Monday," I tell Cody. "Now I gotta listen to the rest of this book, so leave me alone, okay?"

"You're no fun," he says, crossing his arms over his chest.

Sometimes I wish my friends really got how much harder I have to work to keep my grades up. Cody sails by getting Bs and Cs while doing the bare minimum to stay on the team. Meanwhile, I work my butt off and I'm still stuck doing summer school.

I put my earbud in and start the book up again. I'm going to do better next year if it kills me.

Monday afternoon when we're done with camp, Cody and I stop at the gas station to grab some gummy bears, soda, and chips, then head over to Declan's.

"I hope he's in a better mood today than he was the last time I saw him," Cody says.

"Yeah, me too."

When we get to the Taylors' house, Declan's the only one home. He smiles when he sees us, but it's not his usual goofy Declan smile, and he seems oddly stiff when Cody and I bump fists with him.

"I can't get used to the shiny dome," I say, rubbing his head.

He jerks it away. "Makes life easier when you can't lift your arm over your head to shampoo," he says in a grim voice.

I let out a hollow laugh, feeling awful. "Um . . . we brought snacks," I say, holding out the bag of gummy bears.

Declan grabs the bag. "You remembered my favorites!" He smiles, and there it is—a welcome glimpse of pre-accident Declan.

"So, how's it going?" Cody asks as we head up to his room.

"It's going," Declan says. "Doing PT, trying to regain strength and mobility. Working at Big V."

"Mr. M said he saw you there," I say.

Declan's mood changes in a heartbeat, like someone just flicked a switch from happy to mad.

"What did you tell him, Jake? He seemed to think I was never going to play baseball again, and that I'm going to end up stuck in Stafford's Corner for the rest of my life, just like him."

I'm confused. I saw what his arm looked like. How do you come back and pitch at the level he was pitching after an injury like that? I know I'm not a doctor, but still . . .

"I don't know . . . I mean, I'm sorry if I got it wrong," I tell him. "I guess I got the impression from Kayleigh that it wasn't, like, a given that you'd be able to come back."

"Mr. M cares," Cody says. "That's the kind of guy he is."

"My own sister doesn't think I can do it," Declan says through gritted teeth. "I'm working my fricking butt off at PT so I can play again. She knows that."

"C'mon, Dec, you know Kayleigh's always there for you, even if she talks smack," I say. "I just think . . ." I trail off, not sure what to say without pissing Dec off more.

"What, Jake? Go on. Tell me what you think."

It's like he's trying to pick a fight, and that's the last thing I want. We're supposed to be here cheering him up.

"I don't want to fight, Dec. I know that if anyone can do it, it's you," I tell him. "I'm on your side here."

Dec snorts, like he thinks I'm full of it.

"So, Declan, what's this game you're playing? I've never seen it," Cody says with a subtle glance over at me that tells me he's trying to rescue things.

It works. Declan lights up the minute he starts talking about it. "It's this world strategy game called *Imperialist Empires*," he says with the kind of enthusiasm he normally reserves for baseball and Megan Moran. "It's about the Crusades."

"Huh, I never heard of it before," I say. "When did it come out?"

Declan shrugs. "Not sure. Someone I met playing *Force and Fortune* invited me to play."

"Sounds cool," I say.

"It is. And I've met some really great people playing it. They've been helping me a lot." He gives Cody and me a pointed glance. "Like they've been there for me."

Ouch.

"Hey, I'm sorry I haven't been around much," I tell him. "It's just with schoolwork, and camp, and practice, and travel games, things have been kind of crazy this summer."

"But you managed to find time to hang out with Arielle, didn't you?" he says, giving me an icy glare. "After telling me that you were too busy to hang because of homework."

I feel the heat rush to my face.

"I was doing it when you texted me," I say. "Then Ben helped me, so by the time Arielle texted me to hang out, I was done."

"So you were willing to ditch your best friend for some girl you barely know?" Dec spits out. "Nice."

"Look, I'm sorry," I say. "She doesn't know many people around here. I think she's kind of lonely."

"And I'm not?" Dec says, pinning me with those ice-blue eyes of his.

"Face it, Dec, Arielle's a whole lot cuter than you are," Cody says with a grin.

"No offense, Dec, but she is," I say. "I'd much rather kiss her than you."

"Wait, you kissed her?" Cody says.

I nod, feeling my face flush. Dec looks almost mad, like when he thought I was flirting with Megan. I don't know why. It's not like he had a thing for Arielle—at least that I know of.

"Did I or did I not call this on the Fourth of July?" Cody says with a triumphant smirk. He glances over at Dec. "Jake denied making googly eyes at her, but there was serious googlyage going on."

"Are you guys ever going to stop yakking so we can play?" Dec says in a sharp voice.

"Sure," I say, shrugging, with a quick glance at Cody to see if he noticed the edge in Dec's voice, too. But he's too busy picking a Crusader name.

"Can I be Sir Galahad?" he asks. "He's the one who gets the Holy Grail, right?"

"Not in the Monty Python movie," I say. "Speaking of which, can I be a Knight Who Says Ni?"

Dec rolls his eyes. "So glad you're taking this seriously."

What is with him today? Like I know he's mad I blew him off for Arielle, but still.

"Come on, Dec, it's a game," I remind him.

We start playing, and it becomes clear pretty quickly that Declan's been playing at every available opportunity. The three of us are usually well matched on most games, but he's slaughtering people left and right, using swords and maces, and teaming up with some of the others in the chat to use fire arrows and siege weapons like trebuchets.

Imperialist Empires isn't the best game I've ever played. But it's fun enough, and while we're playing, Declan seems happier, almost like his old self.

Then I hear one of the other people playing say, "Yeah! Killed another towelhead!"

Wow.

"Whoa. That's so wrong," I say to Declan in an aside.

"It's just a joke," he says, without even taking his eyes off the screen.

I glance over at Cody, but he's pretty into the game and isn't paying attention to Declan and me.

But that's not all. Peppered throughout the chat are comments about politics and how "we should have killed all the Muslims back in the Crusades" because now "London has become 'Londonistan'" and "Europe is turning into 'Eurabia.'" Someone starts complaining that because the Crusaders ended up losing to the Muslims in medieval times, "we have to prepare for a twenty-first-century crusade in case they start taking over our country with Sharia law."

It's all so blatantly Islamophobic I can't keep listening without saying anything.

"Am I the only one hearing this crap?" I ask, wondering why no one else seems to mind.

"Come on, Jake, it's a game!" Dec says, throwing my own words back

at me, his thumbs working continuously. "Crap! Pay attention! You're letting them break through our flank!"

Ugh, I am.

I try to tune it out, even though there's a heavy feeling in my gut for
doing so. Working with the rest of the group, we manage to use the bat-
tering ram to break down one of the gates of Jerusalem, and our army
floods through, despite the best efforts of Saladin's army to defeat us.

"Yeah! Good work, my brothers!" the one named OdalRune88 says.
"We have reclaimed the Holy City for Christians."

"It's a holy city for Jews and Muslims, too," I mutter to my friends.

"Since when did you become such a social justice warrior, Jake? You
sound like Kayleigh," Declan says. "Like you said, it's just a game."

"I know, but . . . you don't believe this crap about Muslims trying to
take over Europe, like, today, do you?"

"It is kind of a lot," Cody admits.

Declan is ignoring us, totally absorbed in the game, which just makes
me even more pissed.

"Hello?" I say, waving my hand in front of his face. "Do you even
hear us?"

Sighing, Declan finally looks away from the screen. "What happened
to your sense of humor?"

"Wait, so it's our fault for not finding this crap funny?" Cody asks.

"What part of 'it's just a joke' don't you understand?" Declan says in a
tone that implies we're the idiots here for not laughing.

"The part where I know it's not," I say, pushing back.

"You don't even know these guys," Declan protests. "They joke around
a lot. They say crap for the lulz, just to get a reaction."

Then one of the guys in the chat starts talking about globalists. He's droning on about how the "globalists that control the media and the banks are promoting radical feminism and loose immigration policies to emasculate white men and achieve white genocide."

"Whoa!" Cody says, glancing over at me, wide-eyed.

"You've got to be kidding me," I say, tossing the controller down. I'm so angry, I'm about to explode.

Declan puts down his controller and sighs. "What now?" he says. "You're spending more time whining than you are gaming."

"Are you even hearing the things these idiots are saying?" I ask. "You realize by 'globalists' they mean people like me, right?"

"What do you mean, people like you?"

"Jewish people," I bite out between gritted teeth. "That's who."

"No way!" Declan protests. "They're talking about the international group of people who control the banks and the media and—"

"In other words, Jews," I say. "Or at least that's what the antisemitic conspiracy theory claims."

"That's total crap! They haven't used the word *Jews* once," Declan says. He looks at Cody. "Did you hear them say *Jew*? Did you?"

Cody looks like he wants to be anywhere but in the middle of this. "No, but—"

"See!" Declan exclaims, picking up the controller again. "You're getting all worked up about nothing. Lighten up, Jake!"

"They're using *globalist* because it sounds more acceptable," I say, frustrated. "Antisemitic people know what it really means, but most people don't."

Declan's still trying to play along with the game, and that pisses me off.

"Can you stop for a minute and listen to me?" I say, grabbing at his controller. "This is important, Dec!"

"I'm listening," he says. "Are you telling me I'm dumb because I don't get it?"

It's like he's purposely trying not to understand; like he doesn't even care enough about our friendship to try. But I do care, so I explain again.

"No! I'm just saying that I know what *globalist* means, because it's part of some old antisemitic conspiracy theory," I tell him. My chest tightens. Declan's one of my best friends. Why won't he listen?

"That's not what they're saying!" Declan insists.

I put down his controller and stand up. "Stay if you want to, Cody, but I'm out of here."

Declan looks up at me, his brow furrowed, and then the two of us look at Cody, who is wearing a pained expression, like he's torn between Declan and me.

Why isn't this obvious to them? It makes me second-guess myself. Am I overreacting? I mean, I didn't know what *globalist* really meant until recently. But still . . . I can't believe Dec won't even listen.

"I should probably go, too," Cody says. "Since I'm Jake's ride."

A brief, hurt look flashes across Declan's face before he goes back to the game. "Suit yourselves," he says, shrugging.

Wow. I mean . . . just . . . WOW.

"I'll leave the snacks," Cody says, like they're some kind of peace offering.

Declan ignores him.

I don't want to make peace. I'm shaking with anger and anxiety, and I can't wait to get out of here.

"What was that all about?" Cody says when we're both in the car. "That was . . . crazy."

"You think?"

"Is it true what you said about globalists?" Cody asks. "I've heard people say that a lot online, and I never realized that it meant Jews."

"It can have a lot of meanings," I say. "Like it could just mean people who have an international outlook as opposed to, you know, being all 'rah rah, my country first.'"

"So . . . why did you get so pissed?" Cody asks. "I mean, the white genocide stuff seemed kind of out there, but they didn't say Jews."

"Because the minute someone starts talking about controlling the banks and the media, antisemitism is at the root of what they're saying, that's why," I explain. "It's literally straight out of this antisemitic conspiracy theory some dude in Russia made up like over a hundred years ago."

"That's insane," Cody says. "No wonder it set you off."

"Like we could really control the world. There's this joke about how you get two Jews in a room, and you get three opinions. We'd never be able to agree on our secret world-controlling strategy."

Cody laughs. "You aren't the only ones. Try getting the Irish to agree on anything."

It feels good to laugh.

Still, what Cody doesn't see, and might not understand even if he did, is that underneath the humor, I'm still fuming. Declan might think his friends were joking. But unlike him, I know how dangerous their words can be, and it scares the crap out of me.

DECLAN

"My friends are such cucks," I tell my *IE* friends after Jake and Cody leave. "They just walked out because you guys kept talking about globalists."

"That's hilarious," Xtiansoldier503 says.

"One of them is Jewish, and he said that it's antisemitic," I say.

"Figures. They think *everything* is antisemitic," FenrirLupus says. I can practically hear him rolling his eyes.

"Yeah, like this," OdalRune88 says, laughing.

He posts a caricature in the chat of a guy with a big, hooked nose and hooded eyes, clutching a fistful of money.

I mean, that does look kind of antisemitic, if I'm honest, even though I know nobody takes this stuff seriously. It's a good thing Jake isn't here. He'd totally lose it.

"Screw them if they can't take a joke," Xtiansoldier503 says.

Exactly.

At least these guys have a sense of humor. At least these guys are here for me.

Unlike Jake and Cody.

The next morning at work, Charlie asks me what time my shift ends.

"I get off at four," I tell him.

"Same," Finn says.

"My shift ends at four thirty," Charlie says. "Then I'll drive you two out to Ronan's."

I'm supposed to go home after work. It's my turn to get dinner ready, because Mom's got a late client again and Dad's working an extra shift. Kayleigh is going to flip out if I blow it off.

But I'm really dying to meet this Ronan guy.

I send Kayleigh a text: Hanging out w Finn after work. I know it's my turn to make dinner. Can you cover for me?

She sends back a rolling-eye emoji. OK. But you are going to OWE me, big time!

Thank you sis, I text back.

Kayleigh replies, You mean TY brilliant goddess sister, don't you?

I chuckle, and respond: Sure, whatever.

"Okay, I'm in," I tell Charlie.

After work, Finn and I hang out in the break room waiting for Charlie.

In the middle of a conversation about *Imperialist Empires* strategies, he suddenly says, "You know, you're not as much of a Chad as I thought you were."

"What do you mean, a Chad?"

"You know. One of those jerk guys who's always getting some from the hot girls."

I snort with laughter. Finn's lips thin, like he's pissed at me for some reason, so I try to explain why I found it so funny.

"Me? I wish. First of all, I don't get all the girls. If I did, I'd be working at camp with all my teammates, and doing travel baseball, instead of here with my messed-up arm, asking people if it'll be cash or charge," I point out. "And are you calling me a jerk?"

"No," Finn says, looking down at his chewed fingernails. Then he exhales. "I mean, actually, yeah, you were a total jerk in elementary school. You and Mike Sebastian used to rag on me constantly about having clothes from Goodwill. Like shopping at Walmart for your clothes made you so much better."

I have no recollection of doing that—not even a vague memory.

"Um . . . sorry?" I say.

Finn stares at me. "You don't remember, do you?" he says in a clipped voice.

Should I lie so he chills out?

"Don't bother pretending you do," he says. "Because I can tell from the look on your face that you don't."

"You're right, I don't," I say. "But I am sorry. For real."

Finn shrugs. "I gotta admit that when I heard you were injured, I thought you deserved it."

Now it's my turn to be pissed. "Seriously? Finn, that's—"

"Can you blame me?" he asks.

"Yeah!" I tell him.

"Relax! I changed my mind," Finn says. "Anyway, don't you imagine bad things happening to the summer people who treat you like crap?"

Busted.

"Yeah," I admit.

"So give me a fricking break, okay?"

Just then, Charlie comes into the break room, muttering under his breath. "That stupid cow . . . I swear, if she keeps getting on my case about every little thing, something's gonna happen to her."

"I'll help," Finn says. "She's such a man-hater."

"Who?" I ask.

"Rita," Finn says. "Wait till she starts on you."

Rita's been okay to me so far, but maybe it's just because she's a friend of my mom's.

"I should have gotten that manager job," Charlie says, his voice laced with bitterness. "She only got it because they could check off two diversity boxes—brown and woman." He rips off his plastic apron, scrunches it into a ball, and tosses it into the garbage. "Let's get out of here."

We follow him out to his double cab pickup. It's got a bumper sticker on the back window that's the same as OdalRune88's avatar, and the interior smells of coffee, oil, and sweat. Finn takes shotgun and I push aside empty soda cans, coffee cups, and Burger Barn bags to clear room for myself on the back seat.

"What's that sticker?" I ask. "One of my *IE* friends has it as his avatar."

"It's the othala rune," Charlie says. "Sometimes called the odal rune."

"But what does it mean?" I ask.

"It's got a few meanings," he replies with a cryptic nonanswer.

But I don't ask any more because he starts the engine and hatecore blasts from the speakers. Charlie immediately begins to sing along at the top of his lungs, clearly still pissed at Rita. Finn joins in as well as we tear out of the parking lot. I can feel the rapid beat of the drums thrumming along my skin, and suddenly I feel lighter than I have in weeks.

I lean forward and shout, "What band is this?"

"BloodAxe," Charlie says. "You like it?"

"Yeah," I say.

"I'll send you some songs," Charlie says. "You can't get them through any of the usual streaming services, because they're controlled by globalists, like the rest of the media."

Man, these globalists keep coming up everywhere. It's like they really do control the world.

Charlie turns up the volume even more, and we headbang along to the screaming lyrics and driving guitar riffs as we leave Stafford's Corner. It's like this band knows me; like they wrote this music as a soundtrack for my rage.

About ten minutes outside town, Charlie turns right down an unpaved driveway that disappears into the woods. Evergreen trees form a dark canopy overhead, so thick that you can barely see the afternoon sun filtering through. It's kind of eerie, like driving through a dark tunnel toward an alternate universe. I can't imagine living out here. Stafford's Corner is a small town, and living within a hike of its center, I've grown up surrounded by the sights and sounds of neighbors. This place seems lonely and isolated.

Eventually, the driveway widens and there are a couple of cars and pickup trucks parked around an old wooden house.

Charlie pulls in behind a beat-up one, which has an *American Media: the Enemy Within* bumper sticker.

"Welcome to my home away from home," Finn says as we get out of the truck.

"Ronan will be happy to hear that," Charlie says, putting his hand on Finn's shoulder in a fatherly gesture.

We walk up to the house. There's a small flower bed to the right of the front door, with scraggly bushes. It's not all neat and perfect like the houses around the green in the center of town. Like the house the Kramers moved into.

The first thing I see when I walk in are the flags. There's a huge Confederate flag on one wall, and another giant flag on the opposite wall that I don't recognize. In the corner, there's a wood carving of a skull and crossbones, but not the pirate kind. It looks strangely familiar. I think maybe it's someone's avatar in one of the games I've been playing.

There are a few older guys sitting around on worn couches and chairs in the living room, playing *Imperialist Empires* on a huge screen that's larger than any I've seen and looks practically brand-new.

"Look who's here, it's Charlie and Little Brother!" one of the guys says, even though Finn's like a six-foot beanpole who probably towers over him.

"Hey, Luke, what's up?" Finn says. "Hey, Reid. What's up, Ronan?"

"Welcome back, Finn," says a guy with a buzz cut and a close-cropped beard. "Good to see you, as always."

He stands up and puts an arm around Finn's shoulders. Then he looks at me. "So, who is this new recruit you've brought me today?"

Recruit? What is this, the military? Finn said this was a place to chill.

"This here's Declan," Charlie says. "He works with Finn and me at Big V."

Ronan looks like he's in his mid to late thirties. He's not particularly tall, but he's built of solid muscle. He's wearing camo fatigues and a black T-shirt, and he's got a skull and crossbones like the one in the wood carving tattooed on his bicep.

He looks at me with dark eyes that seem to see right through my feeble front of confidence to the loser I feel like underneath. I'm half expecting him to tell me to get out of his house.

But then he smiles, and the crinkle lines around his eyes make him look less intimidating, more welcoming.

"Hey, Declan. Finn's told me good things about you."

"Uh, thanks," I say. "Likewise."

"Why don't you guys go get something from the kitchen?" Ronan says. "Betheney's in there working. She'll hook you up with some snacks, then you can come back and play with us."

I follow Finn into the kitchen. A girl who looks like she's only a few years older than us is sitting at the kitchen table, typing furiously on a laptop with a sticker of that same skull-and-crossbones thing.

"Hey there!" she exclaims when she looks up and sees us. "It's the Finnster and his friend!"

She stands up to greet us. She's really pretty, with long, straight blonde hair and big blue eyes that seem to pop out of her pale skin, like she's an anime dream girl come to life. Her thin arms are covered in tattoos of skulls and flowers and a bunch of symbols I don't recognize.

She wraps her arms around Finn and says, "How have you been? I've missed seeing you."

Finn hugs her back, and when she pulls away, she keeps an arm around his waist.

"So who's McDreamy, Finn?" she asks.

My brain seems to short-circuit. Name. She asked my name.

"Declan," I manage to get out.

She reaches out her hand and touches my cheek. "Welcome, Declan. I'm Betheney. We're glad you're here."

She tilts her head and smiles. "You guys hungry? I can make you some peanut butter sandwiches. Might even have some chips to go with them."

"Sounds good to me," Finn says. I pull myself together enough to say, "Me too."

"Two sandwiches, coming right up," she says, going to grab a loaf of white bread, a jar of peanut butter, and a knife.

"So, tell me about you, Declan," she says as she spreads a thin layer of peanut butter on a slice of bread.

"Um . . . well . . . there's not much to tell. I . . . uh . . . work with Finn and Charlie."

"Finn tells us you used to be some kind of baseball star," she says.

Used to. Even Finn doesn't think I can do it. My fists clench. "I'm working hard to get back to where I was by the time the season starts next spring," I say. "But it's hard when your family and friends"—I throw Finn a pointed glance—"don't think you can do it."

"Well, I believe you can," she says, stopping what she's doing and putting her hand on my bicep. Her fingers are warm and create a tingling in my blood. "We're so glad to have you here. Finnster, can you get Declan a drink while I finish making these sandwiches?"

"You want a soda?" Finn asks, suddenly annoyed.

"Yeah, thanks."

I take the can he offers me, pop it open, and take a swig.

"You got a girlfriend?" Betheney asks.

I start choking. Smooth, Declan. Real smooth.

"Um . . . not at the moment." Probably not ever at this rate. If I couldn't get the girl when I closed the deal at state, how am I ever going to?

"Those high school girls must be idiots," she says. "Good-looking kid like you."

"Don't even talk to me about high school girls," Finn says. "They're a bunch of stuck-up Stacys who are only interested in Chads." He gives me a pointed look. "I used to think Declan was a Chad. But now I know he's not."

"How's that?" Betheney asks.

I tell her the sad story of how I tried to impress Megan and failed, epically.

Betheney shakes her head. "You men," she says. "I just don't know."

"Figures that it was Jake Lehrer flirting with Megan," Finn mutters. "He's a total Chad."

Part of me instinctively wants to defend Jake. But I don't. Megan talks to Jake the way I wanted her to talk to me.

"Your time will come," Betheney says. She takes two plates out of the sink, gives them a little rinse, then puts our sandwiches on them. "There you go. Now I've got to get back to work. These comments aren't going to write themselves!"

I wonder what comments she's talking about. Finn explains on the way back to the living room. "Betheney is a master troll. You wouldn't think a girl would be good at it, but she can start a flame war in no time. She owns SJWs for breakfast."

I'm no stranger to trash talking or social justice warriors (thanks, Kayleigh). It was part of being on the baseball team, a way to get each other pumped to work harder, get stronger, play better.

"Maybe she can give me tips for dealing with Kayleigh," I say.

Finn snorts, and we take seats on either side of Ronan on the sofa, getting right into the game.

After Finn manages to shoot two infidels with a single arrow, Ronan claps him on the back. "Nice work, soldier!"

Finn's face lights up with a proud smile.

In between game playing, Ronan asks me questions.

"Must be hard to lose something that's as important to you as baseball," he says.

Here we go again. Fricking Finn. I'm going to have to tell him to stop saying that.

"It's not entirely lost," I protest. "By next spring, I should be pitching again. At least I hope so. I'm torturing myself with all the PT exercises, so . . ."

"Determination," Ronan says. "I like that." He smiles. "I'm really glad you're here, Declan. I hope you'll come around a lot. You're welcome here, anytime."

The others murmur their agreement.

It's the best time I've had since the accident. I can't wait to come back.

JAKE

"Hey, that new *Star Wars* movie starts at the Plattsfield Mall tonight," Cody says on Friday morning before camp starts. "Wanna go?"

"Is that even a question? Of course I wanna go!" I say.

"I'm going to text Dec and see if he wants to come," Cody says.

"Good luck with that," I say. "I've been trying to hang with him for weeks now. Since our fight. I figured maybe if we could just chill without playing that game, I could get him to understand why the stuff his friends were saying was so out of line." I kick a pebble with my sneaker. "But he keeps blowing me off."

"Huh," Cody says. "I mean, you were both pretty mad, but you'd have thought by now . . ."

"Maybe you'll have better luck," I say.

But later, while we're supervising the campers eating lunch, Cody tells me that Declan says he's working and then he's got other plans.

"Since it's not going to be guys' night, how about I invite Arielle and Kayleigh?" I suggest.

"Why not?" He flashes me a sly grin. "As long as you don't spend the whole movie making out with your girlfriend."

"She's not my girlfriend," I protest. "I mean, yeah, we kissed that one time and we've been flirty texting and stuff, but we haven't really hung out. Either she's working, or I'm working, or I'm at baseball practice."

"But you *want* her to be your girlfriend, right?"

"I mean, yeah. I like her," I say. It feels weird to talk about a relationship I can't even define myself.

"So my condition still stands. We're talking *Star Wars.*"

"Geek," I say, rolling my eyes at him while sending a group text to the girls to see if they want to come.

"Right back at ya," Cody says, then goes to stop a pretzel-throwing incident between two campers, which is threatening to escalate into a major food fight.

That night, Cody picks me up, and I slide into the back seat next to Arielle and give Kayleigh's ponytail a light tug. "Yo, what's up?"

Kayleigh grabs her ponytail and pulls it forward out of my reach. "How old are you again?"

"Old enough to remember when you wrestled me in the sandbox the last time I pulled your hair," I say.

Arielle giggles. "Who won?"

I look at her with mock hurt and disbelief. "How could you have any doubt? It was so definitely me."

Kayleigh turns and rolls her eyes at me. "Sure, Jake. If that's what you need to believe to sleep at night."

Smiling, I turn to Arielle. "The truth is that Mrs. Johnston separated us before we went the full three rounds," I admit. "Then, when I got home, my parents gave me this long lecture about touching another person without their consent. They limited my screen time as a punishment. I couldn't even argue self-defense, because I pulled Kayleigh's ponytail first."

"And yet you still didn't learn," Arielle says, a smile quirking her lips.

"Being smart is Ben's shtick. Baseball is mine."

"Meanwhile, Dad started giving Declan a hard time for not 'protecting' me, even though he was on the other side of the playground when it went down," Kayleigh says. "Anyway, that's beside the point. I couldn't understand why Dad was getting on Declan's case instead of being proud of me for defending myself."

I can tell how much that still bugs her, all these years later.

"Speaking of baseball . . . what's Declan up to tonight?" Cody asks Kayleigh. "I thought he'd be all over coming to see this movie."

She shrugs. "Who knows? I barely see him these days. He's probably hanging out with Finn McCarthy at this dude Ronan's house," Kayleigh says. "He seems to spend his life there at the moment."

"I'd have never pictured Declan and Finn McCarthy hanging out," I say.

"Me neither," Cody agrees.

"They both work at Big V," Kayleigh says. "And they both play that Crusader video game that Declan's totally obsessed with. Something *Empires*."

Cody and I exchange a glance in the rearview mirror. Kayleigh notices. "What?"

So we tell her about all the Islamophobic and antisemitic trash Dec's friends were saying.

She shakes her head. "He's been saying so much random crap lately. I wonder if he's getting it from there, or from hanging out with Finn, or these videos and podcasts he's obsessed with," Kayleigh says. "Oh god, do you know what he had the nerve to say to me this morning?"

"Go on, tell us," Cody says, grinning. "This has got to be good."

"Yeah . . . no," Kayleigh tells him. "He said that white Christians should be paid reparations because Muslim corsairs off the Barbary Coast enslaved them for the Ottoman Empire . . . in like the 1500s!" She rolls her eyes.

"Wow. Never heard that one before," Cody says.

"That's not all," Kayleigh says. "He told me that 'feminazis' like me were trying to 'destroy thousands of years of Western civilization.'" She shakes her head in disgust. "Can you believe it? Do you think twins can get divorced?"

I know it's not funny, but I can't suppress a bark of laughter. "Has Declan developed a sudden death wish?"

"I don't know, but if he keeps saying this stuff, we'll find out," she says as Cody pulls into a space at the mall. "I mean, come on! If women asking to be treated like the intelligent, equal human beings that we are is going to destroy Western civilization, then maybe that civilization wasn't so great in the first place."

"You're not wrong," Cody says.

It still blows my mind that Declan is saying this kind of crap, much less believing it.

Kayleigh kicks a pebble. "Okay, for the rest of tonight, no one is allowed to mention Dec. I need a night where I don't have to think about him."

"Deal," Cody says.

But even though we're not talking about Declan, it's hard to get the stuff he's saying out of my mind.

DECLAN

We're hanging out at Ronan's, gaming and eating pizza on Friday after work when he stands and says, "Listen up. It's time to initiate our newest recruit."

He smiles at me. I hope this isn't like some fraternity initiation where they film me eating a ghost pepper and post it online or whatever.

I'm also not 100 percent sure what I'm being initiated for.

Charlie, Finn, and the others are all grinning, like they're in on some secret that I'm not.

Ronan takes a small bag off the shelf and hands it to me.

I open it up, not sure what to expect, but it's just a bunch of bumper stickers that say *Defend America, Fight Globalists!* in a black Nazi font, but the background is red, white, and blue, so they look totally patriotic.

"Your mission is to sticker as many cars as you can at the Plattsfield Mall tonight," Ronan says. "Charlie and Finn will drop you off." He looks me in the eye. "They'll be there to keep an eye on you."

I can't tell if that's for my protection or what.

He pulls a black gaiter out of his back pocket and hands it to me. "To protect your identity." Gesturing for me to stand up, he slips it over my head, like he's arming me for battle, then pulls it up to cover my mouth and nose before stepping back and smiling. "Charlie and Finn can block a few of the security cameras, but there are a lot so you need to cover up." He puts his hand on my shoulder. "You up for this, Dec?"

I nod slowly. "I won't let you down."

But once I'm in the truck with Charlie and Finn, heading to the mall, I ask, "What happens if I get caught?"

"Don't worry, Finn and I will be keeping watch for you," Charlie says. "We've got your back, brother."

"Even if you do get caught, it's like a misdemeanor," Finn says. "It's not like we're actually hurting anyone."

"Besides, we're in a war for our survival," Charlie says. "We need to wake up our white brothers and sisters, so they understand and join us."

"Red-pill them," Finn says. "You've seen *The Matrix*, right?"

"Of course!" I tell him. "What do you think I am, culturally illiterate?"

"Relax, Dec, I was just checking, man," Finn says.

"Sorry," I mumble. I don't want to admit to being nervous.

"Most Americans are still taking the blue pill: sleeping in their little pods, believing all the crap they're being fed. They don't realize that by the time they finally wake up, whites are going to be a minority in our own country," Charlie says. "But us? We've been red-pilled. We're warriors." He looks up and smiles at me in the rearview mirror. "And the globalists who want to destroy us? They won't know what hit them. Because we're going to fight."

"Okay, I get all that . . . but what's the point of stickering people's cars?" I ask. "Besides initiating me, I mean. Doesn't it just piss people off?"

"We're letting them know we're here," Charlie says. "These bumper stickers are recruitment tools. We're taking the flyer to the next level. People can't just crumple up and toss a sticker."

"That makes sense," I say.

Finn turns around, a broad smile on his face. "I had this idea to add a QR code to the stickers, to make it even easier for people to find us. When we did leafleting on the Fourth of July, our overall site traffic increased by ten percent. The QR code will drive it up even more."

"There's another level to our recruitment," Charlie says. "And that's when people hear about stuff like this on the news, they know they aren't alone. That we're going to fight to protect what's ours."

I'm not sure about the whole white race thing, but I'm super impressed with Finn.

"You should be in like marketing or something, Finn," I say. "That QR code is genius. Bet you could get paid big bucks doing stuff like that."

"What, so I can help companies advertise useless crap for white people to buy so we can be in greater debt to the globalists?" Finn says. "No, thank you."

I think of the medical debt that's crushing my parents. Finn has a point.

"There's one more purpose, Declan," Charlie says, smirking. "And that's to scare our enemies. To let them know that we aren't going to let them get away with it."

"Make sure you get all the Priuses and Subarus," Finn says. "SJWs love those. Slap our stickers over their dumb liberal ones."

"Yeah, and Teslas, because only the summer people can afford those," Charlie says. He turns into the parking lot at the back of the mall, the one near the movie theater, and parks in a spot in one of the darker corners.

He points out all the security cameras. "Stay low. Try to stick between cars as much as you can. We'll keep an eye out for mall security."

Finn switches off the interior light so that it doesn't go on when I open the door. "You ready?"

"Yup," I lie, opening the door and crouching down. Keeping to the shadows, I slip between cars and try to stay as low as I can to avoid getting caught on camera. I go along the row, car by car, slapping stickers on each bumper. If the car has liberal bumper stickers, or if it's a Subaru or a Prius, I put on two, just to make them cry.

Then I come to a familiar minivan. It's Mario.

Cody texted me to go to the movies with him and Jake, but I'd already told Charlie and Finn that I would go to Ronan's.

I hesitate to put a sticker on his mom's car. I know Mrs. Miller. She'll be really mad.

But then I remember how Cody sided with Jake that time they came over a few weeks ago, and I slap two stickers on Mario. Serves Cody right, the traitor.

I've stickered a few rows when I hear people coming. I hide between two cars, hoping that neither of them is the one they're heading for. The pounding of my heart echoes in my ears. As they get closer, I hear them talking. It sounds like a couple on a date, because they're definitely flirting.

Then I hear the woman swear. "Nate, look at this! Some jerk put a sticker on my car!" Then she curses again. "Are you kidding me? It's a white supremacist sticker!"

What kind of guy lets the woman drive on a date? I wonder. On the other hand, at least he *has* a date.

"Crap. So it is," the guy Nate says.

"How did they know I'm Jewish?" she says, and I hear fear in her voice. It gives me a sense of power, like I haven't felt since the last time I struck out a batter, almost two months ago.

I smile behind my mask.

"I don't think they did," Nate says. "Look, all the other cars have them, too."

"Let's get out of here," she says, a tremor in her voice. "What if they're nearby?"

We *are* nearby, lady.

I hear them open the car doors, the engine fires up, and they drive off.

I've still got a few stickers left, and I find a Tesla with a Pride sticker and a *Coexist* sticker. Perfect. I slap on the remaining *Defend America* stickers over the liberal ones and make my way back to the truck.

As soon as I slide into the back seat, I explode with laughter. "Guys, you have to hear this," I say. I tell them about the couple and the woman's reaction.

"'How did they know I was Jewish?'" I say, mimicking her in a falsetto voice.

As Charlie drives us home, we're laughing so hard my ribs start to hurt.

"Hey, brother, since you enjoyed that so much, we'll make sure to include you in some other 'activities' Ronan has planned," Charlie says.

I can't wait.

JAKE

"That movie was perfect summer escapism," Arielle declares as we come out of the theater. "Lots of action, didn't have to think too much, and best of all, good won over evil."

"Yeah, that doesn't seem to happen enough in real life," Cody says.

"Too right," I say. Arielle and I are holding hands, like we did during the movie. We even snuck a kiss or two when Cody wasn't looking.

I stop suddenly, horrified by what I see on the bumper of a nearby car.

It's a sticker for some extremist group. It's red, white, and blue, and says *Defend America, Fight Globalists!* in the same font the Nazis used.

Arielle gasps. She obviously saw it, too.

A rush of fury fills my body, more intense than anything I've ever felt. It scares me, because it feels like the anger is in control, not me.

"It's not just on this car," Kayleigh says. "It's on all the cars nearby. Either there's a group of these white power jerks in the mall or they've vandalized all these cars."

Arielle looks around, and I can feel the anxiety radiating from her. I understand her fear, because underneath the fury, I feel it, too. My family immigrated to the United States from Russia, Poland, and Ukraine over a century ago to get away from this crap. We were supposed to have left antisemitism in the old country. In America, the land my Yiddish-speaking ancestors called the goldene medina, or the golden country, we were supposed to be safe.

"They better not have put one of these on my car," Cody says, taking off. We rush after him.

But they have. And not just one, like on the other cars. There are two of them on the back bumper of Cody's car, ugly hatred masquerading as patriotism. That's the problem with antisemitism—it keeps morphing, trying to hide by using code words like *globalist*. Even when you feel safe, deep down you know it's still there, waiting to rear its ugly head when you least expect it. Like right now.

"It looks like there's one of those QR code things," Kayleigh says.

I open the camera on my phone and hold it up to the sticker. It takes me to a website that makes my skin crawl.

"This is insane," Kayleigh says, looking over my shoulder.

Arielle and Cody are looking over my other shoulder as I click around. There's one page that claims that Jews have this global conspiracy to control the world. The images turn my stomach.

"Those cartoons—and the stuff they're saying on this site—is straight out of Nazi Germany," Arielle says, and the strain in her voice echoes how I feel seeing this antisemitic garbage.

"Group hug," Kayleigh orders, and she and Cody surround Arielle and me with themselves and their arms, like a security blanket.

Arielle's trembling, and I take her hand and give it a squeeze.

"Okay, I'm getting this thing off my car," Cody says, starting to pick at the sticker.

"Do you think we should report it before you do?" I ask.

"I just want to leave," Arielle says. "What if they're still here?"

"Just let us get this off first," Kayleigh says. "We don't want to drive around advertising their hateful crap." She kneels down next to Cody. "Here, let me try. I've got longer nails."

While she's picking at the sticker as best she can, I take pictures of the cars with the stickers, and screenshots of the website. I feel like I'm polluting my phone, but I want evidence that this happened.

"I can't get them off without damaging Mario's paint," Kayleigh says. "You're going to need something more than my nails."

"Great. Now everyone's going to think *I'm* a hater," Cody says, unlocking the door so we can get in.

We're all kind of subdued on the way back to Stafford's Corner.

"Is this new?" Arielle asks suddenly. "Like has stuff like this happened around here before?"

"No!" Kayleigh says.

"No way," Cody agrees. "I mean, sure, there are jerks, just like anywhere else. But mostly good people."

I want to agree with them, to believe that it's true. But I've got memories they don't have. "I . . . don't know . . ." I say slowly. "I remember Rob Oberhulzer and Tim O'Reilly throwing pennies in front of me when we were in first grade, because they heard Jews were penny-pinchers. We were little kids. It's not like they got that watching *Sesame Street*. They got it from someone. And those someones live here."

"Besides, it's not even like Jewish people in medieval Europe had much choice about getting involved in moneylending," Arielle says. "They weren't allowed to own land or join trade guilds, so it was one of the few things they could do."

"Exactly," I say. "And Christians were forbidden to loan money, so they got us Jews to do it, and centuries later, we're still getting all this hateful crap because of it."

"You never told me that about the thing with the pennies, Jake!" Cody exclaims.

"You think it's something I wanted to talk about?" I ask. "I just wanted to be like everyone else."

"I didn't know that, either," Kayleigh says. "I'm . . . sorry."

"Thanks," I say. "But it's not like you did it."

"I know, but—" She cuts herself off, but I'm pretty sure she's thinking about Declan. He's not here, but he's in the air between us.

We drop the girls off first. When Cody finally pulls into my drive-way, he turns to me and says, "Jake, I just want you to know . . . I've got your six."

"Thanks, Cody," I say. "I needed that. This crap makes you feel scared. Alone." I exhale an angry sigh. "Which is probably exactly what they want."

"So don't give it to them," Cody calls out as I shut the car door.

The problem is, it's easier said than done.

Mom, Dad, and Ben are in the living room watching TV.

"Hey, how was the movie?" Dad asks, pausing the show they're watching.

"The movie was great," I tell them, flopping into an armchair. "But finding white nationalist stickers on all the cars in the parking lot afterward? Not so much."

"What?" Mom exclaims. "At the Plattsfield Mall?"

I nod. "Here," I say, pulling up the picture I took on my phone. "And if you swipe forward, you'll see the website where the QR code leads."

Ben scoots over so he can look at the same time as Mom and Dad. I watch the expressions on their faces and see the same anger, disgust, and fear that's making me feel like ants are crawling through my veins.

"I used to think it could never happen here," Mom says.

"When I was younger and thought I knew everything, my grandfather used to warn me that it could happen anywhere, if the conditions were right," Dad says. "I didn't believe him. Neither did my parents. 'This is America,' we used to tell him. 'We're safe here.'"

"Ha," Ben says, his expression grim.

I think about what Cody said about not giving the haters what they want. "Mom, remember Uncle Bernie gave me that Magen David on a chain for my bar mitzvah?"

My uncle Bernie is in the jewelry business, and he literally gives everyone in our family who has a bar or bat mitzvah the same present, a Jewish star.

"You mean the one you refused to wear because you 'didn't want to wear a necklace'?" Ben asks, pulling out his.

"Yeah, that one."

"It's in my jewelry box," Mom says.

"Can I have it?"

"Of course you can have it," Mom says. "It's yours."

"*Now* you want to wear it?" Ben asks, shaking his head.

Dad laughs. "Jake has always done things his own way, and in his own time."

Later, after Mom brings the chain into my room and helps me fasten it around my neck, I look in the mirror, seeing the silver Star of David glinting in the light. Yeah, all this crap makes me scared, but I'm not going to make them happy by giving in to the fear. Instead, I'm going to show them I'm proud to be Jewish. And I'm going to fight this hate, every way I know how.

DECLAN

It's late when I get home from Ronan's. The house is dark, and it looks like everyone is asleep, which suits me just fine. I'm on a high from what we did tonight, and I don't want my family to bring me down.

Stickering those cars in the parking lot felt like I was finally doing something concrete, however small, to fight back against the forces that are trying to keep guys like me down. When we got back to Ronan's, he told me what a great job I did. It feels good to have a purpose again.

I'm in bed checking my phone for any posts about the stickers at the mall when Kayleigh knocks on the door, barging into my room before I even have a chance to say anything.

"You're supposed to wait until I say it's okay," I remind her.

"Yeah, like you ever do," Kayleigh says, taking a leap onto the end of my bed and landing on my foot.

"Owww! Are you trying to destroy my leg so I can't walk or play baseball?"

"I'm Dec, and I'm a whiny brat!" Kayleigh says in a high-pitched voice.

I throw a pillow at her, making the mistake of using my right arm. It hits her, but without the force I intended, and I can't hide the grimace of pain.

"Are you okay?" Kayleigh asks, suddenly serious.

"I'm fine!" I snap, irritated by her concern. "What are you here for, anyway?"

She stares at me. "Oh, I don't know . . . because I felt like talking to my brother for some reason? Because we barely see each other anymore? Because something totally messed up happened at the mall tonight and I need to talk about it?"

I feel a surge of excitement, but work hard to keep it from showing on my face.

"Oh yeah? Like what?" I say, trying to sound totally casual.

"When we came out of the movie—which you would have loved, just so you know—some idiots had put these really awful bumper stickers on people's cars."

My heart beats faster. "Really? Awful how?"

"Like how we should protect America against globalists, which is totally antisemitic," Kayleigh says. "They had this QR code—it went to this website that had really horrific crap on it. Like really hating on Jews, and anyone who isn't white and Christian."

Inside, I'm fist pumping. I can't wait to tell the guys about this. Things are working just the way they're supposed to. But I make sure to keep my expression neutral.

"I was really upset by it, so you can imagine how Arielle and Jake felt," Kayleigh continues. "And I couldn't get the thing off Mario's bumper with my nails, so we had to drive home with that crap on the back of the car. Cody was pissed."

Kayleigh looks down, rolling the drawstring of her pajama bottoms into a tight ball and then releasing it. "I don't want to ask because I'm afraid of the answer," she says, bringing her gaze up to meet mine. "But . . . you didn't do it, did you?"

She doesn't get it, so I know I can't tell her the truth. She's not ready yet. So instead I say, with mock outrage, "Seriously, Kayleigh. Why would you think I'm involved?"

Her eyes search my face for clues, and I'm nervous, because she knows me so well.

"Because when I read some of the awful stuff on that website, I realized that it sounded kind of familiar, like what's been coming out of your mouth lately."

I roll my eyes so I don't have to look at her. "I wasn't even at the mall. I was hanging out at Ronan's house with Finn."

I see the confusion and uncertainty in her eyes. "Dec . . . you don't really believe all that stuff, right?" she asks, almost pleading with me to say no. "You don't really think that there's some secret group that controls everything, do you?"

Maybe here's my chance to get her to understand, to see the danger that we're in, to get her red-pilled. "You don't get what's happening, Kayleigh. The globalists want to dilute the purity of the white race. You should be glad that there are people who do understand and are willing to fight to protect our way of life."

Kayleigh stares at me, open-mouthed. "God, Declan . . . You really *do* believe that crap, don't you?"

I glare at her. I knew she wasn't ready. "I believe it because it's the truth. You're just not awake enough to see it."

She stands up, shaking her head like I'm the one who is ignorant here, not her. "I love you, Declan. I know it's been really tough for you since the accident, and I want to be there for you." Taking a deep breath, she continues. "But hearing that you've bought into this hateful stuff . . . you're making it really, really hard."

Then she turns her back on me and leaves, closing the door behind her.

I'm too riled up to sleep now, so I figure I'll play *Imperialist Empires* for a while. At least there, I know I won't be judged for wanting to protect the American way of life. At least there, I know people care about me, even if my family doesn't.

JAKE

A few days after we went to the movies, the local news shows some grainy video footage of a masked guy that they got off the security cameras at the mall. You can't really see much, but there's something familiar about the way he moves.

I send Kayleigh a link to it. Did you see this?

Yeah, she texts back. Jerk.

I take a deep breath and type, Does it look a little like Dec to you? Like the way the guy moves?

The three dots appear. Then disappear. Then appear. Then disappear again.

Finally, she texts back. It's hard to tell anything from that video, tbh. Anyway, I already asked him. That night. He said he was hanging out at Ronan's house.

I should feel relieved at that, but somehow, the doubt doesn't go away.

The last three weeks of summer pass way too quickly. Before I know it, it's the weekend before school starts. Instead of hanging out and chilling like a normal person would, I'm in the car with my parents, heading to Congregation Anshe Chesed for a special active shooter training before the High Holy Days, Rosh Hashanah and Yom Kippur.

"Isn't it bad enough that I have to suffer through all those active shooter drills at school?" I ask. "Now you're dragging me to one at synagogue, too?"

Mom eyes me in the rearview mirror. "It's not my choice of Sunday activity, either," she says, exhaling a heavy sigh. "Sadly, it's necessary. As president of the synagogue, I've got a responsibility to keep our congregants safe, at all times, but especially for High Holy Days. And after the murders of Jews at prayer . . ."

I see in the mirror she's getting upset, the way she always does when she talks about this stuff. Mom grew up in Pittsburgh, and her family went to the Tree of Life synagogue. The murder of eleven people on a Shabbat morning at a place where she became a bat mitzvah and where she and Dad got married—it was hard for all Jews in America and around the world, but for Mom it was personal.

My dad reaches over and gives her shoulder a comforting squeeze. Now I feel bad for complaining.

"Okay, I get it. We need to be prepared, because the synagogue is going to be full," I say.

I'm not sure what I believe about the whole God business at this point in my life, but with everything that's been happening lately, I've been thinking about it a lot more. Being Jewish has always been part of me, like my dark curly hair, being good at baseball, and having dyslexia.

One thing that all this has shown me is how most people around here don't get what it's like to be in a minority. Like, a few guys on the travel team tried ribbing me the day I showed up to practice wearing the Magen David pendant, and I was pissed. But true to his word, Cody had my back. He put an end to it by listing all the kids on the team who wear crosses at practice and during games without anyone saying squat. That shut my teammates up. They also apologized, which is more than I can say for Declan.

As usual, Tony, our regular armed security guard, is standing by the front door of the synagogue.

I remember one time I went to church with Declan's family after I'd slept over, not long after we met back in T-ball. I was freaked out that the doors were wide open, without a security guard in sight. When I said something about it to Declan and Kayleigh, they looked at me like I was crazy.

"Why would we have a security guard?" Declan asked.

They were shocked that we had buzzers to get into the building and security guards on duty every time there are services, or Hebrew school, or any other big events. Because Mom's the president, I know that in the last few years our congregation has had to raise money to install even more security, because of the increase in antisemitic hate crimes across the country.

I spot Arielle talking to Jordan Goldstein and Naya Luria, two other kids from the youth group.

"Hey, what's up?" I ask them.

"Not sure I'm ready for this," Naya confesses.

"What's the big deal?" Jordan says. "How many of these have we gone through at school?"

"I know," Naya says. "I guess I'm just freaked out by those antisemitic stickers that keep popping up everywhere. They were all over the dumpsters outside Big V on Friday."

"It freaks me out, too," Arielle admits.

Just then, Rabbi Jonas announces that the walkthroughs are about to start. "We welcome our representatives from Centurion, who will be taking through groups of twenty people at a time, so you'll have the opportunity to ask lots of questions," she explains. "Our youth group members will go through first so I can debrief with them afterward."

"Guess that's us," Jordan says, and we all head into the sanctuary, following a seriously ripped dude with a crew cut and Oakley shades pushed up on his head, wearing a black T-shirt with a graphic of a Roman centurion on the front and *Our Training Saves Lives* on the back.

"Good morning, everyone," the guy says when we've taken our seats. "I'm Troy, and I'm about to impart information that may save your life someday, so put your phones on silent and pay close attention." He pauses to give us time to do it. "Can anyone think of another time when you should automatically put your phone on silent?"

"When we're hiding from a shooter," Danielle Fox says, almost wearily. It's one of the things they've pounded into our heads at school.

"Correct," Troy says. He stands on the steps leading up to the bimah, staring us down, like he's evaluating our ability to survive if someone comes in with a gun and he finds us lacking. "Okay, next question: How long do you think the average active shooter incident lasts?"

"It feels like forever when we have to do the drills at school," Joel Kane says.

"In a real active shooter situation, your time perception will be distorted because your amygdala—what we call your lizard brain—becomes activated," Troy says. "But the reality is that seventy percent of active shooter incidents are over in five minutes or less, which means you have mere seconds to make a decision that could save your life."

I look out the window of the sanctuary, where the sun is shining and kids are playing. It seems so bizarre to be in here contemplating death.

Troy tells us that we have three options if a shooter enters the building: run, hide, or take action.

"If you only have seconds to figure out where to run, what should you be aware of at all times?" he asks.

"Where the exits are?" Arielle says.

"Bingo." Troy flashes her a smile, which makes him marginally less intimidating. "In any situation, whether it's here, or at a movie theater, or at a restaurant, or at school, always be aware of where the nearest two exits are, whether it's a door or a window," he continues. "If you've already identified where they are, you'll be able to make a quicker decision when the shooting starts."

When, not *if*. Like this is an inevitable occurrence, and it's just a matter of time before it happens.

I feel the Cheerios I ate for breakfast rise up in the back of my throat, and I swallow hard.

Troy is talking about how we shouldn't stop to help the injured, which seems so incredibly wrong. Like I get that we don't want to get killed ourselves, but I keep thinking about it as Troy leads us out of the sanctuary from one of the back doors behind the bimah, where only the rabbi and the cantor normally go, so we can see all the potential avenues of escape.

"Is it weird that these drills seem so normal?" I ask Arielle as we're walking through an underground corridor that leads past the kosher kitchens that are used to cater synagogue events.

"I know, right?" she says. "Another day, another active shooter drill. It's weird that it doesn't seem weird anymore." Her brow furrows. "Except . . . there's something a little different about this one. Like I wonder how many of the kids at the high school have them where they worship, too?"

"I bet most of them don't have a clue," I say, and tell her about how surprised Declan and Kayleigh were when I told them about our synagogue security all those years ago.

"Lucky them," she says with a soft, sad sigh. "It must be nice to be able to go to pray and not have to think about stuff like this."

I know that what we're learning today could save our lives, but still . . . it's a heavy weight to carry around.

Troy leads us into one of the Hebrew school classrooms to demonstrate how to use the special active shooter locks, and Arielle whispers, "I wonder if the reason I'm such a fast runner is because it's an inherited survival skill developed to escape all the people who want to kill us."

I snort with laughter, which earns me one of Troy's intimidating glares. But Arielle winks, and I realize just how much I like her.

By the time we've gone through the whole building, Troy's succeeded in scaring the crap out of us. He keeps repeating how vulnerable we are.

I kind of knew that already. One of Dad's favorite jokes is about how we can sum up so many Jewish holidays with "They tried to kill us, we survived, let's eat!"

So I'm not sure why this has left me feeling so tied up in knots. That's until we get to the end of the tour and Rabbi Jonas meets with us to ask how we're feeling.

"It seems so . . . not Jewish to leave people who are hurt just to save our own lives," Arielle says. "It's, like, against everything else we've ever been taught."

She just put into words what I couldn't.

"I was thinking the same thing!" I exclaim.

"Me too!" Naya says. "I mean, I understand why we're being told that, but . . . I can't imagine leaving any of my family behind."

"I bet if some guy walked in here with an AR15 and started spraying us with bullets, you'd change your mind," Jordan says.

"You've all raised valid points," Rabbi Jonas says. "As Jordan points out, we never know how we'll react in a given situation until we face it."

Jordan smirks at Naya.

But then Rabbi Jonas continues: "However, Jewish law teaches us that saving a life takes precedence over all the other commandments. For example, we're allowed to break observance of the Sabbath to do it."

"If that's the most important thing, isn't it wrong for us to focus on getting ourselves out without helping others?" I ask.

"That's not an easy question to answer," Rabbi Jonas says. "It's one that the ancient rabbis disagreed on. They had long discussions—"

"Shocker for anyone who has ever been at a seder . . ." Joel quips.

"True," Rabbi Jonas says, chuckling. "But Rabbi Ben Petora and Rabbi Akiva both discussed the ethics of saving oneself versus another by looking at a situation where two people are traveling together in the desert. One of them has a canteen of water. There isn't enough water for both to drink and reach civilization. If they share the water, both will die. If the person with the canteen keeps it for themself, then the other person will die." She scans our group, her eyes resting briefly on each person. "Which action do you think is the right one, and why?"

I have no idea of the answer. Maybe what the rabbi is saying is that there is no "right" answer?

"I would share the water," Arielle says. "I mean, what if the estimates are wrong, and there's a possibility that we could both live? How awful would it be to have even a small chance of saving someone else and not take it?"

"Also, how much of a jerk would you feel like, drinking the water while the other person watches you and is literally dying of thirst?" Danielle asks.

"How does it make it any more ethical if both of you die?" Jordan argues. "If the most important law is to save a life, isn't it better for at least one of you to live?"

Rabbi Jonas smiles. "Without even reading the Talmud, you've illustrated the different arguments. Ben Petora argued that the owner of the canteen should share the water for the reason Danielle brought up—so that they don't have to live with the guilt of having watched their companion die if they don't. Survivor's guilt is real. We saw it with Holocaust survivors and continue to see other communities suffer from it, like war veterans and people who have lived through natural disasters, and, yes, the kind of mass shooting incident that we are training ourselves for today."

I hope I never have to experience that. I don't want to have to ever put any of the things we've been training for today into practice. My fists clench as I realize there's a strong chance that I will.

"Jordan's argument is the one that Rabbi Akiva made years later, using his interpretation of the line in Leviticus chapter twenty-five, verse thirty-six: 'That your kinsman may live with you,'" Rabbi Jonas continues.

We all look at one another, checking in to see if any of us gets how that has anything to do with what Jordan said.

"Um . . . that seems kind of random," I say.

"I hear you, Jake," Rabbi Jonas says. "So let's break it down, Akiva style. He argues that in order for your kinsman to be able to live with you, you have to be alive. Therefore, the owner of the canteen of water should prioritize themselves over their traveling companion."

"Note to self: If I go for a walk in the desert, I'm gonna make sure I'm the one carrying the water canteen," I say.

"Note to self: If I go on a walk in the desert with Jake, make sure to bring my own water canteen," Arielle says, giving me a sideways grin.

I'm glad that we can still joke, even as we talk about ways that we could die.

Maybe that's another part of being Jewish that I wear along with my curly dark hair. Learning to laugh at things that scare me. I guess it's one way of dealing with the anxiety that bubbles up when I think about this stuff.

"You might recognize Rabbi Akiva's argument the next time you're on an airplane and the flight attendant tells parents to put their oxygen mask on first, before putting it on their small children," Rabbi Jonas says. "As with most of the interesting questions of human existence—particularly the ethical ones—much is in the interpretation. That's why it's so important for us to talk about these questions, as unsettling as they are."

"I don't know," Danielle says, twirling a piece of her hair around her finger. "It's kind of sad, but we've been doing active shooter drills ever since I was in kindergarten. By the time you get to high school it's like, yeah, yeah, we know what to do, can we stop sitting in a closet now?"

What Danielle says is depressing but true. There have been so many school shootings since I was in kindergarten, I can't remember them all. You'd think kids getting killed at school should be something so rare that each one would be engraved on our memory.

But still . . . "There's something different about this drill, though," I say, trying to put into words what's causing the unsettled feeling in my gut. "When we do the drills at school, we're not thinking that the kid with the gun in the hall is targeting us specifically because we're Jewish. That's what's freaking me out so much, I think."

"I feel you, Jake," Jordan says.

"Me too," Danielle says. "It's like you've always had this thing hanging over you, even though you can forget it most of the time, until someone says something dumb. But doing this drill forces you to think about it."

"Yes," Rabbi Jonas says. "And to give the thing you were talking about a name, it's called 'intergenerational trauma.' Research shows that descendants of Holocaust survivors suffer from it generations later."

"Like the descendants of enslaved people," Naya says. "Have you ever read *Beloved* by Toni Morrison?"

"Yes!" Arielle says. "It was really powerful."

"Great connection, Naya. It affects all groups that have experienced collective trauma," Rabbi Jonas says. "I want to thank all of you for braving your fears to come here today, even if you were dragged here by your parents." She smiles. "Now I hope you'll go out and enjoy the gorgeous weather for the rest of the day. Remember, when we toast, we say 'l'chaim'—to life!"

As we walk out into the sunshine to wait for our parents to finish, I take a deep breath, wanting to clear my lungs—and my head—of thoughts of death.

"So, that was a cheerful way to start the day!" Arielle says in a bright, high-pitched voice.

I laugh. "Yeah. Well, let's plan something a little more uplifting for our next hangout. Like . . . how about next weekend?"

Arielle tilts her head to the side and gives me a grin that makes her even cuter, if that's possible. "As long as it's funny and not about death."

I grin, and drop a brief kiss on her lips. "You got yourself a deal."

"And you got yourself a date," she says, smiling back at me.

DECLAN

Sometimes I wonder if Cathy, my physical therapist, knows what she's doing. I'm not seeing much progress with mobility and strength, or with the wrist drop, even though I'm religiously doing all the exercises she's given me.

I'm up early on Monday morning, so I have time to do the exercises and play some *IE* before work. I tell my *IE* friends about how badly it's going with PT.

"Lionheartttt, my man, sounds like you need the Alpha Dawg workout," OdalRune88 says.

"Yeah, A-Dawg is da MAN," FenrirLupus adds.

I ask them what the Alpha Dawg workout is.

"He'll whip you into shape," OdalRune88 says. "Prepare you to be a warrior. You can pay him a hundred fifty dollars to create a personalized workout plan, one that'll help you get back to full strength."

One hundred fifty bucks? I've saved some money over the summer, but still . . .

"That's kind of steep," I tell them. "I work at a grocery store making minimum wage. And school starts Wednesday, so I'll have to cut back on hours."

"I hear ya," FenrirLupus says. "But it's worth every penny. Especially because the Dawg doesn't just give you a workout—he gives life advice, too."

"Word," OdalRune88 says. "Alpha Dawg will get you back to a hundred percent in no time. Stronger of body *and* mind."

That afternoon, when I get home from hanging at Ronan's house after work, I look up Alpha Dawg's workout and try a free introductory one. OdalRune88 and FenrirLupus were right. Alpha Dawg doesn't just tell you to do X number of curls and crunches, squats and burpees—which I can't do 100 percent anyway yet because of my stupid arm—he gives you life advice while he's doing it. Like he's talking about stuff that alpha men do right and beta men do wrong, and best of all, the things women really want.

I decide to pay for the personalized plan, even though it's going to put a big dent in my savings. I figure it'll be worth it when I can pitch again and get a scholarship to college.

I set the alarm to get up early the next morning so that I can do another workout as well as my PT exercises. I'm just getting out of the shower when Kayleigh knocks on the bathroom door.

"Hey, Baldilocks, what's taking you so long—you don't even have any hair to wash!" she calls to me. "Can you move your butt so I'm not late for my shift?"

I wrap a towel around my waist and open the door.

"Chill your nuggets!" I say. "The bathroom is yours!"

"What were you doing this morning?" she asks. "It sounded like an elephant was stomping around in your room."

"I was working out, okay?" I say. "Is that a crime?"

"It is if you wake me up before the alarm," she says, yawning and shutting the bathroom door in my face.

As I'm heading downstairs for breakfast, I overhear my parents talking in the kitchen and pause on the third-to-last step so I can listen.

"How are we going to pay all these?" Mom says. "I've called the hospital to see if we can set up some kind of payment plan, but it's hard enough making ends meet as it is. What if Pinnacle—"

"Let's cross that bridge if we come to it," Dad says. "Which I hope we won't. I've worked there a long time, and I've never had a bad performance review. That's got to count for something, right?"

"I hope so," Mom says.

I cough so they know I'm coming and head into the kitchen to grab a Pop-Tart before leaving for work.

They both fake smile and say "Good morning!" like they weren't just stressing out about money.

I guess I should be grateful they're not reminding me that it's all my fault.

Work is the usual boring time. It's busy, which at least makes the time pass quicker. "Hey, Declan, need a ride to Ronan's after work?" Charlie asks as I pass the meat department on the way back from my break.

"Yeah, thanks. That would be awesome."

Charlie winks. "I'm always here to help you young warriors."

I stand a little taller. I like being thought of as a warrior. Not just as an avatar in *Imperialist Empires* fighting the infidel hordes threatening the Western European way of life, but in real life, too, fighting for my people.

Toward the end of my shift, I get a group text from Dad, asking Kayleigh and me to come straight home after work.

Crap. He probably wants to get on my case about something, since that's all he seems to do lately.

What's up? I text back.

We'll talk when you get home.

I consider going to Ronan's anyway. If Dad isn't even going to tell me why he wants me home, why should I go?

I'm still stewing as I scan the groceries for this family who are obviously summer people, judging by their expensive clothes and entitled attitudes. They've got a toddler who is screaming her head off and another kid who is wearing sneakers that I know for a fact cost almost two hundred bucks, because I wanted a pair myself, even though the kid looks like he's six and will probably grow out of them in two months.

Sneaker Boy is whining about how he wants candy and touching all the fancy chocolate bars by the register, the ones that only summer people can afford.

The mom is trying to quiet the toddler. The dad's totally engrossed in his phone, completely unaware his Ray-Bans are about to fall off his head and ignoring both the irritated looks from his wife and Sneaker Boy's whining, which is like a cheese grater being rubbed across my brain.

I'm scanning a bag of coffee that costs five times more than the stuff we have at home when I notice Sneaker Boy has taken a label off one of the fancy chocolate bars and is busy unwrapping it.

"You're going to have to pay for that now," I say, pointing to the kid. The dad is still busy texting, like I never even spoke. The woman turns to Sneaker Boy and talks to him like he's a rational human being instead of a snotty little kid. "Sebastian, you know that sugar makes you hyper. Please put that down or Mommy is going to be upset."

Figures the little twerp has a rich kid name like that.

He ignores her, just like his dad ignored me; he rips off the foil and takes a bite out of it.

"Mason! Do something!" the woman snaps at her husband.

His eyes finally leave his phone. "Bazzer! Put the candy on the belt so Daddy can pay for it," he instructs his son, whose mouth and hands are now covered in evidence. Then he turns to me. "Happy? Can you just do your job and ring us up so we can get out of here, or is that too difficult for someone of your obviously limited intelligence?"

"Jerk," I mutter, feeling the rage knot in my stomach, and this dude who managed to tune out his screaming daughter and whining son this entire time looks up from his phone and says, "What did you say?"

"I said, 'jerk,'" I reply louder, even though there's a part of my brain screaming that I need this job.

But I've been sucking it up all summer, and I'm done.

Then Sneaker Boy with his two-hundred-dollar kicks shoves his chocolaty face in his screaming little sister's face and shouts, "Jerk!" Like even at his age he knows that I'll get in trouble and he won't, because he's a spoiled rich kid and I'm not.

"Where's the manager?" the guy says. "I want to speak to the manager. Now!"

The woman behind him in line, a regular who lives here year-round, rolls her eyes and moves to another cashier. I push the Call Manager button, and the light starts flashing over my head.

I finish ringing up their stuff and say, "The manager is on her way. That'll be $186.44."

The guy pulls out his wallet, whips out a black American Express card, and shoves it into the card reader angrily. I hand him the receipt and say "Thanks for shopping at Big V" in a fake-nice voice, just as Rita arrives.

"What's up?" she asks.

I tilt my head toward Entitled Weekender Dad. Sneaker Boy is now prancing around singing "Jerk, jerk, jerk, you are a jerky jerk jerk," like he's auditioning to be a backup dancer at the Super Bowl halftime show.

"This cashier was extremely rude to us," EWD says.

Rita goes straight into suck-up-to-the-summer-people mode. She assures him that my use of "such language is contrary to the values here at Big V" and that I will "receive appropriate training so that it doesn't happen again," talking about me like I'm not even here and my side of the story doesn't count.

But what makes my head explode, what makes my teeth clench so hard that it feels like my molars are going to shatter, is that she gives them a $25 gift card to "make up for any inconvenience."

She's giving free money to the guy who was an entitled idiot and doesn't even need it, while the guy who really needs money—me—is the one in trouble.

EWD doesn't even thank Rita. He accepts the gift card as his due, slipping it into his wallet next to his collection of credit cards.

When they're out of earshot, Rita says, "Come with me, Declan," her words clipped. I wonder if I'm about to get fired.

I follow her into her tiny closet of an office. She gestures for me to sit and closes the door behind us.

"Why did you reward that guy for being a jerk?" I explode the minute the door shuts.

"Because he's the customer, and that family spends a lot of money here over the summer," Rita says. "And because you should know better than to be rude to him."

"You didn't even ask for my side of the story! Are you telling me rich people just get away with everything?" I say, my fists clenching over my knees. "Even treating us like crap?"

Rita sighs and points up to the sign above her desk, the one with the Big V customer policy: *The customer is always right.*

"I know it's hard sometimes, especially with some of the summer people," she says. "But if you want to keep your job here, you have to remember that."

She tells me to go back to work, and I take my time because I'm so mad, stopping at the meat department to tell Charlie what happened and that I can't go to Ronan's after work.

He curses. "That's why *I* should have been made the store manager. I would've set that guy straight. Rita doesn't have what it takes."

"I know, right? She just folded, without even getting my side of the story." I see Rita coming out of the back. "Gotta get back to the register."

"Hope everything's okay at home," Charlie says.

Me too.

Kayleigh and I end up biking home together because our shifts finish about the same time.

"Do you have any idea what's going on?" I ask her as we ride along, trying to avoid the patches of melting tar.

"No. I mean . . . I hope it's not . . ."

"What?"

"If I tell you what I think, you have to promise not to go off on one of your rants," she says.

"You mean me trying to get you all to wake up to the truth about what's going on?" I say, annoyed.

She rolls her eyes. "And that is exactly what I'm talking about."

"Fine, don't tell me," I say. "I can wait till we get home."

"Fine," she says.

I put in my earbuds and spend the rest of the ride home listening to one of the podcasts that Finn recommended. It talks about how people like me are being screwed because radical feminists are too busy wanting careers. How women should go back to their traditional roles of being wives and mothers, and let men make the decisions instead of trying to usurp our power.

As we ride, the rage that's always simmering inside me is at full boil. More and more, what Ronan says when we hang out at his house makes sense. We need to act, or I won't have a future.

Mom's car is in the driveway when we get home.

"This must be something really big if Mom's already home from work," Kayleigh says, heading to the house. I can tell from the tone of her voice she doesn't think it's anything good.

I follow and we find our parents sitting at the kitchen table, their faces grim.

"Did someone die?" I ask.

"No, thank goodness," Mom says. "But Dad has bad news."

We both turn to Dad, who seems like he's shrunken within himself.

"I got laid off. Pinnacle cut fifty workers, and I'm one of them."

Kayleigh lets out a gasp. "What? No way!"

My dad has worked for Pinnacle since he graduated high school, and they just flushed all his hard work and his loyalty down the toilet.

Just like the baseball team did with me.

And who did this to him?

Arielle's dad.

It's just like what everyone has been telling me. The globalists are trying to destroy us.

"What are we going to do?" Kayleigh asks.

"We'll make it work somehow, like we always do," Mom says. "I've been going through the budget and trying to see where we can cut." She sighs. "We're all going to have to make some sacrifices. I'm going to try to squeeze in more clients and see if I can get some extra wedding party bookings."

"Mom, how?" Kayleigh says. "You're already working super long hours."

"We've all got to do what we have to do," Mom says.

"What can we do?" Kayleigh asks. "Like I know school is starting, so I have to cut back on my hours at Burger Barn, but . . . I guess I could give up soccer."

"No, Kayleigh," Dad says. "Soccer could be your ticket to college. You can't give that up. Mom and I are going to figure this out."

Kayleigh lets out a sigh of relief.

But then Dad looks at me with a pained expression. "Declan, I'm losing our health insurance along with my job. Until I figure out what the options are, we're not going to be able to afford more PT for you, especially on top of all the medical bills we've already got."

This can't be happening.

"But Dr. Molina said I have to have regular PT if I'm going to have any chance of pitching again," I say. "And what if I need more surgery for this stupid wrist drop thing?"

"I'm sorry, Declan," Dad says. "But we could barely keep up with the medical bills when I had a job. There's no way we can swing it now."

A wave of anger crashes over me, thrumming through my entire body.

"You wouldn't have to figure it out if globalists like Kramer weren't trying to destroy the livelihoods of white people like us!"

"Declan, please—give it a rest today, okay?" Dad says. "We've got enough to deal with right now."

"Fine," I say, furious that my family seems to be willfully ignoring the truth. I stomp up to my room and text Charlie, asking him if he's left for Ronan's yet. He says he hasn't, and I ask him if he's willing to give me a ride out there.

Me: My dad just got laid off from Pinnacle.

Charlie: Oh man, I'm sorry.

Charlie: I'm on my way, little brother. We got your back.

At least someone does.

DECLAN

Mom and Dad are still at the kitchen table talking in low, worried voices when I pass by on my way out.

"I get some severance to tide us over, but it's not as much as you'd think it would be after giving Pinnacle over thirty years," Dad says, sounding exhausted.

"Frank, you'll get another job," Mom says. "I have confidence in you."

"Andi, I'm a guy in his late forties with no college education," Dad says. "Who's going to hire me, especially at a wage that will support a family?"

"What about retraining?" Mom asks. "Doesn't the government have programs to help people learn new skills?"

"I wasn't so great at school the first time around," he says. "I'm more of a learn-by-doing kind of guy."

"I know. But we should still look into it," Mom tells him.

I get a text from Charlie, saying he's here to pick me up, so I take the last few steps down to the hallway and poke my head into the kitchen.

"I'm going over to Ronan's. Don't worry about me for dinner."

"Really? You have to go out now?" Mom asks.

"Give me a break, Mom," I say. "School starts tomorrow. I don't have that much freedom left."

"But your father—"

"Let him go, Andi," Dad says, putting his hand on Mom's. "It's not like he can help with this."

Thanks a lot, Dad.

"I'll see you later," I say.

Then I make my escape before anyone changes their mind.

Finn is in the truck with Charlie.

"How's your dad doing?" he asks.

"Not so good," I say. "Mom wanted me to stay home, but I had to get out of there. It makes me so mad that my family doesn't seem to get it."

"Maybe your dad getting laid off is their wake-up call," Charlie says.

"I hope so," I say.

Charlie turns up the volume, blasting BloodAxe. They're telling my story—the story of all the hardworking white Americans like my dad, whose lives are being ruined because of *them*. All of them.

I'm not going to lie down and take it like Dad is.

One of the guys must have already told Ronan what happened, because as soon as I walk into the house, he stands up and says, "Declan, my brother," and enfolds me into a quick hug.

It's comforting to feel his anger and his strength after seeing my dad so diminished.

Ronan lets me go, and I take a seat on the sagging couch.

"This is what I've been warning you about all along, Declan," he says. "Globalists have this all planned. Several of our members were laid off today. It's going to destroy the economy of Stafford's Corner. They're out to replace honest, hardworking white men like us. True patriots. Real Americans." He paces back and forth in front of me. "The numbers don't lie. Their end goal is to exterminate us. How are they doing it? They've been exporting our jobs overseas so we can't make a living wage. Then they opened the floodgates to mass immigration, letting in all these inferior races who take what few jobs remain and hoping we'll mix with them and dilute our white bloodlines."

It's like the news of the layoffs at Pinnacle lit a fire in Ronan. He's always been pretty chill when I've been hanging out here, and I've never seen him this animated and angry before. But it's all starting to make sense to me. All the pieces I've been picking up have fallen into place, and finally I can start to understand why I'm so angry—that there's a reason for it.

"Ronan's throwing down some truth here, boys," Luke says. "Listen up."

"Tell it, Ronan!" Reid agrees.

Ronan doesn't need any encouragement from us. He's revving himself up to a full-on rant, and I'm here for it, because I want to know why all these terrible things keep happening, why our lives are so fricking hard. And here he is laying it all out. Connecting the dots for me, one by one.

"But we're not going to let that happen!" Luke says. "No way. No how."

"That's right, my brother," Ronan says. "We are going to fight them, using all means necessary. Because if we don't, we're going to be a minority in our own country by 2045!"

"That might seem like a long way away when you're fifteen," Charlie tells Finn and me. "But take it from me, you'll be in your thirties before you know it, and how are you gonna feel when you're being bossed around by them like I am at Big V?"

He means Rita. Rita, who rewards the summer people for treating us like crap. Screw that and screw her.

The guys in this room are my people. But more than that, they're my real friends, the ones who have been there for me. They believed in me when I'd stopped believing in myself.

"I don't even want to imagine what it's going to be like being a minority in our own country," Finn says. "One thing I do know is that it would totally suck."

"That's why we're doing what we do," Ronan says. "It's why we have to start doing more. We can't let them replace us. We can't allow white genocide to happen."

"But how do we stop it?" I ask.

Ronan stops in front of the screen and puts his hands on his hips. He smiles and says, "We're working on some plans. But in the meantime, Finn tells me your sister is friends with Kramer's daughter."

"Yeah, she is. And that traitor Arielle didn't even give us any warning that our dad was getting axed. "

"Get us her phone number—without your sister knowing you did it," Ronan instructs me. "Can you do that, Declan?"

"Yeah, I can definitely do that," I assure him. "What for?"

Ronan gives me a long assessing look. I keep looking him dead in the eye.

"Just get it for us," he says. "Better that you have plausible deniability."

"But—"

"Trust us," Ronan says. "You know we're the ones who are really looking after you, right?"

True. I won't let him down.

That night, I stay up till I know Kayleigh's asleep. Then I creep into her room and kneel on the floor by the side of her bed. I lift up her phone and connect it with her thumb, carefully, without waking her up. She pulls her hand away and rolls onto her side, muttering something incomprehensible in her sleep.

But I'm already in. I feel a little twinge of guilt about invading

Kayleigh's privacy. I'd flip out if she did it to me. Still, this my chance to do something for my family, even if they don't seem to appreciate it, to get payback against Mr. Kramer for laying off Dad and so many other guys at the plant.

I see there's a flurry of texts from Arielle that Kayleigh hasn't seen yet. Dad told me they laid off people at Pinnacle today. He couldn't (wouldn't?) tell me if your dad was one of them.

I hope everything is okay! XO

No, Arielle. Everything isn't okay. Screw you, your dad, and your dumb kisses and hugs.

With my phone, I take a picture of Arielle's contact info and send it to Ronan.

I should put Kayleigh's phone back on the bedside table and go.

But I don't.

Instead, I respond to Arielle's text. As Kayleigh. No, you idiot, everything is NOT okay. Thanks to your dad and his globalist friends, my dad is out of a job!

Then I delete the message from Kayleigh's phone and sneak out of her room.

SOPHOMORE YEAR

SEPTEMBER

OCTOBER

NOVEMBER

DECEMBER

JAKE

Arielle and I are on the same bus, but she gets picked up first. I catch a glimpse of her through the window when the bus pulls up at my stop, and she looks kind of . . . anxious. I guess I'd be, too, if I were starting a new school sophomore year.

When I get on, she's saved me a seat and her face brightens a bit when she spots me. But there's still a shadow over her features.

"Hey," I say as I sit, dropping a kiss on her cheek. "Excited for your first day?"

She meets my gaze. "Honestly?"

"No, lie."

She elbows me in the ribs. "Fine. I wanted to crawl back under the covers and stay there," she admits. "Bobby was having a complete meltdown when I left to catch the bus—he kept telling Mom that he wants to go back to his school in New Jersey."

"Poor kid. But I'm sure he'll be okay. Change is just . . . hard."

"Tell me about it!" Arielle says. "Especially because . . ." She leans her head closer to me and lowers her voice to a whisper. "I don't know if you heard, but there were layoffs at Pinnacle."

I immediately think of Declan and Kayleigh. "Ugh. I hope Mr. Taylor survived. They've got enough going on right now."

Arielle shakes her head.

"Wait . . . he got laid off? That's got to hurt."

"I know," Arielle says. "And now Kayleigh hates me."

I stare at her. "She said that? That she hates you?"

She pulls out her phone to show me the text exchange.

When I read the text, I hear the roar of my blood through my veins. There it is again. Someone using that fake antisemitic conspiracy theory. Someone who doesn't sound like Kayleigh—or at least the Kayleigh I know. Someone who sounds like Declan.

"I'm so sorry you had to deal with this crap on your first day of school," I say. "It's so . . . wrong."

"I just can't believe Kayleigh would send me this," Arielle says. "I mean, I totally get that she's upset. From what she's been telling me, things were already pretty bad at home." She sighs. "But I thought she'd at least give me a chance. She *knows* me. And it's not even like it was Dad's decision to lay people off. It came from headquarters."

"Uh . . . I don't think it was Kayleigh. The globalist stuff sounds like something Dec would say. Something he has said. But we're going to find out as soon as we get to school."

And I'm going to have words with Dec if it was him, that's for sure.

As usual on the first day, everyone's outside catching up before the bell. I spot Kayleigh hanging out with some of the girls on the soccer team.

I glance over at Arielle. Her normally animated face is a mask. You gotta admire the girl—I'd never know that she was dreading today by looking at her.

"Come on," I say, grabbing her hand. "We're going to figure this out right now."

"I don't know," she says, pulling her hand away. "Starting a new school is already a lot, without drama on the quad before first period."

"Trust me on this," I say, trying to sound calmer than I feel.

She meets my gaze, and I just want to hug her and tell her it's going to be okay.

But I can't say that. Nothing is okay right now. Still, I'm confident enough that Kayleigh would never text her that crap that at least there's something I *can* do to make her feel better.

"Please," I say.

She puts her hand back in mine and takes a deep breath. "All right."

We walk over to Kayleigh. She doesn't seem as animated as usual, and her shoulders are slumped, but when she turns and sees us, she smiles.

"Hey, cute couple," she says. "What's up?"

"I'm sorry to hear about . . ." I say quietly, trailing off, because I'm not sure if everyone else knows.

"Me too," Arielle says with feeling. "I feel terrible."

A shadow passes across Kayleigh's face, and she moves away from the other girls so that we can speak privately. "It sucks. On top of everything . . ."

"But do you blame me for it?" Arielle asks.

The confused expression on Kayleigh's face tells me I'm right. "What? Why would I blame you?" she asks. "It's not like you had any say about the layoffs."

I feel Arielle exhale.

"I mean, I'll be honest with you: Stuff with my family isn't great," Kayleigh continues. "But it's not your fault."

Arielle and I exchange a glance.

Kayleigh sees it and puts her hands on her hips. "Can one of you tell me what's going on?"

Arielle hands Kayleigh her phone. Kayleigh's eyes widen as she reads the text exchange. "Wait . . . what? This is crazy! I never sent this . . ." Her eyes widen with horror, then narrow with fury. "I'll kill him."

She looks Arielle straight in the eye. "You believe me, right? I'd never write this crap."

There's an awkward moment of silence, then Arielle sighs. "Yeah, I believe you. So . . . you think it was Declan?"

Kayleigh nods, her lips thin with anger and determination. "And I'm going to make him regret it. Big-time."

I don't doubt that. Still, the fact that Declan would send a text like that from Kayleigh's phone makes me even more uneasy about what's going on with him these days.

The usual anxiety creeps over me as we go through the syllabus in each of our classes and I see how much reading there is. I feel overwhelmed already, and it's only the first day of school.

Even though I get accommodations for my dyslexia, by the end of fourth period, I feel like I'm drowning. I'm glad to have the break for lunch. That's until I see Arielle and Kayleigh walking down the hallway toward me, and Arielle is crying. Not like quiet, subdued tears—like major-league sobs.

"What happened?" I ask, with a weird sense of foreboding.

"She's been getting nonstop texts and phone calls," Kayleigh explains, furious. "Like faster than we can block them."

"What kind of texts and phone calls?" I ask, feeling a gaping pit open in my stomach.

Arielle turns on her phone, and almost immediately it starts ringing. She practically throws it into my hand. I press to listen, and a deep voice that sounds like when they use technology to disguise someone's real voice on TV says, "We're watching you, cockroach. We're going to kill you and your entire family, you—"

I hang up, not wanting to listen to any more hateful garbage.

But then a text comes in. It's a picture of piles of skeletal bodies at a concentration camp, and the message is *Camp Auschwitz is waiting for you*.

I feel like I'm going to throw up. I turn the phone off.

"We're going to the principal's office," Kayleigh says.

"I'll come with you," I tell them.

"Thanks," Arielle says, taking a deep breath.

As we head down to the office, anger starts building on top of the fear.

We don't deserve it. This is America. We're supposed to be free to be Jewish here, to live in peace and not be afraid. George Washington literally said so in that letter he wrote to the Hebrew Congregation of Newport, Rhode Island.

Arielle explains what's happening to Ms. Worthy, the school secretary, and turns her phone on for, like, two minutes to show her the kind of filth that's coming her way. Ms. Worthy gasps and says, "Let me see if Principal Gardiner is free."

She goes into Gardiner's office and two minutes later comes out to get Arielle.

"I can give you two passes back to your classes," Ms. Worthy tells Kayleigh and me.

"Are you going to be okay?" Kayleigh asks Arielle. "I mean, stupid question, but . . ."

Arielle shrugs. "I knew it was going to be hard starting a new school, but I never thought it would be this hard," she says. "But . . . thanks. It helps to know that there are at least two people here who don't hate me."

"Everyone doesn't hate you," Kayleigh says. "It's just a few really loud idiots. Give us a chance, okay?"

I'm starting to wonder just how many "few loud idiots" there really are.

"Let me know what happens," I tell Arielle. I raise my arm in a fist. "Chazak!"

That gets me a real smile.

"You too," she says, before following Ms. Worthy to the principal's office.

"What does that mean?" Kayleigh asks me as we head to our classes. "That thing you told Arielle."

"It means 'be strong.' Every time we finish reading one of the books of the Torah in synagogue, everyone stands up and says 'Chazak, chazak, v'nitchazek!'—be strong, be strong, may we be strengthened. My grandpa used to say 'Chazak' when I was freaking out about stuff." I glance over at Kayleigh. "I figured Arielle might need to hear it right about now."

"I'm going to need to chazak up—if that's a thing—to confront Dec," Kayleigh says. "I don't know what to do. I mean, this is *Dec*, like the literal other half of me. And I just don't know what to do, and it's making me—" She lets out a small scream.

I know how she feels—I've never wanted to punch my best friend as much as I do right now. I force myself to uncurl my fist.

"What do your parents say about all this?"

Kayleigh sighs. "They're too busy worrying about how to pay the bills right now. It's like I'm on my own trying to figure this out."

My chest is twisted in knots about Arielle and Dec for totally different reasons—and the worst is that now I'm sure they're related.

JAKE

"Good to see you, Jake," Mr. Morrison says when I get to world history. He's standing outside the classroom door, welcoming people.

"What's up, Mr. M?" I say, high-fiving him before heading inside.

There's Declan, sitting near the back of the classroom, laughing with Finn McCarthy like he isn't responsible for Arielle being bombarded by antisemitic hate on her first day at our school.

I throw my notebook on a random desk with a loud crash that makes Emma Knotts and Katie Jones jump, and I stomp over to where he's sitting.

"Why did you do it, Declan?"

He turns and looks up at me. "Do what?"

His denial adds fuel to my fury.

"You know what," I say through clenched teeth. "Don't play dumb with me, Dec."

"No, I don't know," he says, standing up and facing me without breaking eye contact.

If it wasn't for Finn's smile, I'd have doubted myself. I want to wipe it off his face with my fists so badly, but I don't want to get suspended on the first day of school.

"You sent Arielle that message from Kayleigh's phone. And now she's getting threatening calls and antisemitic texts."

"Jake, I didn't do anything to your girlfriend," Dec says, but his eyes shift away from my face briefly. "Good to know you care more about some girl who showed up a few months ago than your best friend, whose dad just lost his job, which means no health insurance, which means no PT, which means no baseball."

I feel a pang of guilt, but it's not enough for me to back down and let him off the hook for what he did to Arielle. "I'm sorry about your dad, Dec. You know I am. But it's not Arielle's fault, and sending her that anti-semitic crap is way over the line."

"Do you need a Q-tip to clean your ears or something?" Declan says. He thrusts his chest out. "I. Didn't. Do. It."

"Stop lying to me!" I shout, stepping forward so we're practically nose to nose.

"Get out of my face!" he shouts back, shoving me so hard I almost fall backward onto Chloe Miyazaki, who's sitting at her desk trying to mind her own business. Her desk makes a loud screech as it moves.

"What's going on here?"

Mr. Morrison is standing in the doorway, and he is *not* happy. He strides over to us, his expression grim. "I'm greeting students in the hall-way, and you two are fighting?" Looking from me to Declan, he says, "What started this?"

Even though the urge to cause Declan pain to make up for what he did to Arielle still heats my blood, I don't say anything.

Neither does Declan.

"Fine," Mr. M says, his hands on his hips. "You can tell it to the principal. Get out of my classroom. Not a great way to start the school year, guys."

All I want to do is pummel Declan and show him how I really feel about what he did, but that would be a one-way ticket to suspension. We don't speak or make eye contact as we head to the office, sticking to opposite sides of the hallway.

"Twice in one day?" Ms. Worthy says when she sees me.

I glance over at Declan, but he's staring straight ahead. "Mr. Morrison sent us for . . . um . . . shouting."

Giving us a reproachful look, she tells us to take a seat.

We do—as far away from each other as we can get. Dec's looking down at his phone, and something he sees makes him smirk. I force myself to stay put, even though I want to make him pay for smirking about Arielle's pain. About my pain.

I try texting Arielle to see how she's doing, but no response. She's probably still got her phone turned off, but now I've got no way of contacting her to see if she's okay, and there's a constant gnawing feeling in my stomach that won't go away until I know.

Principal Gardiner calls me into her office first.

She gets right to the point. "Is this really how you want to start the school year, Jake?"

"No!" I exclaim. "But getting all that antisemitic garbage wasn't how Arielle wanted to start her school year, either. And it's all Declan's fault."

Gardiner sits up, alert. "You think Declan's responsible for those messages?"

"Yeah." I explain about the message from Kayleigh's phone. "I believe her when she says she didn't send it. I saw her face when Arielle showed it to her."

"But do you have proof that Declan sent the other messages?" Principal Gardiner asks.

"No," I admit. "But . . ." I trail off. I don't have any actual proof, so instead I say, "I just told him to leave Arielle alone."

"I understand the impulse," Gardiner says. "But I can't allow physical confrontation in the classroom. I'm sending you home for the rest of the day. Ms. Worthy will call your parents."

It feels like I'm getting in trouble for doing the right thing. How is that okay?

Mom arrives to take me home while Dec is in with Principal Gardiner. She isn't happy. Not one bit.

"I had to cancel an important client meeting because of this," she says when we're walking to the car. "Getting into a fight on the first day of school? With Declan? Your best friend? What were you thinking?"

"I was doing what you and Dad have always told me I should do," I protest. "Standing up to hate."

"Oh yeah? How's that?" she asks.

"Something really messed up happened to Arielle." I explain about the awful phone calls and texts as we get in the car. "Literally the minute you turned her phone on, it started spewing all this horrible antisemitic crap. Like nonstop."

"Poor Arielle!" Mom exclaims. "What did she do?"

"Kayleigh and I took Arielle to the office to talk to Principal Gardiner, but I haven't heard from her since." I swallow hard. "I'm worried, Mom."

"I'll reach out to the Kramers to see how they're holding up as soon as we get home," Mom says. "But help me to understand what this has to do with Declan, and why I had to pick you up from school for fighting." Her brow furrows. "Come to think of it, we didn't see much of him this summer. What's going on with you two?"

I tell her all that, too. "I can't prove that Dec had anything to do with the calls, only that I know Kayleigh didn't send the globalist text to Arielle. Dec's the only one who could have done that. What was I supposed to do?" I ask. "It's not like I wanted to get into a fight. But I saw how upset Arielle was. You would have been, too, if you'd seen and heard that crap, Mom."

"So how are *you* doing?" Mom asks. "Because I know it must have been hard for you, too. Even more since it's Declan."

I pick up the Magen David that's hanging around my neck and rub it between my fingers. "Not great," I admit. "This whole thing has freaked me out big-time. Especially after seeing those flyers on the Fourth of July and the white nationalist stickers at the mall."

I slide the star from one side of the chain to the other. "Is it my imagination, or are things getting worse? Like, sure, kids at school have said stupid things. Even the teachers, sometimes. But now it feels like it's everywhere. All the time."

Mom flashes me a worried glance.

"There's definitely been a rise in antisemitic incidents, according to statistics we've been getting from the Anti-Defamation League. One of the bad things about those"—she points to my phone—"is that they make it much easier for hate groups to recruit people and spread the same old hateful ideas in a different package, more rapidly than they ever could before."

"Dec's gaming friends were doing that," I tell her. "And not just antisemitic crap. Lots of Islamophobia, too."

"Well, of course not," Mom says. "It never stops with just hating us. Scratch an antisemite and you'll find a whole bunch of other hatreds, too. Basically, people choose to hate the idea of us as a substitute for facing their fears of change in society and the world."

"So you mean we're like the scapegoat? Like we read about in the Torah portion on Yom Kippur? The one they send out into the desert with all the sins and stuff?"

Mom nods. "But there are also people who say things that are antisemitic out of ignorance, not necessarily malice, because they don't know what they don't know."

"What do you mean?"

"Like a girl in my college sorority asked me if I'd had a nose job."

"Wow. That's just rude."

"I know, right?" Mom says. "But I was one of the first Jewish people she'd ever met, and somehow she'd gotten the idea that we all have big, hooked noses—"

"You mean like in Nazi propaganda pictures?"

"Exactly." Mom touches her nose, which is neither big nor hooked. "So to her mind, my nose couldn't possibly be natural. Now, I could have just walked away angry—because trust me, I was—but instead I explained to her how insulting it was for her to ask me that, because it was based on a hurtful stereotype."

"Whoa. How did she react?"

"She was mortified and extremely apologetic."

"But where did she get that idea that we all have big noses?" I ask. "Someone must have given it to her, right?"

"Oh, definitely," Mom says. "Who knows where she got it? Parents. Community. Friends. Church. But here's the thing: She listened, and she learned." She smiles. "We ended up being friends. She came to a seder with me. She loved the matzo balls, and just like you, she was totally grossed out by gefilte fish from a jar."

"As any normal person would be," I point out. "It's yucky and slimy."

"How are you even my son?" Mom says, shaking her head.

"What happens when you try to do what you did with your sorority sister, and it doesn't work?" I ask. "Like what if she told you to lighten up and that it was just a joke?"

"It happens. When you and Ben were in elementary school, and I was on the PTA, the chair suggested that I take on the role of treasurer 'because Jews are good with money.'"

Wow. "I mean, you are good with money, but—"

"Yes, I'm good with money, but it's got nothing to do with being Jewish. And it gets worse," Mom says. "When I pointed out that she was promoting a harmful stereotype—in a way that was much more calm and polite than I felt, because I knew if I didn't, it would become about the way I said it, not what I said—the chair became very defensive. Instead of listening and learning, she said, 'But I meant it as a compliment!' Like that somehow made it okay."

I shake my head, disgusted. "What did you do?"

"I decided not to be on the board of the PTA until they had a new chair."

"I feel so . . ." I search for words to describe all the emotions that are swirling inside me with the force of a tornado. "Angry. Scared. Helpless."

"I know, Jake. I do, too," she admits. I'm not sure if that makes me feel better or worse. I want her to have answers, to tell me everything is going to be okay. I don't want her to be freaked out, too.

"I want to do something," I say. "But I don't know what."

"Well, for one, we need to show our friends support so they know that they aren't alone," Mom says as we pull into the driveway. "I'm going to go inside and call Molly Kramer now."

"Can you ask her to have Arielle call me?"

Mom promises she will, so I go upstairs to my room to get started on homework. Teachers shouldn't be allowed to give homework the first day of school. There should be a law or something. I've gotten through most of it when there's a text from a number I don't recognize.

Hey, Jake. It's me, Arielle.

Got a new phone number.

I call her immediately. "Hey. Dumb question, but . . . how are you doing?"

"I've been better," she says.

"You definitely had to have had one of the worst first days in history."

"I know, right?" I hear her exhale. "Listen, Jake . . . I've got a huge favor to ask you."

"Sure. Anything."

"With everything that's happened . . . I was wondering . . . when we hang out this weekend, could we maybe just watch a movie at my house instead of going out? You'll probably think I'm a coward and maybe even totally paranoid, but getting texts saying that people want to kill you will do that."

"No problem," I say. "I just want to spend time with you—preferably in a hate-free zone, watching a funny movie."

"A funny movie sounds perfect. Maybe even a rom-com."

"Your choice," I say.

"Great," she says. "At least now I have something to look forward to."

"Me too," I say.

"Oh! I'm not going to be on the bus tomorrow," she tells me. "My dad's driving me to school. Meet you outside?"

"Sure," I promise her. "And, Arielle, I know you're scared—I am, too—but it's not cowardly to be afraid of things like this. It's . . . self-preservation."

"I guess," she says. "It just feels like it because I'm literally afraid to go out of our house."

"You know who are the cowards? People who would send crap like that."

I can tell she's not convinced. I understand, though. It could mess with your head, thinking about it all. But I'm not going to let it, because that would be letting the haters win.

DECLAN

After giving me a stern talking-to about fighting in class, Principal Gardiner says, "You said Jake provoked you, but he thought you might have something to do with what happened to Arielle Kramer earlier today."

Fricking Jake.

"Declan, I'm going to ask you this straight up," Gardiner says. "Do you know anything about those texts and phone calls?"

My admiration for Ronan grows, because I can honestly say no, and it's for real. Finn hinted at a few things before Morrison's class, but it wasn't till Jake got in my face that I knew exactly what went down.

Gardiner's eyes search my face like she's looking for truth, and I force myself not to look away.

"I hope that's true, because the Kramers were heading to the police station from here," she says.

She's trying to get a reaction from me, and I'm not about to give it to her. All I did was give Ronan the girl's phone number. What happened from there had nothing to do with me.

Besides, she deserved it. They all do.

"I don't want to start the school year by suspending you, Declan," Gardiner says finally. "But I'm sending you home to cool off, in the hope that you'll come back tomorrow with a fresh outlook and a better attitude." She picks up her pen, dismissing me. "I'll have the school secretary call your mother to pick you up."

"It's okay, I'll walk," I say, planning to hang out somewhere until it's time to go home so my parents don't know I got in trouble.

But Gardiner sees through my game. "Given what's happened, I need you released to a parent."

"Call my dad, then," I tell her. "My mom's working and he's . . . not. He got laid off from Pinnacle."

She puts her pen down, and her face softens. "Yes. I was sorry to hear that. It must be extremely stressful for you and your entire family."

I shrug.

"The school counselor is available if you need someone to talk to," she says.

"Nah, I'm good," I say.

"Let me know if you change your mind," she says, dismissing me with a wave of her hand to go wait for Dad.

Dad is tight-lipped with anger until we get in the car. Then he lets loose.

"What is the matter with you, Declan? You can't even go a full day of school without getting into trouble?"

"It's not my fault!" I protest. "Jake came over and started blaming me for something I had nothing to do with."

"That's not what I heard from school—or from Kayleigh, who sent Mom and me a pretty angry text saying that you'd used her phone to send something hateful to her friend Arielle—and that things escalated from there to the point the poor girl had to leave school." He shoots me a sideways glance. "Are you sure you had nothing to do with this?" he asks. "Who else would have access to Kayleigh's phone?"

"Why are you so focused on what happened to Arielle instead of the

175

bigger picture?" I ask him. "Kramer laid you off! People like him are making our life impossible. If we don't fight them, we won't survive!"

"What do you mean 'people like him'?" Dad asks.

"Globalists. The people who are trying to cause white genocide."

Dad's eyes widen. "Hold on there . . . White genocide? Where are you getting this from?"

"My friends. Online. I've researched it. You don't seem to get it, Dad."

"You're right, I don't get it," Dad says, shaking his head like he's disappointed in me—again. "I'm the one who got laid off. You can be mad at Kramer for doing it—I sure am—but taking things out on his kid like that is just wrong."

Ugh. Why isn't he listening? It's like I'm offering him the key to understanding, but he doesn't want to take it.

"It's affected me, too," I say, wanting him to understand, to wake up and smell the conspiracy to destroy us. "Thanks to Kramer, we don't have health insurance, which means I can't get PT, which means I'm probably never going to be able to play baseball again." I feel sick even saying those words aloud. I don't want to believe them. "How come you aren't pissed about that?"

We're stopped at a light, and Dad puts his head on the steering wheel, his shoulders slumped. I want him to stand up and fight, like the Crusaders in *Imperialist Empires*. I want him to pull out his sword and destroy the people who are doing this to me. To us.

When he raises his head, his face is flushed. "You think I'm not upset about the situation we're in? You think I'm not furious and bitter?" He hits the steering wheel. "Obviously I am—but I've got a family to feed and a mortgage to pay. I can't afford to sit around playing video games and indulging in my self-pity like you do!"

He had to make this about me being a loser. Because of course he did.

"My number one focus has to be on getting a new job," Dad continues. "That's why I've spent the entire morning on that stupid computer trying to figure out how the heck to do it. When I applied for the job at Pinnacle, I filled out a paper form and had an interview with a person. Now you have to submit applications through one of these job websites, and a computer rejects you. No human contact involved." He sighs. "Things have changed so much since I last looked for a job. I'm starting to wonder if workers like me are heading for extinction."

I want to hurt him the way he hurt me just now. He thinks that making me feel like crap will spur me to action. Let's see how it works on him.

"You will be extinct if we don't fight people like Kramer."

Dad rolls his eyes as he pulls the car into our driveway. "There you go again . . . Can you just give it a rest, Declan?"

"Why can't you see the truth when it's as clear as day?" I spit out the words furiously. "If you don't wake up soon, you—and the rest of the white race—will be extinct!"

Nothing like your own dad telling you he thinks you're stupid. I get out of the car, slam the door, and storm toward the house. But then I turn back to say, "I thought you were someone I could look up to."

I get a rush of satisfaction from the hurt expression on Dad's face as I head upstairs and get online to tell my friends about what's been going down.

"That crap is exactly why I got turned on to Jarred Stonepen," FenrirLupus says.

"Yeah. Stonepen is the father figure for our generation," agrees HughdePayens1119.

"You're a warrior, Lionheartttt," OdalRune88 tells me, and I sit up straight with pride. "Your dad should be grateful that you're willing to fight."

"Yeah, especially when he's too much of a cuck to do it," says HughdePayens1119.

"I almost started to feel guilty about what they did to Arielle," I confess. "But why should I? We're the ones being oppressed, right?"

"Right! Don't feel guilty!" OdalRune88 says. "Making you feel bad about being white is all part of the globalist plot. They teach it to you in school, trying to make you all woke so you'll betray your own people. But you're stronger than that, right, Lionheartttt?"

I think I am. By tapping into the rage I feel because my family doesn't understand our peril, I know I will be. I am. Because someone has to fight for us.

"Who needs therapy when I've got you guys?" I say, grateful to have them to set me straight.

I get a group text from Charlie: I'm heading over to Ronan's after my shift. You guys need a ride?

Finn: Yeah. Mom's boyfriend is being complete tool, as usual. Getting on my case nonstop, like he has any right to say anything to me.

I text Charlie back: Yeah! Need to get outta here

Charlie: Great! Dec, I'll be there about 3. Sieg Heil, brothers.

I'm glad Kayleigh's not home yet when I head downstairs. Hopefully I'll miss her so I won't have to deal with her crap till later.

Dad's still in the kitchen, this time watching a cooking video on his phone as he makes dinner. It's really depressing watching him. My dad's a big guy, and he's always stood tall. Now he seems smaller somehow. Diminished.

I should probably be glad he's not wearing a stupid apron.

"I'm heading out," I tell him.

"You get sent home from school, and you think you're going out tonight? You should be thinking about what happened today and how you can do better tomorrow."

"I've been doing that already," I say. It's true, just not in the way he thinks it is. "Anyway, my friend's gonna be here to pick me up in a few minutes."

"Which friend is this?" Dad asks.

"Charlie. I work with him at Big V."

"I don't know. Your mother won't be happy, about any of this. And she's got enough on her plate right now."

I want to remind him that he's the man in this house—or at least he's supposed to be. But I also want to go out. I need to.

Trying to distract him, I move closer to the stove and take an experimental sniff. "Believe it or not, Dad, that actually smells pretty good."

"You think?" he asks, a hopeful look in his eyes. "I figured I could at least have dinner ready for Mom when she gets home." He gets a spoon out of the drawer, scoops up a little of what's in the pot, and points it at my mouth. "Here, taste it and let me know what you think."

Given that Dad's never cooked anything besides scrambled eggs and mac and cheese from a box, I expect it to taste like crap, but I'm pleasantly surprised.

"Not bad!" I say, and his face lights up.

"I'm proud of myself," he says, beaming. "Never been much of a cook—"

"Yeah, I know," I say.

He doesn't get pissed like I thought he would. Instead, he's all excited about these cooking videos Kayleigh showed him. It seems so pathetic after doing actual work at Pinnacle for decades.

"Doesn't it bug you to be doing Mom's work?" The question leaves my lips before I have a chance to think about it.

So many expressions cross his face, I'm not sure what he's thinking. But finally, he just gives me a crooked smile. "Sure, I mind. But what am I going to do about it? Someone's got to make dinner, otherwise we're all gonna starve."

"You could wake up and see what's actually happening here. Join me in the struggle instead of giving me crap for wanting to fight for us."

"Not this again," Dad says, sighing. He turns back to the stove to stir the pot.

Just then, I get a text from Charlie saying he's in the driveway.

"I gotta go," I say, running out the door before my dad can stop me.

JAKE

Late Saturday afternoon, I cycle over to Arielle's house to hang out. It's one of those days where you aren't sure what to wear as we slide from summer into autumn. The sky is clear blue, without that haze of humidity that seemed to hang over us the last few weeks.

I park my bike in the driveway, noticing all the cameras and lights they've added since the last time I was here. There's one of those camera doorbells at the front door. I ring it and then start making funny faces into the camera.

She answers the doorbell, laughing. "You realize my parents have the app on their phones and they can watch your little performance, right?"

"Shoot. Me. Now," I say with a groan. "Can you erase it?"

She shakes her head, grinning. "Why would I do that? It was funny," she says, leading me into the kitchen.

"As long as your parents think it's funny, and not that you're dating some weirdo."

"Well . . ." she says.

"Hilarious," I say, but I can't suppress a smile.

"Can I get you something to drink before we watch the movie?" she asks. "I already made popcorn."

"Water's fine," I say. "Oh! Wait! I have a present for you!"

I reach into my backpack and pull out a small loaf, wrapped in foil with a little ribbon around it. "L'Shanah Tovah. Hopefully the new year will be better than the dumpster fire you've been dealing with since you moved here."

Arielle's eyes soften as she takes it from me. "It has been pretty awful," she agrees. Her lips curve into a smile as she reads the label—*Honey Cake by Jake: Making your life sweeter one bite at a time.*

"Did you make this?" she asks, her eyes wide. "For real?"

I know I'm blushing, because my face suddenly feels like it's a zillion degrees. "Uh . . . yeah."

She unwraps it and takes out a plate and a knife to cut it up, sneaking a little bite to taste after she's cut off the first slice.

"Wow, my life already feels sweeter!" she says. "Is this magic honey cake?"

"I will never tell my secrets!" I say. "But I'm glad . . . I know things have been all kind of messed up since you moved here. I hate what Declan did to you. I just wish I could prove it was him."

She cuts more cake, avoiding my gaze. "My parents were talking about if Mom, Bobby, and I should move in with my grandparents in New Jersey for a little while. Until they can be sure that it's safe for us here."

My fury at Declan flares hotter. If Arielle ends up moving back to Jersey because of him . . . I don't know what I'll do. But right now, I'm alone with her and I refuse to let him ruin it. So I swallow down the anger and focus on the girl standing in front of me.

"This is totally selfish of me—I'll repent for that on Yom Kippur, promise—but I don't want you to go," I admit.

Her eyes meet mine. "You and Kayleigh and getting on the soccer team are pretty much the only things in my 'stay' column right now. Oh wait, and those muffins at Mocha Jenn's."

"There has got to be more," I say. "You haven't been hiking at Seward Park during peak colors in the autumn. Oh, and the youth group is in charge of putting on a Hanukkah play for the kids that's really fun, and we get doughnuts and latkes. Oh, and—"

"Jake, it's okay," Arielle says, putting her hand on my arm. My skin tingles under her fingers. "We're not leaving. My parents decided we should stick together as a family."

"Whew, that's a relief," I say, glad that she's staying.

"Come on, grab the popcorn and I'll take the honey cake," Arielle says. "We've got a rom-com to watch!"

Confession: We spend as much time making out as we do watching the movie. And I don't want to sound like I'm bragging, but I'm pretty sure Arielle doesn't think about all the crap that's been going on for a few hours. I know I don't.

Rosh Hashanah starts Tuesday night at sundown. As synagogue president, Mom's been super stressed out about security for the Jewish New Year, what with the extremist activity that's been going on around here lately.

Arielle comes over when she arrives with her family. I've never seen her dressed up before, and she looks totally amazing. Her cheeks pinken when I tell her that.

"You clean up pretty well yourself," she says. Winking at me, she adds, "I'm going to try not to think about how well so I can focus on my praying."

I feel my own face flushing. "Pray hard," I say. "I want this year to be better."

"Me too," she says before going to sit with her parents.

There are prayers that we only say during the High Holy Days, so you'd think you'd forget them from year to year. But they show up again like familiar old friends.

Like Unetaneh Tokef, which gets repeated a lot throughout the holidays. It's this ancient poem that lays out how it's all going to go, all the awful things that might happen to you if you don't confess but how you can change God's mind through genuine repentance.

The prayer says, "On Rosh Hashanah it is inscribed, and on Yom Kippur it is sealed—how many shall pass away and how many shall be born, who shall live and who shall die, who in good time, and who by an untimely death." Then it goes on to talk about things like who will die and who will be at peace and who will be tormented and who will be poor and who will be rich.

It's weird to think of someone up there with this massive database of who is going to live and die and how, especially when you realize that even if you're down for some terrible untimely death, if you genuinely repent, pray, give to charity, and do good deeds, you've got a chance of changing the outcome—as long as you do it before the end of Yom Kippur, when God's decision becomes final, and you're either sealed in the Book of Life or . . . not.

It all feels more real this year than it has before. I guess I've always assumed that being inscribed and sealed in the Book of Life for the coming year is a no-brainer for a teenager like me. But with all the antisemitic stuff that's been happening around here lately, I realize maybe I shouldn't take that for granted. And it sucks. It makes me mad, and sad, and it feels like a betrayal of what I thought our country was about.

We ate apples and honey before coming to synagogue, as a symbolic wish for a sweet new year. This year, I really hope it works.

DECLAN

When I'm home, it's like I can't do anything right. No one in my family seems to understand what's happening all around us. The worst is Kayleigh, who jumps down my throat telling me how awful I am the minute I open my mouth. It's like living with the chief of the PC Police.

School isn't much better. We're just over halfway through the first marking period, and for once I'm grateful that Mom is so busy working all the hours, because it means that she hasn't logged in to the school portal to check in on my grades like she usually does. If my parents knew my current grade situation, they'd stop me from going to Ronan's all the time, and that would suck. I wouldn't survive. Besides, it's not like my grades matter so much anymore, now that I don't have to worry about keeping them up for the baseball team.

Jake has barely spoken to me since the first day. He's made it clear that he's picked his girlfriend over me. Figures.

I tell myself that I'm better off without him, especially after everything I've been hearing from my online friends and the people at Ronan's. But I'd be lying if I said it didn't hurt.

The one bright spot is that we've finally reached the Crusades in Mr. M's world history class. I'm going to ace this part of class, for sure. I need to so I can pull off a decent grade by the end of the quarter.

"I'm psyched we're finally at the Crusades, aren't you?" I say to Finn as we walk to history. "At least this unit should be easy."

Finn shakes his head. "How can you still be so naive after everything

Ronan's taught us?" he says. "Morrison's going to give us some dumb woke version of history, not what really happened."

"I don't know . . . I had him last year, and he was pretty good."

"The whole education system is about turning us into sheeple so we can be good little workers and do what the government tells us," Finn says. "I already know more than most teachers by being self-taught."

I laugh, thinking he's joking, but then I realize he's not. "I know you're smart and all, but seriously? You think you know more about history than Mr. M? He went to college and studied all this crap."

"College is just another way they try to get us to burden ourselves with debt so we have to become indentured servants for corporations," Finn says. "It's all about them having cheap labor."

What he's saying makes sense . . . Without a baseball scholarship, that's exactly what going to college would mean for me.

"Why do you think the globalists keep pushing for more immigration?" Finn reminds me. "It's so they can lay off guys like your dad and bring in immigrants who will work for less."

Finn's right about that, I think as we walk into the classroom and take our seats next to each other. But I know Morrison from social studies last year and because he helped Coach Kriscoli run baseball practices last spring. I still think he'll give the truth a fair shake.

"Okay, folks, let's get started," Mr. M says. "We've been talking about what we call the Dark Ages of the medieval period, from the fall of the Western Roman Empire to the beginning of the Holy Roman Empire. Now we're going to turn our attention to the Crusades." He goes to the whiteboard and picks up a marker. "There are a lot of misconceptions about this period of history, so let's jot down some of the prior knowledge you have."

"There were a bunch of holy wars between Christians and Muslims," Ryan Peters calls out.

"That's the common belief," Mr. M says. "But the history is actually more complex than that, which we'll discuss as we go through the unit."

Finn throws me an I-told-you-so glance.

"They were ridiculously long," Jake says. "They went on for, like, two centuries."

"It's true the Crusader period went on for two centuries, although there were a number of different Crusades rather than one long one," Mr. M says.

"Yeah, they're like the medieval equivalent of Marvel movies," Jake jokes.

I smile despite myself.

"They were a lengthy franchise, that's for sure," Mr. M says. He looks around the classroom. "Anyone want to add?"

"It was all because the Muslims invaded Europe," Karl Higgins says confidently.

"Okay . . ." Mr. M says. He writes it on the whiteboard, but his questioning tone signals to the rest of the class that it's wrong.

I thought Morrison was better than this. I didn't want Finn to be right about him.

A few people add their ideas to the list, and then Mr. M asks if we notice anything about what people have said so far.

"It's all like Christians are the good guys and Muslims are the bad guys," Arielle says.

Figures she'd say something like that.

"Excellent, Arielle," Morrison says. "One of the things that we don't often consider when learning about the Crusades is that it has historically been taught from a Western European Christian point of view. Europe in medieval times is also portrayed as being homogeneously white, which wasn't the case. It was a much more diverse society than is often pictured in popular culture, particularly in port cities where trading took place."

Finn mutters something under his breath that I don't quite catch.

"We also hear a lot about the Christian Crusaders bringing civilization to the 'infidels,' but we don't hear about how much more advanced medieval Islamic societies were in many ways than the kingdoms of Western Europe," Mr. Morrison says.

"That's total crap," Finn says, loud enough to be heard this time.

"Finn disagrees," Mr. Morrison says, walking down the aisle between desks until he's standing right by him. "Can you tell us why?"

"We don't hear about that, because it isn't true," Finn says, his arms crossed over his chest. "Europe was white, and their society was much more advanced. The Crusades helped to civilize the rest of Europe and the Middle East."

It's true, from what I've read about the Crusades. Noble Crusader knights brought civilization to the Muslim hordes, who were living in squalor and poverty. It's proven historical fact.

"Okay, history scholars. Finn is contending that Western European society was more advanced than the Islamic world." He looks around the class and says, "I'd like to see a show of hands. How many people agree with him?"

I raise my hand slowly, looking around to see how many other people do.

Five of us out of a class of twenty-five. Karl Higgins is one of them.

"How about those who believe that the Islamic society was more advanced during this period?" Mr. M asks.

More people raise their hands—eight people, including Jake and Arielle. Figures.

But that means half the class still hasn't voted.

"I'd like to hear from the folks who didn't raise their hand at all for either choice," Mr. M says. "Why not?"

"I didn't, because I'm not sure," Megan says. "I mean, I've been doing the reading so far, but I still don't know enough about it to judge."

"Fair point," Mr. M says. "Anyone else?"

There's a chorus of "same" from around the room.

"As learners, we shouldn't be afraid to admit what we don't know," Mr. M says. "And even if we think we know, we have to keep an open mind when new evidence comes to light that might contradict our original position."

I hear Finn breathe out a quiet snort behind me. I know how he feels. It seems like Mr. M is speaking directly to those of us who don't buy all that woke crap he's trying to sell.

I raise my hand.

"Yes, Declan?"

"I've been doing a lot of reading and watching all these history videos about the Crusades, because a game I was playing is set during that time period," I say.

"I love that gaming inspired your desire to learn more about history," Mr. M says, showing what seems like genuine enthusiasm. "That's awesome!"

Maybe this will be okay. "So anyway, I voted based on actual facts and historical knowledge."

"Yeah, that's right," Finn agrees.

"I learned about the Muslims attacking Europe by watching all these history videos," Karl says. "'Cause I'm interested in this period, too."

"This is all terrific stuff," Mr. M says. "Because the research paper you're all going to write for this unit will give you a chance to create a reasoned argument using that knowledge." He puts up a slide with our paper assignment. "You have three weeks to research and write a paper answering the following question: Which civilization was more advanced in medieval times—the Christian kingdoms of Western Europe or the Islamic civilizations of the East? Make sure you use your information literacy skills to evaluate sources that you use to back up your assertions and cite them correctly. You'll be using the information you've researched to participate in a classroom debate the day the papers are due."

I think this is the first time in my life that I've been given a school assignment I'm excited about doing.

"Aren't you psyched about the paper?" I ask Finn after class. "Finally, a fun assignment."

"If you consider writing papers fun," Finn says. "I don't."

"Okay, the writing part, maybe not, but researching stuff we're already interested in? I've been watching videos about the Crusades all summer! This is going to be the easiest A ever."

"I bet Morrison won't let us use half the stuff you've watched, though," Finn says. "He'll find some reason to say it's not a 'real' source. Anything to keep the truth from coming out."

Huh. I never thought of that. "There's got to be something out there with our point of view that Mr. M would consider legit. Like some historian or something."

"Trust me. He's going to twist this so that we come out as the bad guys.

Just ask Ronan," Finn says. "Our parents pay taxes so we can be indoctrinated into hating ourselves for being white, even though pretty much all the progress the world has made has been because of white men."

That's exactly what Jarred Stonepen says. I hope Finn's wrong, because I'm psyched for this assignment. I know I can crush this paper, and the debate.

DECLAN

I've spent the last three weeks really focused on researching and writing the paper, so I'm pumped the day of the debate in Mr. Morrison's class. I'm pretty sure this is the best argumentative paper I've ever written, thanks to the sources that my online friends gave me, as well as ones I found myself. If Mr. M doesn't give me an A on this paper, Finn is totally right that we never had a shot, even with all the resources in the world.

"You ready to kick butt?" I ask Finn as we walk down the hall toward Mr. M's classroom.

"As ready as I can be," Finn says. "But it's cute you still think there's the slightest chance of a fair debate with Morrison moderating it."

"Look, I get that he's kind of biased, but we have proof for everything we say, right?" I say.

Finn gives me a pitying look. "Trust me, he'll find a way to promote his agenda instead of the truth," he says before we go into the classroom. "Just you wait."

We take our seats, and I make sure my list of arguments and my works cited are in front of me so that I can blow Mr. M away and wake people up. Hopefully it'll work better here than it has with my family.

"Okay, people, we've got a lot to talk about today, so settle down and let's get started," Mr. Morrison says, waiting for everyone to stop talking. When they do, he says, "You've all done the research on this to write your papers, so I'm looking forward to the lively, respectful, factual debate we're going to have today looking at the relative advances of the two civilizations involved in the Crusades during the medieval period," he says, walking to the whiteboard and picking up a marker. He draws a line down the middle of the board, and labels one half *Christian Kingdoms* and the other half *Islamic Empires*. Then he turns back to us and asks, "Who would like to kick things off?"

"I will," Ryan says. "And I'm going to talk about crap."

People laugh, not sure where he's going with this.

"Uh . . . keep it clean, Ryan," Mr. M says, but he gives a small smile.

"I'll try," Ryan says. "But it won't be easy." He stands and faces everyone. Ryan's a theater geek, and he's leaning into the drama. "Picture yourselves in medieval Europe. All the sanitation advances brought by the Romans have fallen into disrepair. Raw sewage runs down the middle of the street."

"Gross!" Emma exclaims, to murmurs of agreement from around the classroom.

"You think that's bad, wait till you hear this. Rats basically used this crap river as a swimming pool, and diseases like cholera and plague ran rampant."

The idea of rats doing the backstroke in a river of poop running down the middle of the street makes me laugh.

"The worst of these was the Black Death, which killed between thirty to fifty percent of the European population," Ryan says.

"That's insane," Jake says. "So, like . . ." He does the math in his head. "Between eight and thirteen people in this classroom would be dead."

"Pretty sobering thought," Mr. M says. He writes *Bad sanitation, rampant disease* under the Christian Kingdoms column.

"Yeah, but bad sanitation was everywhere at that time," I point out. "Not just in Europe."

"Or so you think!" Ryan exclaims dramatically, pointing his finger in the air. "But you would be wrong! The sanitation in the Muslim-ruled cities of the Iberian Peninsula was waaaaaaaay more advanced. These folks were on it when it came to disposing of their crap."

Mr. M writes *More advanced sanitation* under the Islamic Empires column.

"You can't blame Christian Europe for the Black Death," Finn says. "The Mongol hordes brought it with them from the East."

"Can you tell us more?" Mr. M says, sitting on the corner of his desk.

"The Mongol hordes, led by Janibeg Khan, were besieging the Genoese—that's one of the Italian nation-states that was big into trading—at the port of Kaffa on the Black Sea in Crimea, in what's now Ukraine," Finn says. "His troops brought the Black Death with them. When Janibeg realized he was going to lose because his troops were all dying from the plague, he used biological warfare, catapulting the diseased corpses over the wall into Kaffa. Everyone in the city was vulnerable because they'd been under siege, so they started dying off, too."

"So basically, if the Muslims hadn't flooded the borders of Europe, millions of Europeans wouldn't have died," Karl Higgins adds.

"But that's not the only way the Black Death entered Europe," Jamal Booth argues. "It came from trade along the Silk Road. From rats in ships that were carrying diseased fleas. They thought it just kept coming in waves from Asia, but now scientists think that it mutated in Europe and spread back to the East over a few centuries."

"That's not what I found. Each wave of the plague came from the East. From Muslims. I'm with Finn. You should put *spread disease* in the Muslim column," Karl argues.

"Wow," Jamal says, turning around to look at Karl. "Islamophobic much?"

Karl crosses his arms over his chest with a defiant look on his face. He'd fit right in at Ronan's. We need to try and get him out there sometime.

"We're going to keep this debate focused on facts from reliable sources. Jamal, Finn, and Karl, can you share the sources of your information for these claims so that we can evaluate them?"

One by one, Mr. M projects all three sources on the whiteboard.

Finn's up first. Morrison scrolls around the website and then asks people what they think.

"It's just some rando's blog," Jake says. "What are this person's qualifications? What's their expertise?"

"Good question," Mr. M says. "Let's see if there's an 'About' page, where the author tells us."

He searches the site, but there isn't one.

"Given that we have no idea who this person is and if they have any qualifications in this area, this site doesn't qualify as an appropriate academic source," Mr. M says.

Finn blows out a snort of frustration and gives me a look that says *See what I mean?*

Next, Mr. M puts up Jamal's website. It's a science website, and when Mr. M goes to the "About" page, Jake points out that all the editors have degrees and work experience in science. "This one's more credible."

"I agree," Morrison says. "I would accept this source."

I glance over at Finn, rolling my eyes.

Finally, he goes to Karl's video.

"Again, it's just some rando," Ryan says. "Not an actual scientist or historian."

"Yes, it fails the credibility test," Mr. Morrison says. "You know you can't just use anything you find on the internet as a source. Evaluating the credibility is key." He looks around. "Okay, moving on. Who's got some more arguments for us?"

Emma raises her hand. "So . . . medicine in the Islamic world was way more advanced than in medieval Europe," she says. "This guy called al-Zahrawi was the father of operative surgery. He was some kind of medical genius. And you know what's crazy? Europeans claim that this French dude Ambroise Paré was the one who pioneered using catgut for sutures, but al-Zahrawi was doing it, like, five centuries before he did!"

He looks up Emma's source, and it's deemed credible. Mr. M writes *Medical advances* on the Islamic side.

I try looking up European medicine in the medieval period, but even the British Library website, which you'd think would be all about how advanced Europe was, talks about how the doctors of the time were into bloodletting using leeches and how they based some medicine on astrology. That sounds pretty sketchy, if you ask me. But then I find another site that gives me more information and raise my hand.

"Yes, Declan?"

"Christians started the first hospitals," I say. "In their monasteries."

"Okay, let's look at the source," Mr. M says. "Did they actually 'start' them? I believe they had some form of healing place connected to religious deities in ancient Rome—prior to Christianity."

"But it says they did on this website!" I argue.

He puts the website up for evaluation.

When Katie raises her hand and says it's not reliable, he asks her to explain why.

"Because it's a theological website, not a historical website," she says.

"If you look at the qualifications of the people on the 'About' page, they're all in theology, not history or science."

"I just looked up another one that says they had hospitals in Mesopotamia and in India and Sri Lanka—and this is from the medical school of a famous research hospital," Megan says.

After we look at her source, Mr. M says he's not going to put starting hospitals in either column, because they predated the conflict.

I can't believe I ruined my life for Megan.

It's time to pull out my killer argument.

"Muslims had slaves," I say. "They captured white men for work and women for their harems. The Europeans didn't use slaves."

"Yeah, all we hear about is how Black people want reparations for slavery in America, but what about all the white Europeans who were enslaved by Muslims?" Finn says.

"Seriously, Finn?" Jamal says. "You're gonna go there?"

"The topic of reparations warrants its own discussion," Mr. M says. "Let's stick to the question at hand for now."

He writes *Enslavers* under the Muslim column, then turns back to the class. "It's true that there were enslaved people and harems in medieval Islamic cultures." He looks around the room. "What about Europe? Declan stated that there was no slavery in medieval Europe."

I glance back at Finn, hoping he's got some backup for me.

"They had serfs, not slaves," Finn says. "It's not the same thing."

"Can anyone tell me the difference between a serf and an enslaved person?" Mr. M asks.

I'm ready for this one. "A serf couldn't be bought and sold like a slave. They were tied to the land that they worked."

Arielle raises her hand. "Mr. Morrison, Finn and Declan are wrong about Europeans not having slaves."

I hate that girl. For real. I don't feel bad about giving Ronan her number. She got what she deserved.

"Can you elaborate, Arielle?" Mr. M asks.

"Sure. For one, the Catholic Church enslaved people," Arielle says. "There are all these historical records that prove it. Things were moving more toward serfdom after the fall of the Roman Empire, but after the Black Death decimated the population, they needed labor. So they ended up going back to slavery. Someone had to work the land and harvest the crops, yeah?"

"Guess we're going to have to put that in the European column, too," Mr. M says, writing it on the board after checking her sources.

Crap, that does away with one of my big points—the one I thought would clinch things for our side, because all the woke people couldn't possibly vote for the side that kept slaves, right?

Figures it was a Kramer who screwed us over. Like father, like daughter. We need more stuff in our column.

"I already knew that we got algebra from the Muslim world," says Emily Noether, who is a total math geek.

There's another reason to hate them. Algebra sucks.

"This guy al-Khwārizmī was the father of algebra. What's super cool is that he and these other scholars at this amazing library called the House of Wisdom translated older works about math and astronomy from Greek and Sanskrit into Arabic. Then al-Khwārizmī took all this knowledge from other cultures and was literally doing algebra and using a decimal point centuries before the Europeans."

She's practically jumping out of her seat with enthusiasm as she tells us this. It's hard to imagine getting this excited about math.

Mr. M writes *Algebra, decimal point* under the Muslim column.

"This is like revenge of the nerds," Finn mutters.

I need to get more stuff in the European column, but Jake beats me by raising his hand.

"The Islamic states were much more inclusive than the European states," he says. "Europe was really antisemitic during the Crusades. In one crusade, they slaughtered entire Jewish villages in Germany and France if they didn't convert to Christianity. They also blamed us for the Black Death, just like Karl and Finn are trying to blame Muslims for it."

I've been playing *Imperialist Empires* for months now and watching videos about the Crusades, and I never heard of any mass killing of Jews.

"Where's your proof?" I ask. "I haven't seen anything about that, and I've been doing a lot of research."

Jake gives Mr. M the website, which everyone decides is credible. Morrison disappoints me again, just like Finn warned me he would. "That was a very dark part of the Crusades." He looks around the room with a grave expression. "It's an important reminder that using rhetoric to provoke fear of other people or groups is nothing new, but it's extremely dangerous. There are many examples of how conspiracy theories have deadly consequences."

He leans against his desk. "As a history teacher today, seeing conspiracy theories going viral is . . . worrying. It's why I want you to think carefully and critically about what you read and hear. Take the time to fact-check and evaluate sources before you share, just like we did in class today." He looks up at the clock on the wall. "Unfortunately, we're running out of time, so let's see a show of hands. Who thinks that European culture was more advanced in the medieval period?"

Only three people raise their hands. Finn, Karl, and me.

"Okay, what about Islamic culture?"

Most of the class raise their hands.

"Ryan had me at *crap*," Megan says. "The thought of raw sewage and rats in the street . . . Ugh."

"That and the House of Wisdom stuff," Emma says. "Like how they took knowledge from other places and used it to build new ideas."

"Great point, Emma! We Americans tend to think very ethnocentrically," Mr. M says. "Which means that we judge other nations through the lens of our own. And thanks to a widespread belief in 'American exceptionalism,' we lose out on the opportunity to do what al-Khwārizmī did—build on knowledge from other cultures to create new and exciting discoveries."

"Why are you teaching us to hate our country, Mr. M?" Finn asks. "There's nothing wrong with being proud to be American."

"I'm not teaching you to hate our country, Finn," Morrison says firmly. "We can love our country and be proud of the things that make it special, but still recognize that what we learn from other countries and cultures can help us reach even greater heights of knowledge and discovery— because let's face it, we don't hold a monopoly on good ideas."

As I listen to him talk, I can't help thinking that Ronan was right that our teachers have some kind of agenda.

I mean, seriously. How do you vote on history, anyway?

DECLAN

"Hey, can you give me a ride to Ronan's later?" I ask Charlie when we're at work the Saturday before Halloween. I haven't been able to get there since the debate on Monday, and I'm still fuming about what happened. But it's not like I can talk to my family about it. They'll just tell me how Mr. M is right and I'm wrong.

I always seem to be wrong in their eyes these days.

"Sorry, brother, no can do," he says. "I'm working a late shift."

My heart sinks. Dad's gone to one of Kayleigh's soccer matches, and Mom's working.

"Did you try Luke or Reid or one of the other guys?"

"I don't have their numbers," I say.

"Don't you have Clandestext?" he asks.

"No, what's that?"

"It's a secure messaging app. Safer for us than texting. Download it, and I'll add you to the group chat," Charlie says.

I download it right away. It feels like I'm leveling up, being added to the group chat with all the guys who've been part of this for a while, like I'm really part of the inner circle now.

There's a lot of joking and memes tossed around in the group chat— a lot of stuff that might have bothered me before I realized what was going on.

No one seems to be able to give me a ride out there. So after work, I get on my bike and cycle to Ronan's. I'm dressed for the cold, but even so, by the time I get there I feel like a human icicle.

"Hey, Dec!" Betheney says when I walk in. "Come sit by the wood-stove, and I'll get you something hot to drink."

I shuffle over to the sofa and sit in the spot nearest the stove. Betheney puts a few more logs on, and I stretch my fingers toward the heat.

"Ronan's out right now," Betheney says over her shoulder as she heads to the kitchen. "But he should be back soon."

By the time she brings me a mug of hot chocolate, I can just about feel my toes.

"I can't believe you biked here in this weather," she says, taking a seat next to me, close enough that I can smell the floral scent of her shampoo. "No wonder you're a baseball champ."

"Past tense," I say. "Thanks to you know who."

"And that's why we've got to keep fighting them," she says. "We need guys like you, with purpose and resolve. Guys who understand what we're up against and aren't afraid to fight."

Her words warm me from the inside.

"I hear Ronan's truck," she says. "He's gonna be so happy to see you."

She's right. When Ronan walks in the door carrying a bunch of bags from the hardware store, his face creases into a broad smile. "Declan! Good to see you, brother!"

"Can you believe it? The kid rode his bike here," Betheney says.

"Dec's a good soldier," Ronan says. He sets down the bags and goes behind the sofa to put his hands on my shoulders, giving them a firm squeeze. "That's why I think he's ready to take on a new mission."

"Oh yeah? What's that?" I ask, craning my neck to look up at him.

He walks around to the front of the sofa and starts pacing, like he does when he's about to drop some truth.

"Mocha Jenn's," he says. "The coffee shop with the Pride sticker and

We Believe sign in the window . . . We're gonna send a message. We need to show her that we're not going to stand by while she promotes those ideas."

My heart starts racing with a mixture of excitement and fear. "Like . . . what kind of message?" I'm proud that Ronan trusts me to carry out another mission, to prove myself as a white power warrior. Still, I know Jenn. She makes the best treats in town.

Ronan gives me one of those looks like he can see right down to my soul. I'm afraid that he's not going to like what he sees there, that he's going to think I'm lacking in some way.

But then he smiles. "We're just going to make sure the rest of Stafford's Corner knows what she is."

"How?"

He goes over to the bags he left on the floor and pulls out a can of black spray paint. "You'll use this to decorate the café windows with swastikas and *Jude*."

"So . . . like, just me?" I ask.

He frowns. "What's the matter, Declan? Don't you feel up to the mission?"

"No!" I say. "I mean yes, I'm up to it!"

"Good," he says. "Glad to hear I wasn't mistaken in my confidence. I see your potential. Are you in?"

I want to be the person Ronan sees. "Yeah, I'm in."

"Good man," he says. "If anyone asks you about it, deny everything. Keep your mouth shut about anything to do with me. And remember, the best defense is a good offense. If someone accuses you of being involved, flip the script so that you're the victim. I know I can count on you, Declan."

His praise causes me to puff out my chest and sit up straighter. At least someone sees that I have potential, even without my pitching arm.

While we're waiting for it to get dark, Ronan shows me how to make what he calls a morgenstern, or a morning star, which he tells me is what they called the Crusader weapon that looks like a spiked mace.

When we're finished, he says, "Come on, let's go out back so we can test it out."

Has doing the Alpha Dawg workouts given me enough arm strength? What if my fricking wrist messes me up?

I tighten the brace and pull myself together.

There's a scarecrow with a huge pumpkin head, on which someone's drawn a hooked nose like in those online memes.

Ronan hands me the bat.

"Have at it, my brother. Betheney won't mind."

It's been a while since I've held a bat in my hands. Sure I've been working out as best I can, but I still have to wear the brace on my wrist because of the stupid wrist drop. This feels familiar and comforting, though, like getting into a pair of well-worn sweats. Like I'm the Declan I used to be.

I take a few experimental practice swings, then focus on the pumpkin head and let loose. There's a twinge in my shoulder, but my aim is true. The pumpkin nose caves in, revealing the seeds and fibers within.

But feeling the weakness in my shoulder and wrist, even with all the workouts I've been doing, stokes the embers of my rage. I swing again, and again, hearing Ronan's shouts of encouragement over the blood rushing to my ears.

When there's nothing left to hit, I stop, panting, surrounded by pumpkin guts, then hold the bat out to Ronan.

"Keep it," he says, smiling, his teeth white against his beard. "It's the perfect weapon for you. Injury or no injury, I bet you can break a few skulls with this thing."

I blink a few times, suddenly choked with emotion from this proof that Ronan cares about me—right now it feels like even more than my own dad does.

"Thanks, man," I say, rubbing my shoulder. "That felt good."

Ronan grins, and I follow him back inside. He tells Betheney to get me an ice pack, and then we play *Imperialist Empires* until it's time to go.

When Ronan says it's time, I throw my bike and my bat in the back of the truck, and Betheney drives me over to Mocha Jenn's. She parks down the road, and we go toward to the coffee shop, keeping to the shadows. I pull my hoodie over my head and the gaiter over the lower part of my face. Betheney is wearing a black balaclava; only her blue eyes and pink lips show through the holes.

"You ready?" she asks. "Make it quick. It doesn't have to be pretty."

"Got it," I say, shaking up the can and drawing a test swastika on the pavement.

"Okay, on three," Betheney says. "One . . . two . . . three!"

I start running toward the front window. Over my shoulder, I see Betheney trying to block the cameras on the corners of the building facade to mess with the recording.

Raising my arm as high as I can, wincing at the pain as it comes to shoulder level, I draw a huge swastika on the window. Then I write *Jude* in big letters.

When I'm done, I run back to Betheney, making sure to keep my eyes down on the ground. She turns off the lasers and gives me a high five. We book it back to the truck and she peels out, trying to put as much distance between us and Mocha Jenn's as possible.

"Great work, Dec," Betheney says, turning up Blitzkrieg. "Ronan will be pleased."

Between the adrenaline, the Blitzkrieg, and the praise from Betheney, I feel like I'm flying.

Especially after she hugs me and gives me a kiss on the cheek when she drops me off. I hide the bat in the back of the garage, then walk into the house feeling like the man.

Mom and Dad are in the living room, watching TV. Or at least Dad's watching—Mom's got her head on his shoulder, but her mouth is open and she's snoring softly.

"Where've you been?" Dad asks.

"I went over to Ronan's after work," I tell him.

"And you couldn't text us to let us know?" Dad says. "You're spending a lot of time over there."

I blow out an exasperated sigh. "This is why. Because at Ronan's, people aren't getting on my case all the time. I'm going to bed."

I take the stairs two at a time, wanting to get safely in my room before anyone can give me any more crap.

Unfortunately, Kayleigh's coming out of the bathroom in her pj's just as I get to the top of the steps.

"Hey," she says. "Mom and Dad were losing it because you didn't respond to their texts. Don't you think you've caused them enough stress?"

I don't respond, just shove past her to get to my room.

"Ugh. You smell weird," she says. "Take a shower."

I slam the bedroom door in her face. But once I know she's back in her room, I head to the bathroom to wash up and brush my teeth.

When I'm in bed, I open the Clandestext app. Ronan's told everyone about the great work the newest recruit did tonight. I fall asleep smiling.

I'm dreaming that I'm a Crusader, riding a white warhorse, the Jerusalem cross on my tabard and shield. But instead of wielding a sword, I've got a can of spray paint. One of Saladin's soldiers is riding toward me with a scimitar, and my heart starts racing because it looks like this is it for me, that my life is about to end in pain and bloodshed. But as he swings his scimitar to behead me, I spray him in the face. He loses his balance and topples from his warhorse, to be trampled to death by the knight behind me.

I don't have time to celebrate my escape, though, because someone's grabbing my arm and saying, "Declan, wake up!"

Slowly, I open my eyes, and Kayleigh's standing over me, looking at me with the same determined-to-kill-me expression as the Saracen soldier.

"Was it you?" she says.

"Was what me?" I say, angry that she woke me from my victory.

"Mocha Jenn posted pictures of what she found when she went to open up early this morning," she says. "Some idiot vandalized the store with antisemitic graffiti. Some idiot I'm scared is you."

"Why?" I say, remembering the advice I got at Ronan's to deny everything. "It's not like you have any proof."

"Except that you came back really late, and you smelled weird," she says. "Everyone's totally freaked out by it. Mom, Dad, Jake, Arielle . . . I should tell the police."

I laugh. "Really? What are you going to tell them, Kayleigh? My brother came home late and smelled funny?"

Her face flushes. "Why shouldn't I tell the police I *think* it was you, so they investigate?"

"Because you've got no proof, and I didn't do it," I point out. "And even if I did, you shouldn't, because blood is thicker than water, and all that. Because I'm the one that's fighting for our family."

"Don't give me that crap!" she hisses. "You aren't fighting for us."

Kayleigh turns on her heel and stomps to the door. She pauses in the doorway and turns back. "You have to stop, Dec. Because the next time, I will tell—proof or no proof." She shakes her head. "Where do you think this all ends? Someone's going to get hurt."

I don't answer, because I've already said I didn't do it. But there's no way I'm going to stop. I'm just getting started.

JAKE

"Did you hear what happened at Mocha Jenn's last night?" I ask my parents when I come down to breakfast on Sunday.

Mom nods. "I got a text from Jenn Rosner this morning."

"It's like there's another incident every week," I say, not even hungry for breakfast because I've got that antsy feeling in my stomach.

"You're right," Dad says. "It's . . . disturbing."

"Do they know who did it?" I ask.

"Let me see if there's anything on the local news site yet." Mom reads some more. "Just says that the police are investigating." She sighs. "And the article includes the usual quotes from the town council claiming 'This isn't who we are.'"

"Why do people say that?" I ask. "If anything, all this has made me realize this is who we are. They should be honest and say something like 'This isn't how we want to see ourselves' or 'This isn't who we aspire to be' instead."

"Nailed it," Dad says. "Admitting we have a problem is the first step, as they say in recovery programs. We'll never become the country we aspire to be unless we admit some things are broken."

"It feels like some people are aspiring to make our country a place where only white Christians are welcome," I say.

Mom shakes her head sadly. "I used to think people who thought like that were on the fringes of American life—that there weren't that many of them. Sure, there were always the folks who made the hurtful comments.

But in my experience, most of them were ignorant of how much pain they were causing because they hadn't encountered many Jewish people before."

"What's scaring me is that it's starting to feel like there's more people who feel that way than don't," I say. "People who think that *we're* the problem—us and anyone with black or brown skin."

"I wouldn't go that far," Dad says. "But you're right that antisemitism hasn't just been on the fringes. In fact, it's been promoted by some of the biggest names in American society, like Henry Ford."

"The car company guy?" I ask.

"That's the one," Dad says. "Ford took the conspiracy theories in *The Protocols of the Elders of Zion* and published them in a newspaper he owned, the *Dearborn Independent*, as if they were factual news articles. He also distributed the *Dearborn Independent* in all of his dealerships, like 'Hey, America, have some antisemitic trash with your new car!'"

"So Henry Ford was this all-American antisemite?" I say. "How come we didn't learn *that* in school?"

"People don't like to acknowledge that someone they admire had flaws," Mom says. "Especially a titan of industry like Henry Ford."

"You know who else was an admirer of Henry Ford?" Dad says. "Hitler."

"You know the guy was doing something wrong if Hitler was a fanboy," I say.

I can't help wondering why no one told us about Henry Ford when they were teaching us how he was such a genius for developing the assembly line for mass production of cars. Like, yeah, it's cool that he did that, but it's only part of the story.

•   •   •

The next day after school, Jordan's mom drives a bunch of us to the synagogue youth group meeting in her minivan.

Shira, our youth group adviser, is in like her late twenties, with a cool purple streak in her hair.

When we're all there, she says, "So, listen. I know something disturbing happened yesterday, and I wanted to give you a chance to talk about it—if you want."

We all kind of look around at one another.

"Who would want to do that to Jenn, of all people?" Danielle asks.

"I know, right?" Naya says. "She's, like, one of the nicest people in town."

"What happened at Jenn's is bad enough on its own," I say. "But on top of everything else, like all the stickers and flyers and what happened to Arielle—it's a lot."

"I know," Shira says. "It is a lot. But maybe, given everything that's happening, it's even more important for us to tell the Hanukkah story."

The youth group always puts on a performance at the Hebrew school Hanukkah party, to entertain the younger kids.

"We need to get started, because Hanukkah falls early this year," Shira says.

"Ugh! I hate when it's early," Danielle grumbles. "At least when Hanukkah falls around the same time as Christmas you don't feel like as much of an outsider when everyone's decking the halls and opening presents around the tree."

"I hear you," Shira says. "Christmas is a time when anyone who belongs to a minority faith becomes more acutely aware of their difference. My way of dealing with that is to be even more proud to be Jewish. To be proud of all the ways we've contributed to America in so many different fields."

It's true. We have—in the arts, in science, in sports, and in books that I'll probably never read unless there's an audiobook. That is something to feel good about.

"Yeah, I guess," Danielle says.

"So, does anyone have some creative ideas for how we can tell the Hanukkah story this year?"

"What about telling it through songs people know?" Naya suggests. "Like we could rewrite the lyrics to tell the Hanukkah story."

"I like that idea!" Arielle says.

"As long as the song isn't the one about sharks that the little kids like," Jordan says. "That song drives me nuts."

I laugh and rub my hands together like a cartoon villain. "Now we know how to torture Jordan!"

"Don't. Even. Think. About. It," Jordan says.

But I'm not the only one who's thinking about it.

"Hanukkah . . . do do do do do do, is a time do do do do do do, we spread light do do do do do do for eight nights," Joel sings.

"Make it stooooooop!" Jordan groans, making us all crack up.

We spend the rest of youth group choosing which songs to use. (Not the shark one, thankfully.)

"It's a good thing we still have just over a month before Hanukkah starts," Arielle says. "We're going to need all the time we can get."

"Don't worry," Shira tells us. "I'll put everything we came up with today in a shared document so you can collaborate between meetings."

At six thirty, we head out to the lobby to wait for our parents to pick us up, and all of us—even Jordan, to his disgust—are making up Hanukkah versions of the shark song.

"See you all tomorrow at the Halloween party," Arielle says.

"I'll be there," Jordan tells her. He glares at Joel and me. "Hopefully by then I'll have this stupid song out of my head."

I hope I do, too.

DECLAN

"You got anything planned for Halloween tomorrow?" Charlie asks Finn and me after work on Monday.

"Nah," I say. Last year, Parker Sauda had an epic party. The entire baseball team was there. I don't know if he's having it this year. If he is, he didn't invite me.

"We should do something," Finn says. "Halloween's the perfect cover."

Charlie nods slowly. "Right on, brother."

That's when it hits me. "Pinnacle. We should do something at Pinnacle."

A smile spreads across Charlie's face. "I like the way you think, Declan. I'll drive by and do some recon on the way home. I'll pick you up around seven tomorrow, okay?"

"Sounds good to me. I can't wait to give Pinnacle some payback," I say.

"I'll bet," Finn says.

Charlie claps me on the shoulder. "Don't worry, brother. We'll show them we're not gonna take this lying down," he says.

If only Dad would see things the same way.

The next day after school, I move my bat to a hiding place in the bushes near the driveway, so I can grab it when Charlie picks me up. Dad's putting Halloween candy in a bowl. Mom is still at work, doing some funky Halloween hair for a client who is having a party. I'm coming out of my room dressed in dark jeans and a black hoodie when Kayleigh emerges from hers as Eleven from *Stranger Things*.

"Perfect for you, because you are very strange," I say.

"I wish I really *did* have Eleven's powers," she says. "I'd teach you a thing or two."

"Who are you going out with?" I ask.

"We're not going out," she says. "Because of all the *stuff* that's been happening around here, Arielle's parents are hosting a party at their house."

I shrug, like whatever "stuff" she's talking about has nothing to do with me. But I can't help being pissed I wasn't invited. It's not like I want to go hang out with a bunch of globalists, but I would have been invited to something like this before the accident.

"Dad, I'm leaving!" Kayleigh calls out, putting on her reflective vest. "I'll see you later."

"Call when you're ready to come home," Dad says. "I don't want you riding your bike back. You never know what kind of idiots are out to make mischief on Halloween."

"Yeah, I know. So many idiots," Kayleigh says, giving me a pointed look over her shoulder before leaving.

"What about you, Declan? You going to stay here and help me hand out candy?" Dad asks.

"Nah, I'm heading out," I say. "I'm going to hang out with Finn."

Dad puts his hand on my wrist. I'm wearing the brace, because I know I'm going to need the wrist support to wield my bat. Another thing I can thank the globalists at Pinnacle for.

"Don't do anything stupid," he says.

I wrench my arm away from him. "Why do you just assume it's going to be me doing something stupid?" I head for the door. "You didn't say anything like that to Kayleigh, did you, Dad?"

"Because Kayleigh hasn't been acting up lately like you have," Dad says.

"I'm going to wait outside," I say, wrenching the door open. The

Sullivans from down the street are on the porch with their two little kids, who are dressed like mini superheroes. I want to tell them that there are no superheroes. That we need to learn to fight for our people, because no one is going to swoop in to save us. But I just grumble "What's up?" then brush past them to go wait in the driveway. Luckily, Dad's busy talking to them when Charlie drives up, so I'm able to retrieve my bat from the bushes without anyone noticing.

Finn's in the front seat. "Guess what Charlie got us?"

He hands me what must be the creepiest clown mask I've ever seen.

"This is the stuff of nightmares," I say, trying it on.

"We're just a couple of clowns, out for a good time," Charlie says.

He blasts hatecore to get us pumped up. By the time we get near the Pinnacle plant, I can barely hear through the ear that is nearest the speaker, but I'm 100 percent fired up to fight.

The gate to the plant is locked. Charlie pulls around to a side road and parks the truck, then tells us to put on our masks and follow him. We skirt through the brush on the side of the road and head to the fence hidden in a nearby bush. He pulls out wire cutters and clips the links until there's a small opening.

I'm smaller than Charlie and Finn, so I crawl through first and use my bat to hold the fence clear so they can follow. Then I start swinging the bat around, warming up. Finn whips out a can of spray paint, and Charlie has a heavy wrench.

Wearing our matching clown masks, we approach the building. Charlie and I start swinging at windows, while Finn spray-paints swastikas and anti-globalist slogans.

I know this won't get Dad's job back, but every time I swing the bat and hear the shattering of glass, it feels like justice in a world where people like me don't get any.

We don't stay long, because Charlie's worried about a silent alarm, but it's amazing how much damage you can do in a short time if you're committed.

When we get back in the truck, we're all giddy. Finn can't stop laughing, and I keep punching my good arm in the air along to the music.

As we pass by the green, I see the lights on at Arielle's house and say, "Wait. Stop!"

"What's up, brother?" Charlie asks.

"Can you pull around the corner?" I ask.

"Affirmative," Charlie says. "What's your plan?"

"That house back there is Kramer's," I say. "I want to send him a personal message."

"Finn, you block the doorbell cam. I'll be here as getaway," Charlie continues. "Masks on and make it snappy."

Finn and I put on our creepy clown masks and walk nonchalantly toward the Kramers' house. A couple with two little kids picks them up and crosses the street when they see us. It makes me feel powerful. We sneak into the shadows of the house next door to the Kramers'.

"Okay, now!" I tell Finn.

He blocks the doorbell camera. I run up and take a few swings at the Kramers' front window, reveling in the sound of shattering glass.

Finn and I book it back to the truck, and Charlie peels out, tires screeching. I can't stop laughing. This has been the best night ever.

JAKE

Arielle and I are in the kitchen filling up the snack bowls—and sneaking a kiss—when there's a sound almost like a shot from the front of the house, followed by a terrifying crashing sound. We jump apart, and I rush into the living room to see someone's smashed the front window. Fueled by fear and rage, I run to the front door and throw it open, hoping to catch the culprit, but whoever it was bolted.

Standing there on the sidewalk, hands clenched into fists, I'm filled with anger so explosive it feels like it might break through my skin. The whole reason we're at the Kramers' house in the first place is because Arielle's parents were worried about their kids going out after the crap that's happened lately.

But they couldn't even let us enjoy Halloween in peace. They brought the hate to Arielle's front door.

That's when I remember—the door cam.

I race back into the house. Mr. Kramer, Arielle, and the others are in the front room, surveying the damage.

"Tried to catch them," I say. "Did the doorbell camera catch anything?"

"I hope so," Mr. Kramer says, opening the app on his phone. We crowd around him as he plays back the most recent events.

There's movement, then there's a brief glimpse of a scary clown mask from a distance, but then there's just white flashes and we hear the front window shattering.

Mr. Kramer mutters a curse under his breath.

"But there's that one shot of the scary clown," Arielle says.

"That doesn't give the police a lot to go on, but I guess it's something," Mr. Kramer says.

"What scary clown?"

Arielle's brother is standing in the doorway, his eyes wide as he takes in the broken window.

"Bobby, I told you to wait downstairs with Mom," Mr. Kramer says.

"I had to pee," he says. "Did a scary clown come to our house and do that?" He turns to Arielle. "When I had a nightmare about them, you said that scary clowns aren't real!"

"They aren't." I go over and crouch down so we're at eye level. "It was just some idiot wearing a mask."

"Are you sure?" he asks.

"One hundred percent positive," I say.

He doesn't look totally convinced, but his dad and Arielle circle him in a protective hug.

"I want to move back to New Jersey!" Bobby says quietly. "I don't like it here."

It makes me want to punch things. He shouldn't have to be scared. None of us should.

We go back to the party while Mr. Kramer calls the police, but none of us are in the party mood anymore.

"If I find out Dec had anything to do with this, I am going to destroy him," Kayleigh says.

"Do you know where he is tonight?" Mateo asks.

She laughs bitterly. "Probably with Finn McCarthy, doing something idiotic. That's what he does best lately." Kayleigh looks around at everyone. "I'm sorry this ruined the party."

"Why are you apologizing?" Arielle asks, going over to hug her. "*You* didn't do anything!"

"I know," Kayleigh sighs. "But . . ."

She doesn't say the words, but it's easy enough for the rest of us to fill them in. She thinks Declan did.

DECLAN

"You did it, didn't you?"

Kayleigh is standing in the doorway of my room, dressed in her Eleven costume, fake blood dribbling from her nostril. Or maybe it's real blood. She looks mad enough.

"Did what?" I say, keeping my eyes on the Clandestext chat in front of me, glad that I left my bat and clown mask in Charlie's truck for safekeeping.

"Don't lie to me, Declan!" she shouts. "You know what I'm talking about! When is this going to end?"

"When we've defeated them," I say, finally looking at her.

Her fists clench, and I drop my phone and sit up, because it looks like she's gonna walk in and deck me.

But she just glares at me with disgust and loathing. "I hate you so much right now."

Then she goes to her room and slams the door.

I'd be lying if I said that didn't hurt. But I bury the pain under my ever-present rage.

The attack on Kramer's house and the vandalism at Pinnacle make the local news the next day. When Charlie drives us to Ronan's after school, Ronan is pumped.

"We'll get new recruits from this, I guarantee it," he says, smiling.

"We're getting more hits to the website, that's for sure," Finn says.

Ronan gets up and starts pacing. "It's time to ramp things up—to take it to the next level."

"Like what?" I ask.

Ronan stops midpace and turns to me. "All in good time, Declan, my brother. All in good time."

I'm still fired up from last night. It felt good to fight back. Whatever it is that Ronan's planning, I want to be a part of it.

When Morrison hands back the Crusades paper on Friday, I can't believe my eyes. He gave me a C! I was sure I was going to get an A on it. I did everything I was supposed to do in an argumentative paper. I had an introduction with a clear thesis—that Christian Medieval Europe was more advanced than the Islamic world—three paragraphs with evidence backing up my points, clearly footnoted, and a conclusion.

Finn was right. After how Morrison skewed the debate, it's clear what side he's on. But that doesn't mean he has a right to mark me down.

"Told ya," Finn says when I show him my paper. "Guys like us can't get a fair break. They want to censor us because they're afraid of the truth."

He did even worse than me.

All during class, I'm stewing about my grade. I always thought Mr. M was cool, but it turns out he's just another tool pushing an agenda. As soon as class is over, I stomp up to his desk.

"Why did I get a C?" I ask him. "I backed up all my arguments with facts and footnotes, just like you said."

Mr. M raises an eyebrow, then takes out the rubric. "Here's the thing, Declan—if I were grading your paper just on how you presented your argument in a logical fashion, you would have received the A you think you deserved. You've got a good mind, and you write clearly and concisely."

"So why did I get a C?"

"Because while you presented me with footnotes, you didn't use the information literacy skills we've talked about in class to evaluate the sources." He puts the rubric down and looks up at me. "Did you realize that one of the sources you cited originated on a white nationalist website that had some really despicable—not to mention thoroughly disproven—antisemitic conspiracy theories on the home page?"

"So? As long as it's citing the historical references . . ."

Mr. M's lips thin. "Come on, Declan. Don't play dumb with me. We talked about information literacy last year in class, too. You had several sessions with the media specialist to go over how to evaluate sources. You got a C instead of an A because you created a well-reasoned argument using sources you had to know weren't acceptable for an academic paper."

"I bet if they were unreliable sources that agreed with your point of view, you would have given me an A," I mumble.

He looks me straight in the eye. "Really? Do you honestly think that?" He taps the paper with his finger. "Your assignment was to write an academic paper, and for that your sources need to meet a certain standard. You have to develop the ability to evaluate the sources you use before college, or it won't go well for you."

"Yeah, like I've got any chance of going to college now."

"There are ways," Mr. M says. "Community college. Student loans."

"Yeah, then I'll be saddled with debt and there will still be no jobs."

Morrison gives me the same disappointed look I get from my dad.

He stands up and holds out the paper. "If you want a better grade, you'll have to do a better job evaluating sources."

I grab it and crumple it in my fist.

"I'm worried about you, Declan," Mr. M says, in a gentler voice. "Especially if you're finding your way onto sites like that. I know you're angry about life right now, and that makes you vulnerable to the kind of ideas you'll find there." He pins me with his gaze. "Be careful. Rhetoric like that inevitably leads to violence." He stands and puts his hands on the desk. "And it corrodes your soul. You're better than that, Declan."

He's the one who gave me a C, killing all hope I had of not bombing his class this quarter. So I say "I'm going to be late for my next class" and get out of there, as fast as I can.

Dad's in a good mood for a change when I get home from school. He's in the kitchen, humming as he's following another cooking video, like he doesn't realize how demeaning it is for him to have turned into such a hausfrau.

"Hey, Declan!" he says. "Guess what your old man has going on next Friday!"

"I dunno. What?"

"A j-o-b interview, that's what!" Dad says. "Kayleigh helped me figure out how to use the right keywords in my application. I didn't realize you had to do that so the AI doesn't kick out your résumé before you even start."

"That's great, Dad," I say. "Bet you'll be glad to get out of the kitchen, huh?"

"If I get the job, that is. His face clouds. "This is the first interview I've gotten despite applying for more jobs than I can count." But then he seems to remember that he's supposed to be in Dad mode. "I'll be glad to get back to work for a lot of reasons, but to tell you the truth, I've kind of enjoyed my time in the kitchen," he says, pointing to the casserole dish, where he appears to be attempting lasagna.

Ugh. My dad's turning into such a fricking girlyman. "But still . . . it's kind of demeaning, isn't it? Doing women's work like this?"

Dad rubs his hand over the place on the back of his head where he's starting to get a bald spot. "You know, when I first got laid off, I thought the same thing." He chuckles. "But doing this"—he waves around the kitchen—"it's surprised me. It's given me a sense of accomplishment. I can follow a recipe and make something that's not just edible, but actually tastes good." He smiles. "And the best part is watching my family enjoy what I've made."

"That's cool, but it's still supposed to be women's work, right?"

Dad's eyes narrow, in a way that never bodes well for me. "Declan, drop your backpack, put down your phone, and wash your hands. You're going to help me assemble this lasagna."

"Dad, come on. I've got homework."

"It won't take that long, and it'll be good for you. Just do it."

My first instinct is to fight. But mixed in with Dad's stern look is a hopeful one—like he wants me to bond with him over this stupid pasta dish.

"Fine," I say, reluctantly putting my phone on the table and my backpack on one of the chairs. After I've washed my hands, Dad starts giving me instructions on how to layer the cooked pasta, the ricotta cheese mixture, and the tomato sauce. It's making him way happier than it should that I'm doing this, but whatever. It's no big deal.

I'm busy putting on another layer of pasta when my phone buzzes.

Dad looks down at it before I can do anything, and his expression as he picks it up turns to horror, then anger.

"What did I just see, Declan?" he demands, shoving it under my nose. All I can see is my home screen.

"How am I supposed to know?" I say, hoping it wasn't a Clandestext notification. "I can't see whatever it was you saw."

"I'll tell you what I saw," Dad says, his voice strained. "A picture of a Nazi concentration camp, labeled *Fake News*."

Crap. It *was* a Clandestext notification.

"Tell me you don't actually believe that, Declan," Dad says. It's almost a plea.

But I'm not going to lie and pretend I believe the globalist propaganda just to make him happy. Maybe hearing the truth will finally open his eyes about what's going on. Maybe it'll finally convince him to fight with me.

"It's not fake news that there were camps," I say. "But they were labor camps, not death camps. People tell me that a lot of the stuff you see about the 'history' of the Holocaust has been photoshopped to look so much worse than it really was."

"Oh really? People tell you? What people?" Dad asks.

"My friends. People online. I've watched a lot of videos," I tell him.

He closes his eyes, like he's in pain. When he opens them, he asks, "Tell me this, Declan: Why would anyone make up something that horrific?"

I ignore his question. "I saw online that nowhere near six million Jews died."

I've seen Dad look at me with disappointment so much lately that I've come to expect it. But what I see now is worse than that. It's . . . disgust.

Trying to get him to connect the dots the way Ronan and OdalRune88 and the others did for me, I say, "They make these exaggerated monuments and museums to their victimhood, which they can play off for the rest of time—at our expense."

I thought this would be the thing that finally convinced Dad to see the light, but the pained look on his face and the weighted silence following my words tells me just how wrong I was about that.

"I never thought I'd have to prove to my kid that the Holocaust was real, not 'fake news.'" He stands up, his posture stiff. "Finish that lasagna," he orders as he turns to leave the kitchen. "I'm going to get something from the attic."

"Whatever," I say, but I'm crushed that he still doesn't get it.

As soon as he's gone, I grab my phone and turn off my Clandestext notifications.

By the time Dad gets back, I've finished putting together the lasagna. He's carrying a shoebox that's covered in dust, which he brings over to the table. He gestures for me to sit.

"Open it," Dad says, taking a seat.

Slowly, hesitantly, I lift the lid.

On top is a patch from a uniform. It's in the shape of a triangle, divided into thirds, colored yellow, blue, and red. There's a six at the top and what looks like a tank track, a cannon, and a red lightning bolt in the middle.

Underneath that is a dollar bill with place names scribbled all over it. Some look like they're in England, some in France, and some in Germany. I recognize one name, Buchenwald.

"Where did you get this?" I ask.

"Keep looking," Dad says.

There's a leather box, and when I open it, I find ribbons and medals.

"Wow, this is a Bronze Star," I say. "Whose was it?"

But Dad doesn't answer. He just sits there, his arms crossed.

I set the box of medals on the table and find photographs. There are some of young men in combat uniform, standing in front of a jeep. There's one of them standing in front of the bombed ruins of a building. You can see part of a bedroom, like it was just ripped in two.

I shuffle through those and find more that are facedown. I turn the top one over and it doesn't make sense to me right away. When it does, my stomach turns. They're pictures of stacks of emaciated bodies, piled up like cordwood. The images I see all the time online don't seem real. But there's something different about these black-and-white photographs, yellowed and curled at the edges, which for some reason have been kept in an old shoebox in our attic.

I look up at my dad, confused.

"Go on," he says firmly.

The next photo is even worse. It's a close-up of a skeletal corpse of a woman, her mouth open like she's screaming.

I feel bile rise in my throat.

"How do you even have these?" I ask him. "Who do they belong to?"

"I found the box in the attic of my grandma Brenda's house when I was helping her clean out before she moved into the condo," Dad says. "After my grandpa died."

"So these are Great-Grandpa Eddie's?" I ask. "I knew he was at D-Day, but no one ever told me he was at Buchenwald."

"Because I didn't know, either, until I helped my grandmother clean out her house," Dad explains. "Your great-grandpa didn't like to talk about the war. He always changed the subject when I asked him questions." Dad pins me with his gaze. "A lot of our soldiers were traumatized by the things they saw in those camps. The ones you and your friends claim were just labor camps."

I put the photos back in the box, facedown, and shove it away from me. "It's okay, I don't need to see the rest of them."

"Yes, Declan. You do," Dad says, pushing it back in front of me. "You've been talking a big game, getting down on me because I'm not fighting this so-called white genocide. You need to understand what happens in an actual genocide before you throw that word around."

I start taking more pictures out of the box, one at a time.

I see pictures of the Holocaust all the time online. Jokes about it. Pictures of the latest Destroyer of the White Race photoshopped into pictures of gas chambers. But these aren't the same images I've seen over and over. These are different, and somehow that seems to make them more real.

"I've got to pee," I tell Dad, needing to get away from this.

I shut myself in the bathroom and splash cold water on my face. Conflicting thoughts race around my brain like atoms, and every time they collide, I feel an explosion.

I'm relieved to see Dad's not in the kitchen when I get back and that my great-grandfather's box of horrors is gone. Grabbing my backpack and my phone, I head up to my room. But instead of doing homework or logging in to *Imperialist Empires* or looking at the latest stuff on Clandestext, I start researching the patch that was in the box. It's for the Sixth Armored Division, which fought at D-Day, the Battle of the Bulge, and . . . liberated Buchenwald, which means my great-grandpa Eddie was there. Which means he took those pictures. Which means . . .

I lie down on my bed and stare at the ceiling, trying to make sense of it all and failing.

DECLAN

"Good luck on the interview, Dad!" Kayleigh says as we're about to leave for school on Friday of the following week. She leans down and kisses him on the cheek.

"Thanks, honey," he says.

"Yeah, hope it goes well," I say. I can't resist adding, "Even though you wouldn't be out begging for a new job right now if the globalists weren't working so hard to destroy us."

"Not this again," Kayleigh groans. "Jeez, Dec, give it a rest for a minute and focus on Dad for a change!"

"I am focusing on Dad—"

"Enough!" Dad explodes, standing up and hitting the table with his hands. "I don't need this crap today, of all days!" He turns to me. "I thought maybe you learned something last week, Dec. That maybe a dose of reality would penetrate that fog of garbage in your head. Guess I was wrong."

I storm out of the house, at odds with my own family when they're the ones I'm fighting for.

I hear Kayleigh running to catch up with me and walk faster.

She grabs my arm. "What was that, Declan? Why would you try to get Dad all riled up when he's got a big interview?"

"I was just pointing out the facts, ones that you all seem to ignore, because you'd rather be friends with Arielle and Jake than fight for our people!"

"Arielle and Jake are 'my people,'" Kayleigh says. "Because that's what friends are. If you think you're doing and saying all this awful crap for me, just stop."

"I'm doing it for *me!*" I exclaim. "And Dad! And all the other white men who are being oppressed."

"God, listen to yourself!" Kayleigh shouts.

It's like I scored bonus points for making her lose it.

"Stop being so hysterical," I say, goading her.

She screams with frustration, which is deeply satisfying.

Kayleigh stalks away toward the bus stop. "Just stay away from me," she says, waving a hand behind her in my general direction. "I don't want to even know you right now."

I smile, imagining myself telling this story at Ronan's later and recounting it to my *IE* friends.

Kayleigh won't even look at me as we wait for the bus, or as I walk past her to take a seat in the back.

Whatever. She's still living with her eyes closed.

I choose to be awake.

The further we get into November, the more the atmosphere at Ronan's changes. It's not just a place to chill and play games and learn more about the need to fight for our people. There's a building undercurrent of tension and excitement. Ronan's been spending a lot of time in the back room with Luke, Reid, and Charlie. I don't know what is happening, but I get the impression they're planning something big, something that's going to take our fight to the next level.

Finn and I stepped up in Ronan's eyes because we brought in a few new recruits from school. After the debate in Morrison's class, we started slyly putting up stickers around the halls, with a different QR code.

Karl Higgins is one of the guys we recruited. He does shotput on the track team. The guy has some serious muscle, and he already has his license, which is a plus because it means we don't have to always rely on Charlie.

When we bring him to Ronan's the first time, Betheney's in the kitchen doing her trolling. I introduce Karl to her, and she asks, "Who's this McDreamy?"

It's like a gut punch. I thought I was her McDreamy—well, other than Ronan, obviously. But she's feeling Karl's muscles and making out like he's some Super Aryan.

I leave the room and slump on the sofa next to Finn, who is on a laptop doing something to the website.

"What's the matter with you?" he asks, without taking his eyes off the screen.

"Does Betheney do that to all the new recruits?"

"Do what?"

"Call them McDreamy?"

Finn chuckles. "Awwwww, poor Dec feeling heartbroken because she's giving Karl the treatment?"

"So you're saying she does it to everyone?"

He finally takes his eyes off the screen. "By *it*, do you mean makes them feel welcome and special? Like they are the hottest guy in the history of the Aryan race?"

I nod, feeling my face flush.

Finn laughs. "Yeah, pretty much." He turns back to the laptop. "Hey, it worked on you, didn't it?"

It did. And the fact that I fell for it, just like I see Karl is doing now when I turn and look over the back of the sofa, makes me feel like an idiot. And being made to feel like an idiot here, when this has been the place I've escaped from all that, messes with my head.

It doesn't help that ever since Dad made me look at those photos last week, images from the dusty shoebox in the attic keep popping up in my head like those annoying ads on websites. I need it to stop.

I don't want confusion. I need certainty: the certainty that what I believe is right.

JAKE

The weekend before Thanksgiving, Cody drives us to the last girls' soccer away game in Woodmont Depot. It's in the midforties, so I pack a thermos of hot apple cider in addition to snacks to keep us fortified.

We're setting up our chairs on the sideline when Mr. Taylor comes over.

"Hey, guys!" he says. "Good to see you both! It's been a while since you've been around."

Cody and I exchange a surreptitious glance. Mr. Taylor seems so genuinely glad to see us, I don't want to tell him that the reason we haven't been around is because Dec's turned into the Stafford's Corner version of the Hitler Youth.

"It's good to see you," I say. "Kayleigh's been on a scoring streak this season, huh?"

He smiles proudly. "Yeah, my girl's on a roll."

"She's killing it," Cody agrees.

"But I have to admit, Arielle has been a part of that," Mr. Taylor says. "She set Kayleigh up for some great shots. The whole team has really gelled, you know?"

I do know.

I've got to admit, I could watch Arielle play soccer all day every day. Seeing her dark ponytail streaming behind her as she does all this amazing footwork is insanely hot.

By halftime, the Sabre girls are up 1–0 and my toes are starting to feel numb, despite the cider and thick socks and boots. Cody and I do high knees on the sideline to warm up, while Mr. Taylor goes to sit in his car for a while. Arielle and Kayleigh wave to us before huddling with Coach Carroll.

Mr. Taylor comes back just before the short halftime break ends. "I was thinking, you two should come to the house for some pizza after the match. Got some plain cheese pies and some pepperoni."

Cody looks at me. "You up for it?"

"Heck yeah! Although I'll stick to the plain cheese," I say.

"That's right," Mr. Taylor says. "I forgot you don't eat pepperoni."

My family doesn't separate milk and meat like more observant Jews who keep kosher, but we don't eat pork or shellfish. Sometimes I just tell people I'm vegetarian, because it's easier than explaining the whole thing, but then they get confused when they see me scarfing down a burger.

Five minutes into the second half, Woodmont Depot's striker puts the ball in the back of our net, tying the score.

"Ugh," Cody says. "That's got to hurt."

The Woodmont Depot goalie manages to fend off all our attacks, and it looks like the game could end up a draw. But four minutes before the clock runs out, Kris Jenkins intercepts a Woodmont Depot pass and starts dribbling it back up the field away from our goal. She passes to Abby Sanchez, who passes to Arielle. One of the Woodmont Depot defenders tries to tackle Arielle, but she does some mad footwork and gets the ball to Kayleigh, who shoots and . . . SCORES!

Mr. Taylor, Cody, and I are screaming. The girls are jumping on Kayleigh, just as the whistle blows for the end of the game.

"That was an awesome finish," Cody says.

Arielle spots me and comes running over. She yells "Incoming!" then makes a graceful leap into my arms, wrapping her legs around my waist. "WE WON! WE WON!"

"Um, yeah," I say, laughing. "I figured that out."

She messes up my hair, not that anyone can probably tell the difference, then slides to the ground as Kayleigh comes loping over.

"That was a spectacular goal. Really great teamwork," Mr. Taylor says, giving her a huge hug.

"Kris's interception was *insane!*" Kayleigh says, obviously still on a high from that winning shot.

"I invited these two jokers to come back to the house," Mr. Taylor says. "They said they can't wait to try my pizza."

"Hilarious," Kayleigh says, rolling her eyes.

"We can't!" Cody says. "Really!"

"I'm told the Taylor Pizzeria has a five-star rating in that famous restaurant guide," I add.

"Would you like an appetizer with that crap sandwich, Jake?" Kayleigh asks.

Mr. Taylor laughs. "Okay, okay, I'm not promising five stars. I think my best Yelp review says something like 'It's edible.'"

"That's not true! I told you it's good," Kayleigh says.

"I'll take *good*," Mr. Taylor says. "Grab your gear and we'll hit the road."

Cody drives Arielle and me back to Stafford's Corner. He's talking about the game, and how he's wondering if Abby Sanchez is dating anyone, and I'm listening and responding, but I can feel my muscles tensing up, wondering if Dec will be home. I don't know if I want him to be or not.

Mr. Taylor's pizza is surprisingly good, and it's great to see a smile on his face when we tell him that.

Arielle's started telling him about our Hanukkah play when I hear the front door open. I hope that it's Mrs. Taylor coming home from work.

"Hey, did you make pizza——" Dec breaks off when he sees us all sitting there, his expression guarded. "Um . . . what's up?" he asks, raising his hand in an obviously reluctant greeting.

Arielle grabs my hand under the table. I give hers a squeeze but keep my eyes focused on Dec, challenging him to see me. Me, Jake Lehrer, the guy he was friends with since forever, not some malevolent stereotype.

"Grab a slice, Dec," Mr. Taylor says with forced cheer, passing the plate to him. "I think I've got this recipe perfected."

Dec takes a slice and stands by the sink eating it because there aren't enough chairs.

"Not bad," he says.

"So, this Hanukkah party?" Mr. Taylor says. "You're making it a musical this year? That must be a lot of work."

"No joke," I say.

"We just have to write the lyrics, though," Arielle explains. "We have karaoke versions of the songs we're using."

"Figures we decided to change things up the year Hanukkah falls early, though," I say. "Nothing like adding more pressure!"

"So when do your 'eight crazy nights' start?" Kayleigh asks.

"December eighth," Arielle says. "That's when we're having the party at the synagogue."

"Is that the one with the doughnuts?" Dec asks suddenly.

"Yeah. Sufganiyot," I say. "And the latkes."

"Those doughnuts were sick," he says, and there's a flash of the old Dec smile.

"Sick is what happened after you got home after eating so many of them," Kayleigh reminds him. "It all came up in gross Technicolor spew."

Mr. Taylor starts laughing. "I remember that. Your bedroom looked like a hazmat site."

Dec grimaces, and I can tell he's mad at Kayleigh for bringing it up.

"But you cleaned up on playing dreidels, despite being a newbie," I add, wanting to hold on to that flash of old Declan I saw. "I was pissed!"

He laughs. "Oh yeah, I forgot that part."

Our eyes meet, and for a moment we're just best friends sharing a fun memory. But then, almost as if he remembers that I'm "the enemy," he averts his gaze and the smile fades from his face. "I gotta go," he mumbles before heading upstairs to his room.

Despite everything that's happened, I miss the friendship Dec and I had. Does that make me the idiot? I wonder if somewhere in that shaved head of his, there's any part of Dec that misses it, too.

That's why I say "Excuse me for a sec," then get up and follow him upstairs.

His door is closed. I knock, but there's no answer.

"I can't get away from them anywhere. Now they're in my house," I hear Dec complaining. "The globalist spawn is literally sitting at our kitchen table, eating my dad's pizza like her dad isn't the one who put him out of work . . . I know, right? And Dad and Kayleigh think *I'm* the problem. Why won't they get it?"

Did he just call Arielle "globalist spawn"? I've had enough of this. More than enough.

I throw the door open and storm in.

"What do you want?" he says, pulling off his headset.

I repeat his words back to him. "*They're* in my house? *Globalist spawn?*"

"Now you're eavesdropping on me?" Dec says, looking up at me defiantly, but his cheeks flush pink.

"Eavesdropping!" I exclaim, disgusted. "I knocked, Dec. Because like an idiot, I thought maybe there was a way of saving our friendship."

The pink in his cheeks deepens to a dull red.

"Arielle's a person, not a monster, something that you'd know if you actually took the time to get to know her instead of making her into some evil cartoon character," I say. "And I'm still the same Jake you've been friends with for years." He looks away, like he doesn't want to be reminded of that. I stare him down until he's forced to look me in the eye, then ask the question that's been tying me in knots. "What happened to you, Declan?"

It's like I pushed an invisible button. Dec throws down his controller and stands up, facing me, his fists clenched.

"I'll tell you what happened to me!" he shouts. "You people! Making it impossible for guys like me to succeed!"

In all the years I've known Dec, I've never seen him in a rage like this before. He's glaring at me with narrowed eyes, his mouth twisted in a sneer.

I don't back down.

"*I* make it impossible for you to succeed?" I shout back, just as angry. "You're the one who thought it was a good idea to show off by climbing that rock face. Don't blame your own stupidity on me. Or the layoffs on Arielle."

"It's all part of your plan!" Dec exclaims.

"*My plan?* Come on, Dec, it's me. Jake," I say. "Are you going to look me in the eye and say that you really believe all those antisemitic conspiracy theories?"

He glances away for a moment, and I feel a spark of hope. Maybe I've been able to reach him.

But then he looks me in the eye, raises his hand in a Nazi salute, and says, "Jews will not replace us."

That's when I realize there's nothing left of our former friendship. There's no sliver of anything that I can grasp on to in hope that we can get it back.

"We're done," I say, turning on my heel and slamming the door behind me.

DECLAN

One Thursday in early December, Finn finds me right as school is letting out. He seems electrified, bristling with excitement.

"Did you see the message from Ronan?" he asks me.

"No. What did he say?"

"Just read it," he says. "I can't believe you haven't already."

"I had to turn off notifications for Clandestext after Dad saw one and freaked out," I tell him as I fumble with my phone. I haven't told Finn about what I saw in that dusty box. Ronan doesn't suffer doubters.

The message reads: Be Here. Tonight 17:30.

I feel a surge of excitement. "Do you know what this is about?"

"Of course not," Finn says. "Operational security. Everything's on a need-to-know basis, to protect against snitches."

I stare at him, surprised. "You think we've got snitches? In Ronan's crew?"

Finn shrugs. "Can never be too careful, right? And we've got a bunch of new recruits lately, so . . ."

I nod. I don't know what Ronan has planned, but I'm glad that we're finally taking things to the next level. Maybe it'll help wake people up.

Charlie sends us a Clandestext message saying he'll pick us both up at 16:50 and to wear black.

I'm lucky only Dad is home. He's been waiting to hear about another job he interviewed for, this one about an hour away. He didn't get the first one, which sent him into a total funk for a few weeks. I thought

I could convince him to join our fight then, but he got angry every time I brought it up.

"I'm heading out," I tell him.

"You going to Ronan's house again?"

I shrug. "If you already think you know, why are you asking me?"

"What's with wearing all black? You pretending to be a Nazi storm trooper now?"

"The Nazi storm troopers, the SA, wore brown shirts, not black," I say.

Dad rolls his eyes. "Didn't you learn anything from seeing those pictures?" he says. "Are you so convinced that you know everything at age fifteen that you're not willing to open your mind and learn something?"

"I could ask you the same question."

Dad mutters a curse and turns away. I take it as a victory.

Charlie's truck is in the driveway, with Finn already in the front seat. I slide into the back, and Charlie turns down the music. "You ready to rock and roll?"

"Oh yeah," Finn says.

"Totally," I say.

Charlie smiles, then turns up the music so loud that the bass feels like it's rattling the chambers of my heart.

The hatecore music normally gets me fired up. It's like a catalyst activating the fury that runs constantly beneath the surface of my skin, like that crazy reaction with dishwashing soap, hydrogen peroxide, and potassium iodide that Mrs. Mirviss showed us in chemistry.

But today the screaming lyrics slice across my nerve endings; everything feels too raw. I close my eyes, trying to get those pictures from the attic out of my head.

. . .

The atmosphere in the house is different than usual. Ronan, Charlie, and Luke are clustered around the kitchen table, talking in low, urgent voices. Betheney is leaning against the counter, listening. None of the newer recruits are here.

Finn tries to go into the kitchen, but Reid, who is standing guard by the doorway, shakes his head and points to the couch, telling us both to sit.

As Finn turns to join me, his face is contorted with hurt and anger.

I flop onto the worn sofa and pick at a hole in the fabric. Finn folds his long frame next to me and whispers, "No one died and made Reid in charge! Who is he to boss me around? He's treating me like a stupid kid. Ronan said I'm his junior lieutenant!"

"What do you think they're planning?" I whisper back.

"I don't know. But it feels like something big," he says.

Finn's leg starts to bounce up and down repeatedly, and because he's sitting so close to me, it feels like there's a jackhammer next to me, which only ups the nerve jangles.

We sit there for half an hour before the guys come out of the kitchen.

"So, what's the plan?" Finn asks, his leg pumping even faster. Ronan stares at it, as if he's trying to will it to stop with his eyes, but it keeps moving. Ronan finally squats down in front of Finn, putting a hand on the moving knee.

"Stay cool, brother," Ronan says. "The plan will be revealed shortly." He stands up and goes down the hall into his bedroom-slash-office. He comes out carrying a large dark duffel, which he places on the coffee table in front of us.

"Luke, the site plan, please?"

Luke walks over and holds up a large piece of paper so we can all see it. It's a plan of the Congregation Anshe Chesed property.

Jake's synagogue.

"My brothers, we've been building up slowly. We've let our enemies know that we're here, and that we're watching them, waiting for the right moment," Ronan says, starting to pace like he always does when he's going off. "Now it's time to strike with a mighty fist. To send a message that we're at war with those who seek to destroy the white race, and to inspire other groups to take action."

I should be more excited. This is what I've been waiting for. Action, not just words. A way of fighting back. But instead . . . I feel queasy.

"Tonight provides us with the perfect opportunity to do that," he continues. "To strike at those who seek to control us. The people who have been promoting policies that seek to diminish white men."

White men like my dad, who got laid off by Kramer the globalist but was horrified by that Clandestext meme calling the Holocaust fake news. There were no such things as death camps, they were just labor camps, but my great-grandfather was there when the US Army liberated Buchenwald, and he took pictures of bodies so emaciated you can see almost every bone, stacked up, waiting to be bulldozed into a burial pit.

My head feels like it's about to explode from these conflicting ideas. They can't all be true. Right?

"Ideally we would have struck earlier, during their 'High Holy Days,'" Ronan says, using air quotes. "Because that's when we'd get a bigger body count. But our reconnaissance told us that's when security is at its highest. The odds wouldn't be in our favor, no matter how well prepared we were." He pauses, and his lips curve into a smile that reminds me of the Grinch when he gets the idea to steal Christmas. "Tonight, there's only one security guard, and we've taken him into account. But there's some kind of party."

Body count? Does he mean the Hanukkah party?

Ronan stops pacing by the site plan that Luke's holding.

As he goes over the plan for the attack, I start to feel pain in my forehead, like my brain is being crushed between two hard surfaces. Like in the trash compactor scene in *Star Wars*. Which I watched with Jake. And Jake's going to be there tonight for that party.

I rub my hand over my head, trying to stop my thoughts and focus on what Ronan is saying.

"And we're well prepared," Ronan says. "Reid, Charlie, show them what we've got."

Reid brings over a rifle case and opens it. Inside are several AR15s.

I swallow a gasp and try to blank off any show of emotion from my face.

Then Ronan nods at Charlie, who opens a duffel bag. Inside are a bunch of devices that look like . . . pipe bombs.

We've been damaging property, and I'm down with that. But . . . killing people?

I think of those little kids all excited for doughnuts being ripped to pieces by bullets or blown to pieces by these bombs if they try to escape.

I think about Jake.

Images run through my head, of the two of us, tight as two friends can be, teammates, celebrating wins, commiserating after losses. I see that picture on my shelf of the two of us bursting with pride, our arms around each other's necks when the Stafford's Corner Cheetahs won the championship.

Keep it together, Declan.

If anyone realizes how freaked out I am, I'm screwed. Worse than screwed. Ronan would literally kill me.

We all head out to the driveway except for Ronan, who stands in the doorway watching us. He raises his arm in a Nazi salute, and we return it before getting into Charlie's truck.

"Ronan isn't coming?" I ask.

"Come on, use your head, kid. You don't send your general out to the front line," Luke says.

I've watched enough war movies to know that's true. But there's a part of me that can't help thinking that we're being sent out as sacrificial lambs for the cause, while Ronan is safe at home with Betheney.

Finn doesn't seem to share any of my doubts. Ronan is the dad he never had. Finn would do anything for the guy's approval.

What I realize, in this moment, is that I won't.

Because Ronan wants us to commit cold-blooded murder.

Because this is Jake.

I inch my phone out of my pocket.

Do soldiers ever have doubts about the war they're being asked to fight? If I were in the army, would doing what I'm about to do make me a traitor or a hero?

As Blitzkrieg shouts about the superiority of white people and the need to cleanse the country of our foes, Finn screams along.

I thumb out a quick text to Kayleigh.

Call 911 NOW. Anshe Chesed. 4 ppl AR15s and pipe bombs. Get there FAST.

Then I turn off my phone because I can't risk her texting me back.

      •   •   •

As we get close to the synagogue, Charlie flips off the music.

"Y'all ready?" he asks.

"Oh yeah!" Finn says.

"Ready as I'll ever be," I mumble.

Luke switches off his headlights as he pulls into the synagogue's exit driveway. He backs into a spot near the street "to make a hasty exit."

He's obviously optimistic that Ronan's plan is going to work. They all are.

They don't know what I just did—and if they find out, I'm dead.

JAKE

"I'm Judah Mac-B, MC Hammer of the Jews, gonna lay some Hanukkah truths on you—wait, or is it Chanukah with a C?" I say to my youth group crew while we wait in the passage behind the bimah for the play to begin. "If people without dyslexia can't figure out how to spell it, how am I supposed to know?"

"In other news, you can't rap," Naya says.

She has a point. Still, I strike what I hope is a noble warrior pose with my fake spear made from a broom handle and the shield we made from an old silver garbage can lid onto which we painted a big blue Magen David.

"Are you impressed?" I ask, glancing around to assess the general level of impressedness.

"I gotta say, the garbage can lid shield is—" Jordan does a chef's kiss.

"Hey, there weren't a lot of shield stores in the Judean hills!" I point out.

"I'm soooooo impressed," Arielle says, batting her eyelashes exaggeratedly and hanging off my shoulder with one leg kicked up behind her. Then she reverts to normal. "Now can you finish your sick beats so these kids can get their doughnuts?"

"Sick, but not in a good way," Jordan says.

"Don't insult me, or I'll sing the shark song," I warn him.

"No!" Jordan groans. "It took me a week to get it out of my head last time!"

Rabbi Jonas asks us if we're ready, then goes out onto the bimah to start the program.

"Welcome, and happy Hanukkah!" she says.

"Happy Hanukkah!" the kids shout.

Then we all come out, to lead everyone in a round of "Hinei Mah Tov," a song I love because (a) it has very few words to remember, and (b) the lyrics mean "Behold, how good and how pleasant it is for brethren to dwell together in unity," the first line of Psalm 133. It would be cool if people could really do that.

"We're here to celebrate Hanukkah, a holiday dedicated to light," Rabbi Jonas says. "*Hanukkah* means 'dedication' or 'rededication,' because we're celebrating the reconsecration of the Second Temple in Jerusalem after it had been defiled by the Greek-Syrian king Antiochus the Fourth." Glancing out the window of the sanctuary at the darkened sky, she continues. "In a moment we're going to celebrate by lighting the hanukkiah, but first I want us all to think about ways we can share light in the world, even when the eight days of Hanukkah are over." She smiles out over the sanctuary. It's not nearly as full as it was on the High Holy Days, but there's a decent crowd, mostly parents who are here with the younger Hebrew school kids.

"Can anyone share a way they are going to help spread light?" Rabbi Jonas asks.

Lots of hands go up, and a few little kids stand with their arms raised, jumping up and down so that Rabbi Jonas will pick them. She does, one by one, and they call out their ideas.

"Share toys with my friends!"

"Be kind!"

"Give compliments to people!"

"Put some of my allowance in the tzedakah box!"

"Stand up for anyone who is being bullied!"

"Wow, these kids are much better people than I am," I murmur to Arielle as Rabbi Jonas continues taking answers.

Arielle covers her mouth with her hand, suppressing her giggles.

Rabbi Jonas take the matches and lights the shamash, the "helper candle" we use to light the other candles, and she kindles the first candle of the eight. Each night, we'll add another candle, until on the last night of Hanukkah, all of them are lit.

Then she recites the blessings over the lights.

בָּרוּךְ אַתָּה ה' אֱלֹקֵינוּ מֶלֶךְ הָעוֹלָם אֲשֶׁר קִדְּשָׁנוּ בְּמִצְוֹתָיו
וְצִוָּנוּ לְהַדְלִיק נֵר שֶׁל חֲנֻכָּה.

"Blessed are You, Eternal One, Sovereign of the universe, who hallows us with mitzvot, commanding us to kindle the Hanukkah lights."

בָּרוּךְ אַתָּה ה' אֱלֹקֵינוּ מֶלֶךְ הָעוֹלָם שֶׁעָשָׂה נִסִּים לַאֲבוֹתֵינוּ
בַּיָּמִים הָהֵם בַּזְּמַן הַזֶּה.

"Blessed are You, Eternal One, Sovereign of the universe, who performed wondrous deeds for our ancestors in days of old at this season."

I can't help hoping God does some wondrous deeds to stop all bad stuff that's going on lately.

Finally, Rabbi Jonas recites the Shehecheyanu, first in Hebrew, then in English.

בָּרוּךְ אַתָּה ה' אֱלֹקֵינוּ מֶלֶךְ הָעוֹלָם שֶׁהֶחֱיָנוּ וְקִיְּמָנוּ וְהִגִּיעָנוּ
לַזְּמַן הַזֶּה.

"Blessed are You, Eternal One, Sovereign of the universe, who has granted us life, sustained us, and enabled us to reach this occasion."

I've heard that prayer so many times before in my life, but I say "Amen" with extra feeling this year. With antisemites seeming to grow louder by the day, I finally get why it's important to say a prayer expressing gratitude for just being able to be here, celebrating.

"And now I'm going to hand it over to the youth group for tonight's entertainment," Rabbi Jonas says. She takes a place in the first row, and Arielle goes to the mic.

She's wearing a top she found online by googling "ugly Hanukkah sweaters." She kept texting me pictures of the over-the-top stuff she found, one more ugly-yet-hilarious than the next. She settled on one that has light-up LED candles and says *Hanukkah Is Lit*.

In my expert, totally unbiased opinion, Arielle looks way cute, even in that ridiculous ugly sweater.

"We're going to be eating latkes and doughnuts in a little while, and we want to do a poll beforehand. We're doing research on a very important cultural issue." She glances around the room, her expression serious. "Are you willing to help us with our research?"

"Yes!" the kids shout. They'll agree to anything at this point if it gets them closer to eating.

"Are you ready?" Arielle asks.

"YEEEEESSS!" they shout even louder.

"Great!" Arielle exclaims. "So here we go. We're hoping to settle a long-standing debate in the Jewish community about the correct topping for latkes. So we want to know: Are you Team Applesauce, Team Sour Cream, or Team Both?" Arielle asks.

Kids start shouting out, but Arielle holds up her hand asking them to stop. "Naya and Danielle are going to act as our Applause-O-Meter judges, so be sure to make some noise when I say your favorite latke topping, okay?"

The kids are practically bouncing off their seats in excitement.

"Okay, here we go," Arielle says. "Let's hear from Team Sour Cream!"

There's a decent amount of noise, but Team Sour Cream is definitely out-shouted by Team Applesauce. Team Both, the one I'm on as a true connoisseur of latke eating, comes in a distant third.

"Heathens," I mutter to Jordan, who is wearing a crown and a cape because he's playing King Antiochus IV. "The only correct answer is both."

"Don't look at me, I'm Team Sour Cream," Jordan says.

Team Applesauce cheers, and Arielle starts her narration. Our first song is about the villain of the story, Antiochus IV. He's this all-around bad dude who stole the throne of Syria from his nephew Demetrius. The Seleucid Greek Empire also controlled Jerusalem, and Antiochus banned observant Jews from practicing their faith. But it gets worse . . .

"I'm gonna turn your temple into Zeus's shrine and use it to sacrifice lots of swine," Jordan sings, making Antiochus all campy and evil, like how Jonathan Groff played George III in *Hamilton*.

Out of the corner of my eye, I see Rabbi Jonas jump up, looking kind of freaked out. She runs from the sanctuary.

My stomach drops.

The kids don't seem to notice anything is wrong, but the parents do. I try to keep going, but now my brain is heading to all the dark places on this festival of light.

"That Antiochus is a pain in the tuchus," sings Joel, inspiring giggles from the kids, who start whispering, "He said *tuchus*!"

Rabbi Jonas comes jogging back into the sanctuary. The expression on her face tells me something is going down, and it's not good. She rushes up the three steps to the bimah and holds out her hand for the mic.

"Sorry to interrupt the show, but we've had notification of a potential security threat," Rabbi Jonas says the minute the mic is in her hand. The tension in her voice gives me chills. There's a collective gasp. "The police are on their way. Stay calm and move quickly and quietly through the door behind the bimah to the Hebrew school classrooms. Once inside, we will secure the special locks. Do not open these unless a police officer has identified themself and told you it's all clear."

I'm playing a warrior, but I don't feel like one. My heart is thumping in my chest. I look over at Arielle, and her face is pale with shock. Some of the younger kids start crying.

Seeing the little ones so freaked out gives me an idea. Raising my broom handle spear and my garbage can lid shield above my head, I say, "Yo, kids! It's J-Dog Mac, Hammer of the Jews! Follow me 'cause I'm gonna take care of you!"

Under the circumstances, I hope they'll forgive my awful rhymes.

The rabbi starts ushering kids to follow me, and I lead the way through the door behind the bimah. When we get to the first classroom, I hold the door open for as many people as we can fit, activate the special safety locks, the way that Troy showed us, and pull down the shade over the reinforced glass.

"Everyone, make sure you have your cell phones on silent," Jordan reminds people, who are taking seats on the floor behind desks.

I text my parents and Ben: Security threat at Anshe Chesed, don't know what. I love you.

We turn off the lights and I sit next to Arielle, our hips and shoulders touching.

"I can't believe this is happening," Arielle whispers. "I should have expected it with everything going on, but . . ."

I feel tremors going through her body, so I put my arm around her and squeeze her tight. She puts her head on my shoulder.

My mouth is dry with fear, making it hard to swallow.

This is real.

This is not a drill.

DECLAN

"Okay. You two understand your part in the plan?" Charlie asks in a low voice, turning to look at Finn and me.

"Roger that," Finn says.

I just nod because I'm afraid of what my voice will sound like when I speak.

"Phones on vibrate, everyone," Reid says.

I pretend to check mine, leaving it off.

We pull up our gaiters. The fabric mask sticks to my face, and I'm afraid I'm going to suffocate. *Don't lose it, Declan. Deep breaths.*

But inhaling makes it worse.

"You okay?" Finn whispers.

I nod because it's too hard to speak.

Charlie overhears Finn and turns to me. "You're not going beta on us, are you?"

"No way," I say, hoping to sound like a true alpha male, but my voice comes out in an embarrassing squeak.

"Good. Because this is war, brother," Charlie says.

I'm freaking out about the people inside that building. I hope Kayleigh called 911, and that the police come in time. If they don't . . . I can't think about that.

Charlie looks around at our group and stands to attention, like he's some kind of drill sergeant. Clicking the heels of his steel-toed boots together, he lifts his right arm. "Sieg Heil!"

We copy him, keeping our arms straight and even, like we're at our own mini–Nuremberg Rally, instead of hiding in the shadows of Congregation Anshe Chesed.

Luke turns on each of the superbright LED flashlights he has duct-taped to the bill of his black trucker hat. Charlie has the same setup. They both have pistols in holsters on their belts, and they've got on tactical vests with fully loaded magazines and AR15s over their shoulders.

"You ready?" Luke asks Finn and me. He picks up the bag with the pipe bombs.

"Yeah!" Finn says.

He and I start creeping toward the front parking lot of the synagogue, sticking to the shadows. My heart pounds so hard I can hear blood rushing in my ears, and cold sweat on the back of my neck makes me shiver, despite the thick hoodie I'm wearing.

The security guard is standing outside the front doors of the synagogue. I've walked through those doors. I've sat in that sanctuary, watching Jake read from the Torah for his bar mitzvah. Others, too. There weren't many Jewish kids in our middle school, but I got invited to all the bar and bat mitzvahs that year.

That was before.

Staying low, Finn and I sneak behind some parked cars.

"Ready to start the distraction tactics?" Finn asks me.

I nod.

Finn starts to stand up but then ducks down. "Did you hear that? It sounds like a car just turned in."

I look around nervously. "Should we bounce?"

"We can't. Ronan is counting on us," he says.

Finn doesn't have the slightest doubt that what we're doing here is right.

He stands up to start the distraction plan. I start to rise, but suddenly Finn is bathed in bright white light, and red-and-blue lights start a blinding, rotating show.

"FREEZE! POLICE! GET YOUR HANDS IN THE AIR!"

Finn swears and I panic, wondering if I can crawl away and escape before they walk over to handcuff Finn.

No. It's too risky.

My heart pounds so hard in my chest I can hear blood rushing in my ears.

Rising slowly, I make sure my empty hands are visible before the rest of me.

The light is so bright that I can only see the outlines of the officers, but I know that there are guns pointed on us.

Then I remember that Charlie and Luke are armed. I hear Ronan's voice ranting about how "acceleration is the last resort of the white man." He might be sitting at home, but I can imagine him recounting to his next recruit, another angry guy like me, how Stafford's Corner became the new Lexington, Massachusetts.

"PLACE ONE KNEE ON THE GROUND! KEEP YOUR HANDS VISIBLE AT ALL TIMES!"

My eyes are squinting in the blinding light, and I'm trembling as I follow the instructions to kneel. The officer cuffs my left wrist, then grabs my right and twists it behind my back, forcing my bad shoulder to a place it doesn't want to go, ignoring my shout of pain.

"General" Ronan would want us to go down fighting, so we're heroes to inspire others in the movement. He's willing to sacrifice us.

But I don't want to die.

I don't want Jake to die, either.

My head is turned toward Finn, and our eyes meet. He looks as terrified as I feel.

I hear shouting and swearing from the other side of the building, but thankfully no gunshots.

"You're under arrest," the officer says. He reads me my rights, just like they do on TV.

Then he grabs my arm so tightly it's almost painful, and leads me toward a waiting black-and-white police car.

He puts me into the back seat and slams the door.

I am so screwed.

JAKE

The blinds in the classroom are closed, but even so, we can see the strobe-like blue-and-red lights shining through them. Arielle and I are holding each other close, and there's comfort in feeling her warmth by my side.

What is happening out there?

My heart is beating fast and hard, and my chest is clamped in a vise, making it hard to breathe. Is this what it feels like to have a heart attack?

Not knowing just makes it all scarier. Who is out there? Who hates us so much they want to attack us?

There's fury mixed with my fear. I force myself to take some deep breaths, to loosen the grip on my chest.

"You okay?" Arielle whispers.

"Yeah. You?"

She gives me this crazy fake smile and whispers, "Great! Never been better."

I snort loudly, unable to contain myself, and get some dirty looks and shushes.

It feels like we've been in here for half my life, but when I check the time on my phone, it's only been an hour. Texts are coming in from my family.

> Mom: I love you, Jake.
> Mom: Call us, please! As soon as you can.
>
> Dad: I'm so proud to be your father, Jake. I hope you know that. Love you.

Ben: Jake, please be okay.

Mom: I've been notified the police are there. Please let us know you're okay.

Me: Locked down in a classroom. Okay so far. I love you.

The little kids are getting restless, and a few are crying and being comforted by their parents, who are trying to quiet them without freaking them out more.

Then it strikes me, a realization like a knife in my heart.

"Declan . . . he knew about the Hanukkah party," I whisper. "We talked about it when we were at their house after the soccer game."

Arielle's eyes widen. "You think . . ."

It's like she knows saying the words aloud will split me in two.

He wouldn't go this far—or would he?

There was a time when I would have been able to answer that question. Now I can't.

Eventually, a police officer knocks and shows us her badge through the window in the door, telling us that it's all clear.

One of the parents opens the lock, and we file out. The officer leads us through the lobby and into the parking lot. Then someone tells us they've set up a zone outside "the crime scene perimeter" in the next-door parking lot for us to meet relatives, but we're not allowed to leave the scene until we've given contact details so that we can be interviewed.

As we're walking over there, I dial Mom. She picks up before I even hear it ring on my end.

"JAKE!" she exclaims. I hear a wobble in her voice. "Are you okay? Is everyone okay?"

"Pretty freaked out, but . . . we're all okay, as far as I know," I tell her. "It felt like we were there for a long time, but the police got here fast."

"Dad and I are on our way," she says. "I love you, Jake."

I tell her where we are, then add, "Love you, too, Mom."

It feels like I should tell everyone I care about that I love them, just in case. After what happened tonight, the future seems as fragile as it does infinite.

JAKE

After the police officers have taken our names, addresses, and phone numbers so they can follow up for interviews, Arielle and I stand holding each other in the parking lot adjacent to the synagogue waiting for our parents to come pick us up. I feel her body trembling and realize I'm shaking, too.

We sit down on the curb.

"I'm so tired of this," Arielle says. "Tired of being scared. Tired of being hated."

I'm tired, too. Exhausted. Like I just want to curl up under the covers and go to sleep and hopefully wake up to find out this was all a bad dream.

"Do you think we'll ever be able to light candles on the first night of Hanukkah without this sick fear?" Arielle asks, a hitch in her voice.

"I don't know. My brain . . . isn't working so well right now," I reply.

"Mine isn't, either. I think it's shock. Like this." She holds up her hand, which is shaking like crazy, then touches my leg, which seems to have taken on a life of its own.

"Do you want me to take you over to the EMTs?" I ask her. There are two ambulances in the lot, and EMTs are going around checking on people.

"No. I'm okay," she says. "Well, not okay, but . . ."

I put my arm around her.

"I love Hanukkah too much to let them ruin it for me," I say. "Seeing all the candles lit up gives me hope."

"Even though we're literally celebrating a holiday where they wanted us to give up being Jewish and worship Zeus and all the rest of the Greek gods?" Arielle says dryly. "To force us to be something we're not or be killed. You know, like Purim, Pesach . . ." Her shoulders slump. "It's all history repeating. Over and over and over again. Why won't it just stop already?"

"I don't know. I guess because we make a convenient scapegoat. Because people keep believing in conspiracy theories." My head drops into my hands. Arielle puts her hand on my back and rubs it slowly, and for a moment I allow myself to give in to the comforting sensation. But then I lift my head and let out a bitter chuckle. "Am I an idiot for wanting to believe that things can get better, despite all that?"

"Maybe," Arielle says. "But I love that about you."

There are so many things I love about her, but my brain still feels like it's short-circuiting. I'll tell her later, when I'm thinking more clearly. But I am going to tell her, because I'm so grateful there's going to be a later. Tonight could have ended very differently. It could have ended . . . everything.

The thought makes me shake again.

Just then, they allow our parents into the parking lot. I start running toward Mom and Dad. The two of them squeeze me so tightly in relief that I can barely breathe.

Dad whispers, "Love you, Jake."

"Thank god you're okay!" Mom says.

We all have tears on our faces.

"Let's go home," Mom says, holding my arm like she's never going to let me out of her sight ever again.

We're all quiet during the drive home. Mom keeps looking at me in the rearview mirror, and Dad reaches his hand back to give mine a squeeze. It's like they both want to make sure I'm still here.

When we get home, I tell them that I want to take a shower. I need to be alone for a little while, because their obvious fear that they could have lost me tonight just amps up my own anxiety.

Turning up the water as hot as I can stand it, I let it wash over me. I hear the faint buzz of my phone against the sink but focus on the flow of water, white noise to shut out the world.

It's not till I'm dressed in sweats and heading downstairs that I see the text Kayleigh sent to Arielle and me.

> Declan was arrested. I am soooooooooo sorry. ☹

I'm choked by a sense of betrayal so strong I have to sit down on the top step. Even though I had my suspicions about his involvement, having it confirmed makes me question my judgment about people. I never thought he would go this far. That he'd try to kill me. Try to kill all of us.

I should probably text Kayleigh back to tell her it's not her job to apologize for Dec. But I don't have it in me right now.

I find my parents huddled together on the sofa, talking in low voices. Holding out my phone, I show them the text and see a mix of emotions cross their faces.

"How am I ever supposed to trust people again?" I ask them. "How many of my other friends and teammates are antisemitic under the surface?"

My parents exchange a glance, like, *Okay, you take this one.*

Mom moves away from Dad and pats the sofa in between them. I sit down and they both put their arms around me. I feel sheltered by them, but deep down I know this feeling is an illusion. How am I ever supposed to feel safe in a world where my best friend can be convinced to try to kill me?

"It's easy to feel paranoid at a time like this, Jake," Mom says. "But it's important to remember that there are good people in the world, too. The people who attacked the synagogue tonight are extremists. Their beliefs are on the fringe."

"Are they, though?" I ask.

"They used to be," Dad mutters.

Mom gives him a look. "Dan, you're not helping."

"It's all right, Mom," I say. "You don't have to pretend things are going to be okay. I wasn't a little kid before tonight, and I'm definitely not after what happened." I shudder involuntarily.

Mom strokes my curls back from my face. "I know, Jake. I just don't want you to lose hope."

"But Mom's right," my dad says. "Even though it's hard with so many bad things happening, we can't let it destroy our desire for tikkun olam. We still have to keep trying to repair our broken world. To paraphrase *Ethics of Our Fathers*, it is not our duty to finish the work, but we can't blow it off, either."

"While taking every protective measure we possibly can," Mom adds. "So that we're not overcome by fear and anxiety."

"Yeah, I'm having problems with that not-being-overcome-by-fear-and-anxiety part right now," I say. "Can we just watch TV? I promise I won't give up on tikkun olam, but I need to blow off the work tonight."

Dad gives me a hug. "Of course," he says. "Just don't lose hope, okay?"

I nod, and Dad switches on the TV.

Despite watching a funny comedy special, I still lie awake reliving what happened. I think about how today could have been the last day of my life. I'm fifteen. There's so much more I want to do.

I'm angry at the people who want to deny me that chance to live my life—to live, period—just because I happen to be Jewish.

Most of all, I'm angry at Declan. With him, it's personal.

I hear more details about what happened from Mom before I leave for school the next morning. She's been in touch with the police, the FBI, Rabbi Jonas, and the synagogue board. Last night they sent out an email to all the congregants alerting them to what they knew so far, and telling them that the board would be reviewing safety measures—again.

"The detective said they were going for body count," Mom says, her face grim and pale opposite me at the kitchen table. "If they'd succeeded . . ." She shudders.

Going for body count. Our bodies. The bodies of little kids. Of parents. Of me.

And Declan was one of them.

"Despite all the money we've already spent on security, we're probably going to apply for federal aid to beef it up even more," Mom says with a heavy sigh. "And fundraise more from the congregation. We've got an emergency board meeting tonight."

It's so unfair that we have to spend all this money just to pray safely. They should make Declan and his friends pay for it as part of their punishment.

"Are you okay with going to school?" Mom asks. "I'm happy to call you in for a mental health day if you want."

"No. I want to go. If I stay here, I'm just going to think about last night on a loop. School will be a welcome distraction."

"You might find you have a hard time focusing," Mom warns me. "That's okay. And if you find it's all too much, just call me."

"I hope Declan isn't there," I say. "I'm not sure what I'll do if and when I see him. I'd like to punch him in the face right about now."

"He won't be there. He's still in police custody," Mom says.

I exhale in relief.

"But even if he was, violence isn't the answer," she continues.

"It is sometimes, though, right?" I argue. "Like, wasn't it the right thing to fight the Nazis in World War Two?"

"It was," Dad agrees. "But it should be the last resort, not the first one. Let the legal system deal with Declan and his extremist friends."

I know my parents are right, but I can't help feeling like punching Declan would be a lot more immediate and satisfying than waiting for the legal system to work.

DECLAN

Because Finn and I are fifteen, they don't keep us at the local police station for long. They put us in a van and drive us to a juvenile facility an hour and a half away.

"What's going to happen to us?" I whisper to Finn. "My parents can't afford bail."

"You think my mom can?" Finn mutters. He lets out a bitter chuckle. "Even if she could, her boyfriend would probably tell her not to pay it, because he likes it better when I'm not around."

"I don't know if I can take being in prison," I say, hitting my head on the back of the seat in front of me in despair.

"Ronan will have a plan," Finn whispers with a confidence I don't feel. "They're going to try to scare you into ratting out the others. Don't buy it." He leans over and reminds me that "snitches get stitches."

Ronan was supposed to have a plan for tonight. Would it have worked if I hadn't texted Kayleigh? Did she even call 911? Or did the police already know somehow? Maybe they were watching Ronan, and that's why he didn't come tonight?

We don't talk for the rest of the ride, each of us sunk into our own thoughts. I wish I had the same faith in Ronan that Finn does. But I don't.

When we get to the county juvenile detention center, we're strip-searched, which is beyond humiliating, and then made to shower. I'm not allowed to take anything into the shower with me, not even soap; the guard passes me stuff through a two-way door. Even though the hot water feels good against my clammy skin, I take the quickest shower ever, feeling self-conscious because there's probably a camera somewhere.

After I dress in my uniform of T-shirt, sweatpants, and a sweatshirt, they hand me bedding and lead me to a cell.

The sound of those doors clanking shut, even more than being arrested, is when I realize what serious trouble I'm in.

I throw the sheet over the mattress and curl up under the blanket in the fetal position, wondering how I got here. Being locked in this cell without any distractions means I'm also stuck with the whirlwind inside my head. Wondering if my parents are going to come see me or leave me here to rot. The police said they were going to contact them when they brought me here. Where are they? I have no idea what time it is because they took my phone and there aren't any windows to see if it's day or night.

Despite the fear about my future, exhaustion takes over and I drift off to sleep on the hard bench.

I wake when the cell door slides open, and there's a guard standing there.

"Your lawyer's here," he says. "Get up and come with me."

Grabbing my arm, he handcuffs my hands in front of me, then leads me to another room with a metal table and two chairs. He cuffs me to the table, leaving me in there to stew. Why haven't my parents come yet? Have they given up on me?

The door finally opens and a gray-haired white lady in a suit holding a stuffed briefcase comes in.

"I'm Tricia Lewis, your court-appointed attorney," she says, plopping her briefcase on the table wearily and pulling out a yellow pad and a pen. "You've been charged with some very serious crimes."

I eye her warily. "Are my parents coming? Am I going to jail?"

"I've asked them to alert me if your parents arrive," she says. "As to your question about jail—are you facing time in juvenile detention? Yes, you most certainly are."

Crap.

"That's why I need you to be totally honest with me and tell me everything you know. Are we clear?"

I nod to acknowledge her but hear Ronan's voice telling me to deny everything. If I spill to Tricia, it's going to be worse for my friends. For Finn. For Charlie. For Luke. For Reid. For Ronan and Betheney. For the people who understand me and support me. I just met this woman. How do I know she's really on my side?

"Okay, let's start from the beginning. When and how did you get involved with the North Country Militia?"

"North Country Militia? I've never even heard of it," I say. It's the truth. Sure, Ronan used words like *recruit* and called us soldiers and warriors and stuff, but militia?

Her brows are raised with obvious skepticism. "The NCM is a known neo-Nazi group operating in our area, with links to violent extremist groups across the country. The FBI has been interested in Ronan Bachmann for a while now."

I want to cross my arms over my chest, but I'm chained to the table, so instead my hands clench into fists. "I don't know anything about this militia business," I say. "I just hung out at Ronan's because the people there understood me. Because it was better than hanging out at home."

That seems to get her attention. "You had issues at home?"

I figure telling her about all the crap with my family is safe enough. So I explain about the accident, and how Dad losing his job meant this whole health insurance struggle and how my parents couldn't afford to pay for

PT in the meantime on top of all the other medical bills. How mad that made me because no PT meant killing my hope of playing baseball again.

"Was there any physical abuse?" she asks.

"What? No! Nothing like that," I say. "They just gave up on me. Didn't believe that I could get back to playing baseball. They were always on my case, and made me feel like crap because of the medical bills."

"How did you first meet Ronan?"

There's no way to tell her that without throwing Charlie and Finn under the bus. I can't rat out my friends. I know they'll have my back, so I need to have theirs. I'm a minor. I'm not going to go to prison. Except this place is bad enough. Crap, I don't know what to do.

Tricia becomes frustrated with my silence.

"You may think you're doing yourself a favor by keeping quiet," she says, "but you're not. Don't fool yourself into thinking that your 'friends' are going to have your back. They're not. They're going to be out for themselves. Nothing would make them happier than to have you be their fall guy."

She's lying. They wouldn't do that to me. She's just trying to make her own job easier by getting me to snitch.

But Tricia's not done. "Declan, I want you to understand how serious things are for you. There's a strong possibility that the Feds will threaten to try you as an adult given the seriousness of the charges."

My stomach turns over. "The Feds? What do you mean?"

She pins me with her gaze. "I mean that even though you were arrested by the local police, you were engaging in a hate crime, which is a federal offense. The FBI is very interested in NCM. There are going to be serious charges brought in this case." Putting her pen down, she adds, "You want the cold, hard truth, Declan?"

I nod, slowly, even though I'm suddenly afraid to hear it.

"The more information you can share with the Feds, the better chance you have of avoiding doing hard time," Tricia says. "Don't throw your life away out of loyalty for these people, Declan. They *want* you to take the fall."

Hard time.

There's a demolition derby going on inside my head; so many conflicting thoughts crashing into one another.

Stay quiet. Don't betray your friends.

Save yourself.

Ronan will have a plan.

Ronan said the Holocaust was exaggerated. That they were just work camps, not death camps. If he lied about that, what else could he have lied about?

"Help me to help you, Declan," Tricia says.

As mad as I am at my parents, I wish they were here now so I could ask them what to do. There are no good choices. If I snitch, I'll have a target on my back. If I don't, I could be charged as an adult and do hard time.

"Okay," I mumble.

"Okay what?" Tricia asks.

"I'll tell you what I know."

She nods and picks up her pen. "You're making the right decision, Declan."

I wish I could be sure about that. But I tell her about how FenrirLupus gave me the link to *Imperialist Empires*, and how when Finn and Charlie learned that I was playing it, they took me to meet Ronan. She asks me lots of questions about Ronan and what we did at his house, and anything I might have noticed while hanging out there. I tell her about the stickering and about Finn's QR codes. I even admit that I spray-painted the swastikas at Mocha Jenn's, smashed the Kramers' window, and vandalized the Pinnacle plant.

I feel guilty as I answer her questions. Guilty that I'm betraying my friends, and the cause. But still . . . it would have felt a lot worse if people had died.

Tricia is scribbling furiously on her notepad the whole time. "Tell me what happened leading up to your arrest at the synagogue, in as much detail as you can," she says. "When did you first learn about the plan to attack?"

"Ronan had been talking about doing something big to make people pay attention. You know, so they'd wake up to the threat to the white race and all," I tell her. "But I had no idea what he was planning. Finn told me they were keeping it on the down low for operational security. The first I heard about it was when Finn told me there was a Clandestext message in school this morning. Or maybe it was yesterday morning by now."

She stops me several times, like when I mention Clandestext. She's never heard of it before, so I explain that it's an encrypted messaging app.

"It wasn't till we got to his house that I found out the actual plan. That we were going to attack the synagogue. With guns . . . and pipe bombs."

"Would you be able to access this Clandestext group chat so that investigators could view any and all conversations?" Tricia asks.

"Yeah, if I have my phone," I say. "The police took it."

She makes a note. "So you found out that they were planning to attack the synagogue. Then what happened?"

"I guess . . . I mean, I wanted to fight back and all, but all the other stuff I did was just, you know, hurting property. Like spray-painting and breaking a few windows. This seemed . . . different. Like it was actually going to hurt people. Kill them, even."

Tricia puts her pen down. "You don't think it hurts anyone when you spray-paint a symbol associated with the genocide of six million Jews on a Jewish business owner's coffee shop?" She looks at me over her glasses. "I hate to break it to you, Declan, but it does. And it's considered a hate crime."

Crap. I just admitted to more hate crimes?

"But it's not like *killing people*," I say. "And I knew . . . I knew Jake, my best friend"—I swallow—"I mean, my former best friend . . . was going to be there."

"What happened after you found out the plan?" Tricia asks.

"I sent a text to my sister to call 911 and tell them there was going to be an armed attack at the synagogue as soon as I could without being caught," I tell her, looking down at my cuffed hands. "I had to be careful, because I was afraid of what they would do to a snitch if they were planning something like this."

"We'll get your sister's phone records to see if we can prove that you texted her—and that she then called in the threat," Tricia says. "That might help—it's not going to get you off the hook, but it could go toward mitigating your sentence." She looks me in the eye. "The best thing you can offer is information on other members of the militia. Anything you can give that might help lead to their conviction could work in your favor."

"I told you pretty much everything I know," I say.

"You've been hanging out with these people for months now. There's got to be more you can tell me. The more you give the Feds, the better things will be for you."

"But isn't this going to make it dangerous for me? Maybe even for my family?"

She nods slowly. "Yes, it makes it dangerous. But like I said, they're prob-ably going to threaten to try you as an adult. If you're willing to provide information and testify, there's a chance you might get off with probation. In that event, they'll move you and your family away from here to make sure you're kept out of harm's way until you can testify at the trial."

"What about after the trial?" I ask. "Then do we come back here?"

"After the trial, they'd place you in a more permanent witness protec-tion program." She pauses. "Which means you wouldn't be able to contact people from your life here. Not friends. Not family."

Maybe a completely new identity is what I need since I've done such a great job of messing up being Declan Taylor.

But then I try to picture my family's reaction to having to leave Stafford's Corner, and it's almost as scary as thinking about what might happen if I testify.

I tell her everything I can think of, then ask, "What happens now that I've told you all this stuff?"

"You will appear before a judge later today," she says. "That's where we'll hear the charges, and you'll enter a plea."

"Then what?" I ask. "Do I get to go home?"

"Then I set up what's called a proffer," she explains. "We meet with prosecutors and the FBI and you'll tell them everything you know, and that you're willing to cooperate. I'm going to do that as soon as possi-ble. In a few days you'll have your detention hearing. The prosecution is probably going to ask that you be held due to the serious nature of your crimes."

"You mean . . . I have to stay here?"

She sighs and shakes her head, like I'm exhausting her with my idiocy.

"You were involved in a very serious hate crime, Declan. Domestic terrorism. What did you think would happen?"

I didn't think enough, I guess. And now I've screwed up my life even more than when I started climbing the rock face. I didn't think enough then, either.

"If the judge does set bail, you might be released with an ankle monitor," Tricia says, giving me a tiny ray of hope. "But there's no guarantee."

I put my head down on my arms on the table, overwhelmed by everything that's happened. I don't know what's scaring me most—the thought of being locked up, or having to face my parents.

Right now, it's a toss-up.

DECLAN

After Tricia leaves, I'm taken back to my cell, where I've got nothing to do but think and hope that when she tells the Feds that I'm willing to tell them everything I know, I'll be able to avoid jail time.

I stare at the concrete-brick walls and pass the time trying to count all of them. One-two-three-four-five-six-what-is-my-family-going-to-say-seven-eight-nine-are-they-going-to-disown-me-ten-eleven-twelve-thirteen-what-if-the-entire-family-has-to-go-into-witness-protection-before-the-trial-fourteen-fifteen-sixteen-if-we-have-to-go-into-the-witness-protection-program-after-the-trial-we-can-never-talk-to-our-extended-family-or-our-friends-again.

I give up counting and cover my head with the blanket, trying to shut everything out. But a blanket isn't enough to shut out the disaster I've made of my life. Can anything?

A guard knocks on the door and speaks through the little window. "You've got visitors."

My heart starts beating faster, with a mixture of nerves and excitement. Maybe my family doesn't hate me after all.

Maybe they will after we talk.

The guard cuffs me, then unlocks the door and brings me to a visitation room.

My parents are there. Both of them. They look older. Tired. Like I've disappointed them in every way a kid can.

I want to hear them say everything is going to be okay. But I stand still, uncertain how they feel about me.

Mom steps forward and enfolds me in a hug. I relax into it for a second, but then I hear the voices that have been in my head for so long. *What are you, some kind of beta? Alpha males don't cry. Alpha males fight.*

I stiffen and pull away, stuffing down the guilt I feel from seeing her reddened, swollen eyes.

My dad is standing next to her, his posture stiff and unyielding, but he puts a hand on my shoulder. "Are you okay?"

"What do you think, Dad? I'm locked up in fricking juvie."

I expect him to go off on me for being disrespectful. I want him to.

"Declan——" Mom starts to be the peacemaker, to tell me not to speak to him that way, but Dad puts his hand on her arm and she stops.

He's not playing according to the usual script. Instead of blowing up at me, like I'd expect him to, he just stands there. The weight of his silence presses in on my chest. *Come on, Dad, bring it.*

He doesn't. Instead, he finally speaks to me in a calm, quiet voice. "Are we angry? Yes. Do we understand how you could do this? No, not in a million years."

"Yeah, yeah, I'm the screwup, as usual."

Dad takes a deep breath, and it's almost a relief to see that he's having to fight his anger. I've been mad for so long that it's my comfort zone.

"That's not what I said," Dad says, still calmly, but with an edge. "What I was about to say was that we love you, even if we're devastated by some of the choices you've made lately. Mom, Kayleigh, and me . . . we're here for you——"

"You mean like you were here for me after the accident? Like when you and Mom and Kayleigh were working all the time? Like when I really needed you, and you weren't there?"

"We weren't there, because we were working to pay off the hospital bills from your stupidity!"

Shattering his calm facade feels like a win.

"Yeah, yeah, I'm the stupid one, Kayleigh's the perfect one, whatever," I say. I have the upper hand now, and I've managed to flip the script, making myself the victim.

"You talk to him, Andi," Dad says, walking to the corner of the room like he needs to be as far away from me as possible.

Mom sits at the metal table and gestures for me to sit, too. She tries to take my hand, but I pull my cuffed wrists away.

"We spoke to the public defender," Mom says. "She told us that the only chance you have of avoiding prison is to tell the Feds everything you know about this group."

"Which you're gonna do, not just because it'll help you get off easier, but because it's the right thing," Dad says from the corner, his hands jammed in his pockets.

"Oh yeah? Did she tell you what happens if I do that?" I say. "Did she tell you that I wouldn't be the only one in danger? That you all would, too? Did she tell you that they're going to move us all somewhere for protection, so that I can testify against all the others? How does Kayleigh feel about having to up and move in the middle of the school year, without being able to tell any of her friends where she's going?"

Mom is frowning, and now Dad's pacing.

"How do you feel about having to leave all your clients, Mom?"

Dad's the one I expected to explode, so I'm shocked when Mom slams her hands on the table so loudly I jump.

"What do you think, Declan? I'm devastated," she shouts, her voice trembling with rage. "I've been working to build up my clients for years. Years, Declan! And now, thanks to you, I'm going to have to leave all my customers in the lurch without even telling them why, and start all over again who knows where!"

I want to be the victim, filled with righteous rage and purpose. But right now, I feel like the absolute worst.

"We haven't told Kayleigh yet," Dad says. "We don't want to upset her unless it's definitely happening."

"It wouldn't be happening if Kramer—"

"STOP!" Dad shouts.

This time Mom and I are the ones who jump.

"You think you're some kind of big man, Declan? A warrior for the white race, or some crap like that?" Dad bites the words out through clenched teeth. "A person with integrity owns up to their mistakes, takes responsibility for the things they've done wrong. And if you don't think attacking a synagogue with the goal of killing people is wrong, I just—"

He breaks off, shaking his head, and the righteous anger I'd managed to whip up starts draining from me. What's left is a mess of guilt and shame and . . . loneliness. Because if I testify, not only am I putting my family at risk, but I'll lose the friends I still have left. If my old friends didn't already hate me for laying down the truth they refused to see, they'll hate me for being a part of the attack on the synagogue.

Suddenly, it's all too much. Lack of sleep, the chaos in my head, uncertainty about the future, being locked up here, missing baseball . . . I lower my head to my arms on the table and start crying like a total beta.

Maybe that's what I am after all.

I feel Mom's hand stroking my hair, and Dad comes to stand next to me and rubs my back.

"We've got you, Dec," Dad says. "We'll figure this out . . . together."

Maybe it makes me even more of a beta that hearing that makes me cry harder, but right now, in this sterile visiting room with flickering fluorescent lights, I can't find it within myself to care.

JUNIOR
YEAR

AUGUST

DECLAN

To say that I've been in a dark place for a long time is an understatement. It's been almost two years since the attempted attack on the synagogue. As soon as I agreed to testify, the Feds moved us from Stafford's Corner to another tiny town in middle-of-nowhere Nevada.

One day we were home; the next day we'd vanished. We couldn't say goodbye to our friends—not that I had any friends left at that point—or even our family.

For the first six months or so, Kayleigh barely spoke to me. When she did, it was to list all the ways I ruined her life, how she missed her friends, and how the only way she could keep up with them was by basically stalking their social media accounts. But she can't like or comment or post anything herself. We're supposed to have vaporized.

She totally freaked when they showed pictures of the arrested militia members on one of the New York news sites.

I heard her scream, "Oh my god! It's Creepy Chuck." She came running into my room, brandishing her phone. "Your *buddy* Charlie is Creepy freaking Chuck, the guy who harassed us all the time at Burger Barn," she said, like I was an accomplice to his creeping.

"How was I supposed to know?" I said, immediately defensive.

"Oh, I don't know—maybe because he was feeding you misogynist crap or something?" she said, before stomping away in disgust.

Things are only a little better now. I miss how we used to be—even her insults. We've been tiptoeing around each other tentatively to avoid any explosions, growing further apart every day.

Until the trial is over, I have to wear an ankle monitor, which is both uncomfortable and a total pain. I have to charge it twice a day, and that means I can't go hiking in the national parks with my family. The first time we went, the charge on the thing got too low and went off, and people looked at me funny, like I was suddenly going to attack them or steal their wallets.

We ended up having to leave. Kayleigh was furious, and I felt even more like crap than usual.

It was easier for Kayleigh to make new friends at school than it was for me. She still had soccer. I didn't have baseball or the militia. I had nothing, and I didn't want to talk about what I'd done. From the comments I heard around the halls, in class, and in the cafeteria, there were definitely guys at school who would have considered me a hero for being part of the militia, but I knew enough to stay away from them. I didn't spend that long in juvenile detention, but it was enough for me.

As part of my staying-out-of-prison deal, I had to take an anger management class and I've been doing court-ordered therapy with this guy named Dave.

Dave put me in contact with this organization called Love Not Hate, which helps people get out of extremist groups. It's turned out to be pretty dope. They talk to me like I'm a human being, not some evil loser who deserves whatever he got. Now I have a "former" named Chris as my mentor. He's in his late thirties and used to belong to a neo-Nazi group. What made him leave was when his kid was born. He started thinking about how he'd grown up surrounded by anger and hate. He didn't want that for his kid—or for his kid to grow up and be shunned because his dad was in a hate group.

Chris showed me where he used to have neo-Nazi tattoos. Love Not Hate helped him get them covered so he could move past that life and so he wouldn't freak out the other parents at his son's preschool.

We talk at least once a week, sometimes more if things are really going to crap. Chris warned me in the beginning that loneliness is one of the biggest challenges when you're leaving extremism. "You've lost your identity—again," he told me.

It's true. I'm not a baseball player or a soldier for the white race. I don't know who I am anymore.

"See, when you're part of the group, you develop this intense bonding through intolerance of anyone who isn't like you," he said. "But that hatred also makes you isolated from the rest of the world. That's what you're experiencing now, on top of physical things like that."

He pointed to the bulge on my ankle, the one that no pants can 100 percent hide.

"Is this what I've got to look forward to for the rest of my life? Being some kind of . . . outcast?" I asked him.

"Declan, that kind of thinking isn't going to get you anywhere," Chris told me. "First you gotta deal with your crap, because let's face it, most of us joined an extremist group because we were lacking something in our lives. It wasn't the ideology that attracted us—it was being accepted into a community, feeling like we had a purpose greater than ourselves. It gave us our identity."

"I guess." I wasn't convinced. At that point, I was still sure it was the ideology.

"You got involved after you realized your baseball career was over, right?" Chris continued. "You had this whole story about who you were and what your future looked like. And then that got taken away, leaving you adrift. That's when recruiters are most successful. They look for kids like you so they can feed you a new, hateful narrative."

That's when a light bulb went on. Between Chris and my work with Dave, I've gradually started to realize that even though I thought I was a smart critical thinker who was "doing my own research," I was being manipulated. Like when I thought I was learning legit stuff about the Crusades, my "friends" were feeding me links to white nationalist propaganda videos that told a selective view of history—just like Mr. Morrison said.

I wish I could go back and talk to Mr. M. To thank him for trying to get me to talk about stuff and for offering to listen. To tell him that I finally realize how cool it was that he let us research and debate the ideas we had, instead of straight-out telling Finn, me, and the others we were wrong. I can't help wondering, if I'd taken advantage of his offer to listen, to talk to a school counselor, would my life be better than it is now?

Dave, my therapist, has been helping me with the dealing-with-my-crap part. He's way cooler than I thought he'd be. I was dreading going to "talk out my feelings." The first three times I went, I sat in the chair with my arms crossed, convinced it wouldn't do anything for me. Dave didn't say a word, either. Just waited for me to start talking.

But when Dave asks questions about the stuff I've said, it helps me think about things in a different way. Like when I finally started talking, and complained that my life was ruined, and I was never going to be given another chance.

"And it's not like I actually hurt anyone. As a matter of fact, I was the one who stopped people from getting hurt!" I told him.

He leaned back in his chair, tapping his pen against his chin.

"What I'm hearing you say is that you want credit for being a hero because no one was hurt in the synagogue attack," he said. "Is that accurate?"

I got the feeling it was kind of a trick question and wasn't sure what to say.

"Not a hero, exactly. But it's like no one even appreciates that it could have been a lot worse if not for me."

"That's true," he said. "But if you light the match to start a fire, are you a hero for calling the fire department to put it out?"

I never thought of it that way.

In another session he said, "I want us to focus on the idea of being hurt. Do you think things like putting antisemitic leaflets on cars or sharing memes making fun of the Holocaust online hurts people?"

"No." I saw the expression on his face. "I mean . . . yeah. But, I mean, it's not like getting *killed*."

"That's true. Let's imagine that there's a scale of hurt from one to ten and getting killed is a ten," Dave said. "Where would you put sharing memes that disparage people of another race or religion?"

"A one or a two?"

"What about sharing a conspiracy theory that Jews control the world?" he asked.

I tried to weigh that against a meme. "A three or four?"

I waited for him to tell me if I was right or wrong, but he didn't. Instead he suggested I think about how someone from the communities that I hurt would rate it. "Better yet, try to talk to some people from those communities."

"Who's going to want to talk to me?" I asked, with no small amount of self-pity. "The only people who talk to me are my family, you, and Chris, and you're getting paid to do it."

"All you can do is try," he said. "People from groups that you've hurt aren't obligated to speak to you, or even to listen if you want to say you're sorry." He tapped his pen against his notepad and looked me straight in the eye. "I haven't actually heard you say that you're sorry about any of this—except for how it's affected your life. I haven't heard you talk about wanting forgiveness from the communities the militia targeted. From your friend . . ." He checked his notes. "Jake, for example."

I realized he was right. I'd been wrapped up in guilt for how this all affected my family but hadn't given enough thought to the other people I hurt.

That's one of the reasons I have such mixed feelings about going back to New York for the trial next month. Like I want to get this whole nightmare over with, but I've realized testifying against Ronan and the others isn't enough. I need to do more, however much it scares me.

I'm sitting in Dave's office for my weekly appointment. My security guy is standing guard outside the door, because I'm not allowed to go anywhere without him, another reason I don't get out much.

"What do you think you'd need to be happy?" Dave asks me.

Wow. Ask me a deep question, why don't you?

"Baseball, but I can't have that anymore."

"Is that true?"

I thought you needed some medical training to be a shrink. I spent all these sessions with him talking about the accident and what it did to my arm, and how that was what sent me down the rabbit hole. I feel the familiar drug of anger start to bubble up in my chest.

"Yeah, it's true! You know I'll never be able to pitch like I did before the accident!"

But then I take a deep breath, in through my nose and out through my mouth like they taught me at anger management. One of the things I learned there was that you can get addicted to anger just like people get addicted to drugs and alcohol; that anger is tied up in all of that.

Dave waits while I take several deep breaths.

"Declan, I know playing baseball at the level you did is lost to you, and how painful that is."

It feels good to hear him acknowledge it again. But then he's right there with another question. "Tell me, do you think everyone who works at a professional baseball franchise can play competitively?"

"No," I admit reluctantly.

"So there's no reason you can't be involved with baseball even if you don't play," Dave reminds me. "Coaching. Learning the business aspects of the game. Scouting. We've talked about this before."

"I guess. It's hard to think about anything beyond the trial right now."

"Remember we talked about cognitive distortions—especially black-and-white, all-or-nothing thinking?" Dave asks me.

"Yeah." Cognitive distortions are his favorite subject. I seem to make a lot of them.

"You seem unwilling to open your mind to anything that might make you happy," Dave says. He gives me a moment to deny it like I usually would, but this time, for some reason, the words sink in. He continues in a gentle voice: "I'm wondering if guilt and shame have anything to do with that. If you feel like you need to be punished."

"Of course not! I'm already being punished! I have no life, and my twin sister hates me."

He does another one of the silence things, and I start to fidget in my chair, because I've learned that he usually gives me time to think before he drops an uncomfortable truth bomb.

"Have you apologized to her? Really given her—and the rest of your family—a heartfelt apology where you don't talk at all about the reasons why you were the victim? Where you own your actions and express contrition without making it about you?"

Ouch.

"You make me sound like a selfish jerk."

"That wasn't my intention," Dave says. He sounds genuinely apologetic. "I'm pointing out that I haven't heard much from you in the way of regret and repentance, where you acknowledge how you hurt people, where you listen to them and learn, rather than focusing on your own pain." He leans forward, his elbows on his knees. "Going back for the trial offers you an opportunity. Genuinely repenting and trying to make things right is an important part of your own healing."

When I get home that afternoon, I'm still thinking about what Dave said. About how I have this opportunity—even if the thought of facing everyone makes me want to puke.

But I need to start closer to home. I need to start with my sister.

The door to her room is closed, like it has been most of the time since we moved here. Like the person I've always been closest to wants to shut me out.

I knock on the door.

"Yeah?" she shouts over the latest hit by Oversized Aviators.

"It's me. Dec."

She ignores me, and I almost go back to my room. But then I remember what Dad said about how people with integrity have the courage to own their mistakes. What Dave said about needing to apologize before I can move on.

"Can I come in?"

She turns down the music. "If you must."

I open the door. She's on the bed reading a book and doesn't even look up as she says, "What?"

"I . . . I . . ." Breaking off, I wonder if I'm man enough for this after all.

"God, Declan, either spit it out or leave, okay?"

I take a deep breath. "I'm sorry. I want to say I'm sorry. For ruining the last two years for you. For making it so you had to leave all your friends, and the team and—"

That gets Kayleigh's attention. She stares at me. Then her brow furrows. "Why now?" she asks.

Not the response I expected.

"What do you mean?"

"I mean that you've had almost two years to apologize, but even though you've kind of done it, it's usually immediately followed by how much *you've* suffered. How *your* life is ruined, like the rest of us weren't totally upended because of what you did."

Kayleigh doesn't have a degree in counseling, but she's kind of saying the same thing Dave did, which means I need to own it.

"You know I've never been the sharpest tool in the shed," I say, hoping that if I do it in a humorous way, maybe we'll get back to our easy way of talking to each other. "You of all people should know that."

"True," she agrees.

"But it's also that I've been thinking about what happened a lot, what with having to go back there to testify," I explain. "And I've realized that the trial being over isn't enough for me to really move on. I need to apologize to people I hurt."

"So it's all about you again," she says.

"No! I *want* to apologize for what I did."

Her eyes search my face, and I force myself to maintain eye contact so that she knows I mean it. If anyone can read whether I'm telling the truth, it's Kayleigh.

I don't realize I've been holding my breath till she stands up, punches my arm, and then hugs me.

"It's about time, you jerk," she mumbles into my shoulder.

I exhale, hope bubbling in my chest.

She flops back down on her bed, and I sit at the foot of it.

"Are you scared to go back and testify?" she asks.

"Of course I am," I say. "I'd be an idiot not to be." I stare down at the scar on my arm. "But I'm not sure if I'm more afraid of testifying or trying to apologize to people like Jenn, and Arielle, and Jake."

"Do you want to know what I hate most?" she asks.

I'm not sure if I do, but I nod.

"I feel guilty," she says.

That blows me away.

"What? Why would *you* feel guilty? You didn't do anything wrong!"

"Oh, but I did," she says. "I ignored some stuff when I shouldn't have. Because it was you, and I didn't want that to be you." Her shoulders slump. "I have to live knowing that if you hadn't texted me, two of my best friends—not to mention a whole bunch of other people—might have been killed because I didn't say anything. I should have spoken up."

"Why didn't you?"

"Because I love you, you loser, even though you can be a total idiot."

I have to swallow a lump. Kayleigh hasn't called me a loser in a long time. Hearing her say that, and that she still loves me, makes me feel like a winner—even after everything I did.

"I don't deserve it, but I'll take it. Love you, too."

"Now can you get out of here and leave me to read in peace?" she says.

I salute her. "Yes, ma'am."

"Ugh, the patriarchy strikes again," she says. "'Yes, boss' will do."

Laughing, I head back to my room and grab my cell to send a text to Jake. I've been able to keep up with Jake a little by reading the sports page of the local news website. I wonder if he'll be captaining this coming year now that he'll be a senior and if he's still dating Arielle.

I type out a text but hesitate before hitting send. We've been told not to communicate with anyone in Stafford's Corner for our safety. Am I about to put my family at risk again?

Hitting the backspace button, I start deleting what I wrote. But my finger pauses halfway through. I'll be there next month. I want to apologize to everyone, but to Jake most of all. So I retype what I'd erased and press send.

Hey, it's me, Declan.

I'm coming back to testify in the trial next month, and I was hoping we could meet.

I'm sorry.

SENIOR
YEAR

SEPTEMBER

DECLAN

Dad and I are in the motel room watching a movie when we both get a news alert on our phones that the jury came back with a guilty verdict in the North Country Militia trial.

I heave a sigh of relief that, despite everything, is tinged with guilt. But still . . .

"I'm glad it's finally over," I tell Dad.

Although it isn't, not really. When we go back, I'll finally get the ankle monitor off, and we'll be moved to our permanent witness protection location, complete with new names and IDs. Maybe then I can really start again. I can become someone else, someone better.

But no one I meet from now on is going to know my history. I won't be able to share memories of growing up in Stafford's Corner with anyone besides my family.

"How did it feel to see your former friends in the courtroom?" Dad asks.

"Scary," I confess. "Especially Ronan. Talk about if looks could kill."

"Well, he's going to be locked up for decades now," Dad says.

"Yeah, but I know how this works," I say. "There's probably someone online in a gaming chat right this very minute persuading a miserable kid that killing a traitor like me would make him a hero."

"I'm proud of you, Dec," Dad says. "It took courage to testify."

That makes me squirm, because it didn't feel like courage. It felt like the very least I could do to make up for the harm I caused.

"You know what's weird?" I say to Dad. "When I look at Ronan now, I can't believe I thought so much of him. Like that he held all the answers."

"I'm sorry that I wasn't around for you enough when you needed it," Dad says. "I was so worried about getting laid off and how to pay the bills."

It feels good to have him acknowledge that—like he's owning up to his stuff, too.

"I wish I knew what to do about Jake," I say. "I've tried texting him a bunch of times, but he doesn't respond. I don't even know if he's going to show up at the synagogue on Saturday."

Tricia, who is still my defense attorney, encouraged me when I asked her if I could try to apologize to people back in New York. When I told her I was having no luck with Jake, she said, "Jake's not the only one. You hurt an entire faith community. Maybe you could reach out to the rabbi?"

So I did. Rabbi Jonas was cautious at first, but we had a few video chats, and eventually she invited me to speak at Congregation Anshe Chesed this Saturday, Shabbat Shuvah, the sabbath between Rosh Hashanah and Yom Kippur. She told me that in Hebrew, *teshuvah* means "return," as in return to God, so it would be "an auspicious time" to make my apology.

"You can't control what Jake does," Dad reminds me. "The only person you can control is you."

"I know," I say with a sigh.

"What about seeing if you can apologize to some of the other people you hurt while we're here?" Dad asks.

I realize it's a good idea. I ask Rabbi Jonas if she can reach out to Jenn from Mocha Jenn's, and Arielle and her family.

She comes back saying that I can meet Jenn at the café the following afternoon, but the Kramers don't want to meet with me. They'd rather wait to hear what I have to say on Saturday.

So I'm surprised when I get to Mocha Jenn's the next day and Arielle is sitting at a table. I wonder if it's just a weird coincidence, but after I offer my apologies to Jenn for the hateful graffiti, she tells me that Arielle is here because she wants to speak to me.

I've got serious dry mouth as I walk over to where she's sitting.

"Hi," I say awkwardly. "I thought you didn't want to talk to me. At least, that's what Rabbi Jonas said."

She gestures for me to sit and then leans forward, her chin on her hands. "My parents didn't want you at our house. My brother, Bobby . . . he still suffers from anxiety because of everything that happened. Especially the stuff on Halloween."

I look away, feeling my face flush with shame, remembering how proud I was that night. How it felt so great to get back at the people I thought were responsible for all my problems. How I basked in Ronan's praise the next day.

"Bobby thought he was safe at home," Arielle continues. "You smashing our front window made him scared he wasn't safe anywhere. My parents had to homeschool him for the rest of the school year."

She sighs, and I force myself to meet her gaze. "It made me feel that way, too," she says.

My chest constricts, and I feel like the absolute worst. I thought I was just vandalizing property. Just sending a message. I never thought about how it would affect the people I was sending that message to.

No, that's a lie. I thought they deserved it. And if I'm honest, I didn't think about Arielle and her family as real people. They were the enemy.

I realize that rating the things I did so low on Dave's hurt scale showed how clueless I was. How clueless I still am about so many things.

I remember Jake coming up to my bedroom. How he told me that Arielle was a person, not a monster.

He was right.

"I'm so sorry," I tell her. "What I did was wrong. I realize that now."

She leans back and scrutinizes my face.

"You know what's weird? I hardly know you—especially compared to Jake. But . . . I think I believe you."

The tightness in my chest loosens a little. Knowing that she believes me makes me even more willing to answer her questions about how I got involved with Ronan's group and why.

"Can I ask *you* a question?" I say.

She nods.

"Do you think Jake will ever forgive me?"

She doesn't answer right away, and the seconds weigh heavy.

"I can't speak for him. We're not dating anymore—it all got to be too much for me after what happened—but we're still good friends," she says finally. "I honestly don't know." Looking at me, she admits, "I didn't tell him I was meeting with you today. I didn't tell my parents, either."

"So why did you come?"

"I guess because . . . my need to know was greater than my fear." She gives me a brief smile. "Insert something about curiosity and cats."

I laugh. Jake was right. Arielle is pretty cool. I never even gave her a chance because I was so busy feeling sorry for myself.

She asks me how Kayleigh's doing and tells me how much she and all the girls on the soccer team miss her.

After Arielle leaves, I sit finishing my now-cold chocolate and think about Bobby and how my actions stole his sense of safety. Saying sorry isn't enough to fix that. I'm not sure what is. I also wonder if Jake's curiosity will ever be enough to make him want to talk to me. But like everyone keeps reminding me, that's out of my control. All I can do is keep trying.

JAKE

The first time I got a text from someone claiming to be Declan years after the Taylors disappeared, I couldn't help wondering if it was one of his extremist friends trying to troll me.

Two years ago, I tried texting Kayleigh when she didn't show up at school, but . . . nothing. Arielle's dad said Declan probably agreed to testify against his friends in exchange for a reduced jail sentence or probation, and they were moved to keep them safe.

Sure enough, Dec showed up in the coverage of the trial this week as a "deradicalized former member of the North Country Militia" who had been moved into witness protection with his family. Even though the guy wasn't named, it's obviously Declan.

I wonder if he still keeps his head shaved.

I wonder why I even care enough to wonder.

In his testimony, Dec tried to make it sound like he became a Jew-hating extremist because he lost his identity as a pitcher and that made him vulnerable to people who were offering him a new one.

I wasn't impressed by that excuse. "Lots of people have bad stuff happen to them without going full Nazi," I complained to Mom and Dad. "Declan made a choice to hang out with people who want to kill us."

Mom said something about empathy and trying to put myself in Dec's head, but I wasn't having any of it. The trial made all the anger and fear that I'd thought I'd dealt with come roaring back to the surface.

"All I'm saying is that it's important to understand how someone like Declan became radicalized. There's a lot of research trying to figure out what makes young people vulnerable to extremism—of every kind," Mom said. "Not just right-wing extremism."

"I have to go to his fricking apology tour stop, don't I?" I grumbled.

Mom frowned at my characterization. "It's your choice, Jake."

But I know she and Dad think I should go.

I'm not the only one who's unhappy about Declan speaking at Anshe Chesed. Rabbi Jonas has had concerns from other congregants.

Weirdly enough, Arielle isn't one of them. When I complain about it on the way to school on Friday morning, she asks, "Aren't you at all curious about what he has to say? Isn't it worth hearing him out?"

"Would *you* meet with him if he texted you saying he wanted to apologize?"

"Actually, Jake, I have to tell you something."

The way she's not quite meeting my eyes makes my stomach flip.

"I met Declan yesterday afternoon," Arielle confesses. "At Mocha Jenn's."

"What! Why would you do that?"

"Because I wanted to know what made him do it," she says.

"He did it because they're all antisemitic, that's why. Because they believe some old conspiracy theory."

"But what made Declan fall for it?" Arielle says. "He and Kayleigh are twins. They grew up in the same house with the same parents. And you know Kayleigh wasn't buying into all that, right?"

"Yeah." I'm reluctant to admit that what Arielle's saying makes sense.

What I don't understand is how she could stand to be in the same room with him when she was targeted by those creeps after the layoffs. Dec was the one who gave them her number.

"I really think you should meet with him," she says.

"No. I don't want to have anything to do with the guy," I say, shaking my head. "It's bad enough I have to listen to him pretending to be sorry during services tomorrow."

I can't help feeling like I've disappointed Arielle somehow.

Still, here I am, sitting at Shabbat services next to Dad, about to hear Declan's "apology."

Rabbi Jonas usually gives her sermon between the Shacharit service we do in the morning and the Mincha service we do after the Torah reading. But today we pray straight through, and then she speaks to us from the bimah.

"Declan Taylor was involved with the extremist militia that attempted a terrorist attack on our congregation two years ago. When he reached out to me asking if he could make a public apology, I had serious misgivings," Rabbi Jonas says. "While we were thankfully spared any deaths or physical harm to life or property, no one should underestimate the tremendous, lasting harm suffered when a Jewish community is attacked this way—not just to our immediate congregation, but to Jews everywhere."

Declan stares down at his shoes like he's ashamed to face the congregation, which is packed almost as full as it is on Rosh Hashanah and Yom Kippur, despite the objections to having him speak.

"But here we are on Shabbat Shuvah, a time we are confessing our own sins and asking for forgiveness. During the Unetaneh Tokef prayer on Rosh Hashanah last week, we repeated that we can avert the severity of God's decree through repentance, prayer, and charity. After extensive conversations with Declan, I believe that he's genuine in his desire to do teshuvah, to heal the wounds that he helped create," Rabbi Jonas continues. "Declan has already been doing community service as a condition of his probation, but he knows that he has to do more to earn forgiveness. That's why he asked to speak to you today. I hope you'll listen to what he has to say, with open minds and open hearts, even though we feel pain whenever we think about what he did." She turns to Mom. "And now, I'd like to hand over to Melissa Lehrer."

My mother walks to the podium and surveys the crowded room.

"Shabbat Shalom and L'Shanah Tovah," Mom says, smiling. But the smile fades as she continues. "We're living in challenging times, where it sometimes feels like hatred and divisiveness are going to win the battle against love, empathy, and understanding," she says. "I truly believe that part of overcoming that is learning to reach beyond our fear—not an easy ask, I'll grant you. I know many of us are struggling with this. I'm wrestling with it myself, if I'm totally honest."

It feels like she's speaking directly to me as she says this. Like she knows that seeing Declan up there on the bimah is bringing up feelings.

"Our community was targeted. We have a right to be angry about it. I want to make it perfectly clear—it is not our responsibility to forgive. However . . . it is our choice."

Mom looks around, letting that sink in. "Some of us will be able to make the choice to forgive. Others might not. As the targeted community, it isn't our job to make things right when people have done hateful acts toward us. But just as God listens to us as we confess during the Days of Awe, I hope you will join me in giving Declan your attention."

Now that I'm here, I guess I'm curious to hear what Declan has to say. It's easier to be here as part of the crowd instead of meeting him one-on-one. But I'm still afraid that there are too many people like his former friends, who hate us so much they want to kill us. And I'm mad that I'm scared. I shouldn't have to be afraid just because of my religion.

Mom is clearly a better person than I am, because she shakes Declan's hand and whispers something to him that the mic doesn't catch.

"How can she be so nice to him?" I whisper to Dad, my hands fisted on my knees.

"Your mother is a very special woman. You should know that by now." He puts his hand on my clenched fingers. "Hear Declan out. And remember: If you don't let go of this"—he taps my angrily clenched fingers—"in the long run, the person it will hurt the most is you."

I look up at Declan, who is taking a sip of the water Mom poured for him with an obviously trembling hand, and against my will feel a pang of sympathy for him. I remember how intimidating it was standing up at that very podium at my bar mitzvah, and that was when the room was filled with family and friends who love me.

He's up there facing a crowd of people who for the most part only know one thing about him—that he was involved with an extremist group that came to our synagogue with pipe bombs and AR15s with the intent to do us serious harm. Now he says he's not. Most of the people in the audience don't have the kind of history with Declan that I do. They haven't shared wins and losses together as part of a baseball team. They haven't shared sleepovers and birthday parties, or just hanging out and chilling.

Declan stands at the podium, tall, blue-eyed, his blond hair fully grown in again, and I can't help wondering, if we'd both been born in another time, in another country, would he have joined the Hitler Youth and gone around in packs with his Nazi friends, vandalizing Jewish stores and beating up Jewish kids like me—or at least trying to? Is the fact that we were best friends and teammates only possible because we happened to be born in this time and place?

The thought makes me shudder.

Declan clears his throat, and his gaze sweeps the room, landing on me. I stare back, not giving anything away.

But the look in his eyes is so familiar, so seemingly genuine, that I can't help myself—despite everything, it's a reflex reaction to give him the same kind of encouraging smile I'd have flashed from first base if he was about to throw the winning pitch.

I realize that Mom is right. That underneath the fear, the anger, the sense of betrayal, is the need to answer the burning question: Why?

As Declan starts to speak, my biggest hope is that he'll tell us.

DECLAN

Listening to Jake's mom introduce me, I want to crawl out of my own skin. Sitting up here in front of all these people I harmed is terrifying. What if they don't believe me when I say that I'm sorry? What if they still hate me for the things I did, and the even worse things that I almost did?

I take a deep breath and remind myself of what both Dave and Chris kept reminding me: that no one is obligated to forgive me just because I ask for it. All I can do is speak from my heart.

"Declan, welcome back to Congregation Anshe Chesed," Mrs. Lehrer says.

With a shallow breath, I walk over to the podium with my notes in my hand, hoping that it's not obvious to everyone in the audience that I'm trembling.

Mrs. Lehrer shakes my hand. Before this happened, she would have given me a hug.

But then she whispers in my ear, "You can do this, Declan."

I know I don't deserve her belief in me, but having it gives me the strength to look out into the crowded sanctuary at the faces of all the people I've hurt, including Dad, whose life was totally upended because of me. I know he's worried that if this doesn't go well, it will set me back. That I'll go back to that dark place I was in after the accident, the one that led me into the even darker place where embracing hate made sense.

I clear my throat and search for Jake in the crowd. When I find him, our eyes meet, and I want him to know this means something to me—being here—even if it's terrifying.

He must see something, because he gives me the same you-got-this smile he used to give me before I made a pitch that really counted.

It's a smile I never thought I'd see from him again. It gives me hope.

I take a deep breath and begin.

"I want to thank Rabbi Jonas and all of you for being willing to have me here tonight. I know not everyone was happy about it. I don't blame you. I caused you pain. I was involved with people who wanted to cause you serious harm.

"When we got here earlier, I noticed that there isn't just the usual security guard, like I remember. Tonight, the security guard is there, but there's also a police presence. When I walked into the synagogue entrance, I noticed those large concrete flowerpots to prevent anyone from ramming a car through the front door.

"Seeing those changes was another reminder of how my actions have had a long-term impact on your community, both emotionally and financially."

The words I'm about to speak are for everyone, but I'm aiming them at Jake.

"I'm here to do teshuvah, to ask your forgiveness, and hopefully to continue to earn it through my words and actions."

I was encouraged by the smile Jake gave me earlier, but now his face is unreadable. My heart sinks. Maybe this is all one great big waste of everyone's time.

But even if no one forgives me, apologizing is part of my own journey to get out of a place of hate. Without that step, I can't move forward.

"So how did it happen? How did I go from an all-star baseball pitcher who counted a Jewish teammate as his best friend to becoming part of the North Country Militia?"

Some of the faces looking back at me are hot with anger. Other people are listening with their arms crossed, like they're closed off to anything I might say and there is no way I'm going to change their minds. I'm scared that Jake is one of those people, but I have to try. I miss him. I miss our friendship. I'm afraid I've damaged it so badly I might never get it back.

"The short version is: I lost myself. I can tell you all the things that went wrong in my life; they matter in some ways to the path I ended up on, but they also don't matter. I was in a bad place, a place of loss and pain. But then I found what I thought were answers to why I ended up there—answers that said none of it was my fault.

"Extremism gave me a narrative for why these bad things were happening—one that didn't force me to look in the mirror and take ownership of the things I did. It was so much easier to blame everyone else." I look around at the audience. "It's hard to admit this standing here on the bimah at Congregation Anshe Chesed, whose name literally means 'people of loving-kindness,' but the people I was led to blame most were Jews. I didn't realize I was being taught to believe age-old antisemitic stereotypes."

There's rustling and an undercurrent of whispers. It makes me want to run, to hide, to be anywhere but here. But I force myself to be brave; to stay and face what comes at me.

"But part of it was also ignorance. I didn't recognize that when people I was gaming with said 'globalists,' they meant Jews—and when my best friend tried to tell me, I told him to lighten up, that it was just a joke."

I glance at Jake, but he's looking down at his hands.

"I should have listened. He knew it was no joke." I take a deep breath and keep going. "Then a classmate took me to hang out with the North Country Militia. They treated me like an adult with legitimate ideas, not as a stupid teenager.

"If you take one thing from what I say to you today, it should be that being accepted and respected was way more important to me than any ideology. That's what was missing in my life after I lost baseball."

I see a few people nodding thoughtfully as I start to wrap it up.

"I know this is Shabbat Shuvah, and teshuvah is about repentance. I'm here because I'm truly sorry for the harm that I caused you and so many others. I hope that even if you don't forgive me, that at least this has helped you to understand. Thank you for listening."

JAKE

When Declan finishes, there's a quiet buzz of people in the sanctuary starting to discuss what he said. I hear a couple sitting behind us asking each other if he's genuinely repentant or just saying it to get out of trouble.

I'm not sure what to believe.

Rabbi Jonas comes over and puts her hand on Dec's shoulder. He gives her a faint smile and goes back to his seat, his head bowed and shoulders slumped.

She looks around the sanctuary like she's trying to take the emotional pulse of the congregation. I wonder if everyone else feels as mixed up about this as I do.

She turns to Declan. "Declan, I can't speak for everyone in the community, because the choice to forgive is up to each individual. But I am reaching out the hand of friendship to you. I hope you will take it."

I see that Declan is getting choked up. He ducks his head, his blond hair falling over his face.

"I want to thank Declan for helping us to understand how young people become radicalized. Let's all strive to become instruments of love, empathy, and understanding," Rabbi Jonas says.

Then she does the blessing over the wine and the challah, and invites everyone to the kiddush in the social hall.

"So, what do you think?" Dad asks me as we stand up to leave the sanctuary.

"That's it?" I say in an undertone laced with bitterness. "Declan says he's sorry, and now we're all supposed to forget what he did? Like I'm supposed to be his best friend again just like that?"

"No one is saying that you have to forget," Dad tells me. "No one is saying that you have to be friends with Declan again, either."

"Sounds like it," I mutter.

Dad spots Mom, who is talking to Mr. Taylor and Declan. "I'm going to go join your mother." He looks at me expectantly, like, *Come on, Jake, now's a good opportunity.*

Then Declan glances over. Our eyes meet. I look away, because I'm not ready to talk to him. I still don't know how I feel.

"I'm going to go find Arielle," I mumble, ignoring Dad's disappointment. It just makes me angrier. How am I the bad guy here?

Arielle is talking to Rabbi Jonas, and I join them, feeling suffocated by my confused emotions.

"How are you doing, Jake?" Rabbi Jonas asks, her eyes kind and concerned, like she knows that I'm struggling.

"Honestly? I feel like I'm being forced to forgive Declan for something that still makes me mad."

"Forgiveness, if you choose it, is a complicated process," Rabbi Jonas says. "But the Talmud tells us there are three levels of forgiveness. Right now, maybe you're at the first level, which is where you still feel hurt and anger toward Declan, but you don't wish him harm."

"I'm not even sure I'm there yet, if I'm totally honest," I admit. "I thought he should have more consequences."

"What kind of consequences?" Rabbi Jonas asks.

"I don't know," I admit.

"He already lost baseball, his teammates, his home, his whole life as he knew it," Arielle points out. "And he's had to come to terms with the fact that those people he thought were his friends weren't really."

"Welcome to my world," I say. "That's how I feel about him. I thought he was my friend, but he wasn't."

"I understand why you feel that way, Jake," Rabbi Jonas says. "Let's talk about the second level of forgiveness, which is where you let go of your anger. That would mean a great deal to Declan, obviously, but it's more important for you."

"Because . . . otherwise . . . it eats away inside?" I say slowly.

"Exactly. Like the old saying goes, holding on to anger and resentment is like taking poison and expecting the person you're angry at to die," Rabbi Jonas says.

I'm definitely not there yet. Every time I think about Declan's betrayal, fury courses through me. "So, what's stage three?" I ask.

"Stage three is when you're ready to forgive and accept the person completely," Rabbi Jonas explains. "It's not like you forget what happened, but you're able to move beyond it and restore the relationship. Some people might never get to that point, and that's okay. Stage two is the most important one for your future health and happiness."

I look over to where Declan is standing with his dad, greeting other members of the congregation. "I'm not sure I can ever get to stage three," I confess. "I'll be happy if I ever make it to stage two."

"Remember, I'm here if you want to talk about it," Rabbi Jonas says quietly.

Someone comes up to ask her a question, and Arielle and I walk off the bimah to head for the social hall.

"I know you don't want to hear this, but I think you should spend five minutes with Dec," Arielle tells me. "For your sake more than his. Even if it's just to get some closure."

I realize she's right. There's still a Declan-shaped hole inside me—one that's been there since everything happened.

"Maybe," I admit.

"I'm usually right," she says, smiling.

I flash her a brief smile. "Can you do me a favor? I don't want to talk with all these people around. Can you tell him I'll be out on the playground?"

"Of course," she says. Then she adds, "You can do this, Jake."

"We'll see," I tell her as I head out of the building. I say hi to Tony, the security guard, and give a grateful nod to the police officer in the black-and-white car sitting in the parking lot.

It's warm for an evening in early September. I make a beeline for one of the little rocking horses on a spring. I used to love this particular horse when I was a kid. I named it Bullseye, after the horse in *Toy Story 2*. Now I can't put my feet on the pegs without hitting my chin with my knees. Instead, I sit sideways on his saddle and wonder how it's going to go with Declan. Still not sure I'm ready for this.

But then I see him come out of the main synagogue doors, and as soon as he spots me, he jogs over, despite being in a coat and tie. As he gets closer, I see that his eyes are hopeful, his mouth twisted into an awkward attempt at a smile. I notice the security officer trailing him. Declan turns and stops to talk to the guy. The officer hangs back, but he's obviously on alert.

"Hey," Declan says, half waving with what used to be his pitching arm.

"Hey," I say back.

We used to speak to each other so easily. Now there's this distance, this wall between us, and I'm not sure if we can ever cross it, or if I even want to.

"I can't go anywhere without my tail while we're back here," Declan says, gesturing at the security guy. He gives a brief, bitter chuckle. "The militia folks aren't big fans after I testified at the trial."

"So why did you?" I ask. "For the get-out-of-jail-free card?"

A brief, hurt expression crosses Declan's face. He inhales, then exhales slowly and loudly through his mouth. He does it again and then says, "Okay, I guess that's a fair question. And yeah . . . that was probably most of it in the beginning. But not at the end. Things changed."

"Changed how?" I ask.

Declan toes the wood chips. "So as part of my deal, I had to do anger management and therapy, which helped me realize a lot of stuff." He looks up, meeting my gaze. "Like that testifying was the right thing to do. That the people I'd betrayed the most weren't my militia friends, but people like you, and Arielle, and Jenn, and all the people in that building." He waves back at the synagogue.

There's an awkward silence.

"I need to ask you something," I say finally. "And I need you to be honest when you answer me."

"Okay." He gives me a wary look.

Declan's acting like *I'm* the one who hung out with guys who wanted to kill *him*.

I thought I could get through this calmly, but I don't think it's possible. Maybe I'm still stuck in stage one. Maybe I'll be stuck there forever.

Still, I have to ask this. I need to hear Declan's answer.

"I get that you were in a bad place after the accident. But you knew me, Declan—or at least I thought you did. So how could you start believing all that antisemitic stuff? How could you think anything about those people you started hanging out with was okay?"

I expect Declan to get defensive, but he looks me in the eye.

"After the accident, I was looking for anyone to blame but myself, and that's what the militia gave me," he says. "Something—someone to blame. I was also jealous that you and Cody and Jeff and Mateo and all the guys on the team were living the life that was supposed to be mine."

I can't help reminding him, "I was the one who was telling you to be careful when you climbed that rock face."

"I know. And part of the whole counseling thing has been learning how to take responsibility for my own crap instead of blaming everyone else for it."

"That's good and all, but I gotta tell you, Declan, I'm still having a hard time getting over the fact that despite everything you knew about me, all our years of friendship, you bought into that antisemitic conspiracy crap."

Declan's face flushes. His hands clench into fists at his sides, and he looks away and takes another deep breath. Then, almost like he's willing himself to be calm, he meets my gaze. "I understand. All I can say is that I'm sorry."

He starts to walk away, and I'm angry all over again. *I'm sorry* doesn't feel like enough after what he did.

But then Declan turns back. "You were the reason I texted Kayleigh to dial 911, Jake. I . . . want you to know. No matter how much I'd bought into everything, I couldn't let something happen to you. Or anyone in that building. But especially you."

I search his face for clues that he's just saying that, but all I see is truth and regret.

"Thanks for telling me that," I say. "It . . . helps."

His tense posture relaxes, like I've just given him what he needs to hear, too. "I really miss our friendship, Jake. I know there's a good chance that you won't ever want to talk to me again, but if you do . . . I'll be there. You've got my number." Then he turns and walks away.

I watch him head back to the synagogue entrance, where his dad and his security guy are waiting.

I do feel better for having done this. Maybe being able to listen to the apology of the person who hurt you is part of the stages of forgiveness. Maybe doing this was as much for me as it was for Declan.

I don't know if he and I will ever be friends again. It's not something I can see right now, or any time soon.

But who knows? Maybe someday in the future, the memory of the good times we had together will outweigh the pain he caused.

If it does, I know Declan will be there, waiting.

AUTHOR'S NOTE

I was nine years old when a classmate I considered a friend shouted, "You killed Jesus!" at another Jewish girl and me. As an adult, I can still see the hatred in her eyes as she confronted us. It was hurtful, but it also didn't make any sense. As I pointed out to her, it was impossible for us to have killed Jesus because his death happened long before we were born.

That was my first personal encounter with irrational hatred; sadly, it's nowhere near the last.

I grew up in a family that was affected by Holocaust trauma. My great-grandparents were murdered when the Nazis invaded Ukraine in 1941. Other relatives were murdered in Treblinka, a Nazi extermination camp near Warsaw. So it's probably not surprising, then, that I've always been hyperalert to antisemitism around me. In 2019, when I first started thinking about this book, I'd already grown extremely anxious about the rise in antisemitism, both in the US and worldwide. That anxiety has only intensified. A March 2021 Anti-Defamation League survey of Jewish Americans found that in the previous five years, 63 percent of those surveyed had either experienced or witnessed some form of antisemitism, up from 54 percent the previous year. More than half (59 percent) of those polled said they feel Jews are less safe in the US today than they were a decade ago.

I needed to know why. As an author, the way I answer questions is to write a book. To do that, I was going to have to follow Declan on his journey into antisemitism. Reading was one of the ways I first got into his head: how to understand the appeal of giving one's mind over to a worldview that promotes hatred of anyone considered "other." It helped me figure out what questions to ask when I interviewed former extremists. Because listening was the next step. I had to ensure I was listening with an open mind, even when people I was interviewing said things that were harmful and made me angry. Listening is a skill, and like all skills (playing baseball or soccer, writing, playing an instrument), it takes practice.

One thing I've learned is if we can listen to each other better, if we can have genuine conversations, we can find points of commonality in places we'd never expect. Unfortunately, technology often works to prevent those conversations. Social media companies encourage us to talk *at* one another rather than to listen. We know from both research and whistleblower testimony how they promote content that creates outrage and indignation, because it increases user engagement with their sites.

A common thread of both the interviews and readings was that it was community, identity, and purpose that drew people into the movement far more than ideology; hate came later. As one person I interviewed said, antisemitism is so widespread because it's entwined with all the other hatreds. It boils down to the belief in some version of the debunked conspiracy laid out in *The Protocols of the Elders of Zion* over a century ago: that us Jews have a grand master plan to destroy the white race through immigration and intermarriage. There's usually an economic thread thrown in—that we're pushing for some kind of "ism": Marxism, socialism, communism, or, most recently, "globalism." The various "isms" are often used interchangeably, with no regard for actual meaning. When people are hurting economically, they're more susceptible to conspiracy theories that give them someone to blame. As the COVID-19 pandemic unfolded in 2020, so did the antisemitic conspiracy theories claiming that

Jews were behind the spread of the virus—similar to bogus medieval claims about Jews being responsible for the spread of the Black Death.

What helped people renounce extremism? For some, it was family, not wanting to see the cycle of hatred and violence repeated. But more than one "former" said that the first crack in their beliefs happened when someone from whom they least deserved kindness gave it to them anyway. Which gives us something to think about: How can we offer people community, identity, and purpose in a way that leads to love and acceptance rather than hatred of anyone different?

It's been nearly eighty years since the end of the Holocaust, but it's important to understand that genocides don't occur quickly. The road to Auschwitz and Treblinka was gradual and insidious; it happened because people who weren't targets of Nazi hatred were willing to turn their gaze away. That's why it's so important to use your voice whenever you see someone being targeted.

It can be scary to take a stand, especially when the people causing the injustice are powerful adults. But if we have learned anything from history, it's that staying silent in the face of hatred and injustice is complicity. Every one of us has a responsibility to create understanding, to help protect groups that are targeted, to continually learn and grow no matter how old we are. Change doesn't happen overnight, but it can happen if we all work toward a more compassionate, equal, and just society. I have faith in you, dear readers. As my late father used to say to me when I needed courage: "Chazak!"

For a list of further readings and resources on how you can help to combat hate in your community, go to somekindofh8.com.

ACKNOWLEDGMENTS

I've written about difficult subjects before, but *Some Kind of Hate* is one of the hardest novels I've ever researched and written. It wouldn't have happened without help.

First and foremost, I want to thank my brilliant editor, Jody Corbett. I emailed her with a vague idea, and thanks to her expert editorial input and her unending patience, that idea became a novel.

I'm unutterably grateful to be a part of the Scholastic family. Thank you to Janell Harris, Maeve Norton, David Levithan, Erin Berger, Seale Ballenger, Lizette Serrano, Emily Heddleson, Sabrina Montenigro, Rachel Feld, Shannon Pender, and the entire Trade sales force, as well as the Scholastic Clubs and Fairs.

Behind every successful writer is a fantastic agent. I'm so lucky to have Jennifer Laughran in my corner, and to be a part of the Andrea Brown Literary family.

Thank you to the "formers" who left various extremist movements and wrote books, gave talks, and/or were willing to speak with me personally about their journeys: Christian Picciolini, Jeff Schoep, Tony McAleer, Caleb Cain, Arno Michaelis, R. Derek Black, and "Sam."

Writing this book required a lot of research, and I'm fortunate to have had help from experts in many different fields. Any errors are mine.

Thanks to Megan Condis, assistant professor of game studies at Texas Tech University, for her research on how young people are being radicalized through gaming, and to Jonathan Holden for collecting screenshots of examples he encountered.

Sincere thanks to Christopher C. Kain, MD, and Rafael G. Magana, MD, for helping me to figure out all the injuries I could give Declan to mess up his future as a baseball player.

The legal knowledge I gleaned from Law & Order wasn't sufficient, so I'm fortunate to have had help from Heather Crimmins, Esq.; Amy D'Amico, Esq.; and former US Attorney David M. DeVillers (thanks, Julia!). Cantor Michael Shochet and Captain Mark Kordick (ret.) helped with policing issues.

Ken Borsuk, Jeff Seale, and Matt Miller answered my baseball questions and made sure I didn't embarrass myself by using the wrong terminology.

Sincere thanks to my critique group, Joan Riordan, Stacy Barnett Mozer, Nina Haberli, and Trevor Macomber for your feedback. I promise to write something lighthearted next.

A special thank-you to teen readers Annie Mozer, Lilly Weisz, Samuel Rodrigue, and Dylan and Daniel Davis.

I'm grateful for the support of Heidi Rabinowitz, Susan Kusel, Joanne Levy, and members of the Jewish Kidlit Mavens group, as well as Cindy L. Otis, Karen Ball, Debbi Michiko Florence, the WOMG, and my synagogue communities, especially Rabbi Joshua Hammerman. I owe you all, big-time, for helping to preserve my sanity—or what's left of it!

An especially big thank-you to Liza Wiemer and Gae Polisner for their encouragement and incredible words, and to Todd Gutnick and Jonathan A. Greenblatt of the Anti-Defamation League for their feedback and for all they do to fight hatred of any kind.

Parents teach their children, but likewise, children teach their parents. Josh and Amie, your reminders to listen, learn, and grow make me proud to be your mama.

This book is dedicated to my husband, Hank, who if there were such a thing as a Jewish atheist saint, would be canonized immediately for putting up with me as I researched, wrote, and rewrote (and rewrote and rewrote) this book. Thank you, my love, for . . . everything.

Last, but certainly not least, thank you, dear readers, teachers, librarians, and booksellers. Your support gives me the courage to face things that scare me and write books about them. Read on!

ABOUT THE AUTHOR

Sarah Darer Littman is the critically acclaimed author of *Deepfake*; *Backlash*; *Want to Go Private?*; *Anything But Okay*; *In Case You Missed It*; *Life, After*; and *Purge*. She is also an award-winning news columnist and teaches writing in the MFA program at Western Connecticut State University and with the Yale Writers' Workshop. Sarah lives in Connecticut in a house that never seems to have enough bookshelves. You can visit her online at sarahdarerlittman.com.